Seven for the Revolution

A Collection of Short Stories

By

Rudy Ruiz

SA PL

MILAGROS
PRESS

Milagros Press
A division of Victory Boulevard Corporation
4021 Broadway
San Antonio, Texas 78209

Milagros Press is a registered trademark of Victory Boulevard Corporation.
The Milagros Press logo is a trademark of Victory Boulevard Corporation.

First Milagros Press hardcover edition: 2013
First Milagros Press trade paperback edition: 2013

ISBN 978-1-304-06489-9

Library of Congress Control Number: 2011904857

Ruiz, Rudy, 2013.
        Seven for the Revolution / Rudy Ruiz

ISBN 978-0-9844345-0-3

1.   Hispanic Americans–Fiction.

Printed in the United States

"We love with our hearts. We think with our minds. But we are defined by our borders."

—*Rudy Ruiz*

For Heather, Paloma, Lorenzo & Isabella

Contents

The Colonel and His Bridge

Since his days as a child on the Gulf coast of Mexico, Enrique yearned to build structures that would make life better for people, but he always felt confounded by the world's refusal to cooperate.

He first noticed this infernal dynamic at the age of seven. His widowed mother, Elena, took him to the beach to stay with her friends at a rustic beach house perched on stilts over the dunes near the mouth of the Rio Grande. Long after the other children tired of the scorching sun, stinging waves and burning salt in their eyes, Enrique toiled at the water's rising edge, racing against the setting sun.

"Come, Enrique," his mother urged, her blue eyes darting anxiously towards the beach house on stilts beyond the dunes, which he regarded with disdain.

"I'm almost done. You'll see, *Mamá*," he replied, packing sand tightly as he completed a turret at the end of a long wall facing the ocean, intermittently looking out over the river to the north. The waters were deceptively calm at the point where the Rio Grande flowed into the Gulf. "Tonight my walls will protect us from the waves. And the bridge I am building will cross this river." He pointed at the various structures arrayed within the sprawling complex he had erected. "And tomorrow when we all wake up, my castle will still be standing."

Elena, also known as "*La Viuda Shulz*," surveyed the intricate network of canals, walls, and towers her son had sculpted in the dark brown sand, for a moment losing her train of thought within the maze. Then her gaze drifted to her only child, working diligently while chewing on his sand-sprinkled lip. What could she say? He was inspired, building his own river just so he could span it with his bridge and protect it with his walls. Ah, to be a child again, so full of hope and imagination, still undefeated by the insurmountable currents and cycles of the world. Sighing in resignation, she settled on a boulder nearby and watched the waves as the sun disappeared beyond the dunes, streaking the sky with bands of gold and purple reflected on the water.

The merry voices of her friends, their husbands and children wafted down from the house, stirring Elena from her gentle slide into sleep. She'd been dreaming that she was a little girl again, her skin smooth and pearly as imported Bavarian porcelain, her golden curls gleaming in the sun, her whole future an uncharted ocean, before the heavy but hollow crush of widowhood had been draped upon her like a black *mantilla* she could never put back in a wardrobe. As her eyes fluttered open she caught a glimpse of Enrique beaming proudly in the moonlight at his masterpiece. Behind her the warm, inviting light of kerosene lamps flickered in the windows.

"Can we stay up all night and watch it fight off the ocean?" He asked eagerly.

She stared back at the house, squinting through the darkness. She knew that the others did not miss them, did not need them, a fading widow and her orphan son. They were invited by the other families of German heritage purely out of pity for their situation, their sudden fall from promise into poverty upon the death of her husband during a construction accident. Truthfully, she preferred sitting alone with Enrique next to the waves. While there was no chair and the parasol flapping in the evening breeze was an annoying reminder of another day behind her, she was more comfortable here. Still, they could not spend the whole night out in the elements. It would not be sensible.

"*Ay, mi hijo,*" the widow answered reluctantly, sorry to smother his dreams but sensing guiltily that it was also her obligation to set his expectations honestly. "Nothing made by man can beat the tide." She stared sullenly out over the white crests of the waves glowing in the pale light of the crescent moon.

"We'll see, *Mamá,*" Enrique declared defiantly, allowing her to finally tow him up to the house after a good long while of watching the waves slow but methodical advance. Up rickety stairs, the children all slept in a neat row on the wooden kitchen floor and the adults had slinked off to their tiny but private rooms.

The next morning, as the sun rose over the waves and warmed the beach, the children laughed, pointing cruelly at the tears streaming down Enrique's sunburned cheeks, his bleached hair floating in the morning breeze.

"*Mira el mariquita*," they chanted. "*Pobrecito.*"

Enrique didn't listen to their insults. He wasn't crying because of their taunts and jeers or because of the sting of the redness that had eclipsed his honey-toned skin. He mourned for his fortress and levees, which had been washed away just as his mother had prognosticated.

On the trolley ride home, he squinted mournfully out the window in the stifling heat as his mother snored lightly in the seat beside him.

Maybe his walls had fallen because they were not built strongly enough. Surely the tides could be defeated. His mother concluded his obstinacy and obsession with engineering were "results of the German" in him, passed on through both of his parents' genes, but the Jesuit priest with the cropped bowl-cut hair at his school opined confidently that it was the Mexican in him.

"You see, my son, Mexicans are builders. We love to build," Padre Raúl ran his dark weathered hand through the boy's hair gently. "Even though you are a *güerito* with *ojos azules*, you're still a *Mexicano.*"

The Jesuit had known his father, one of the darkest skinned Germans he had ever seen, the son of an immigrant and a Huasteca Indian woman.

"And Mexicans, we love to create and build more than we like to maintain or inhabit," Padre Raúl explained. "We build houses and barely bother living in them because before they're even finished we're off building more. Why do you think the Aztecs and the Mayas erected all those pyramids and then vanished?"

Enrique wasn't so sure. Had the Mayans gotten bored of Chichén Itzá and Uxmal and decided to head south for Tikal and Copán? Had disease wiped them out? Or—more likely—had the Spaniards killed them all? The history books in the dingy school library were little more than shells and spines with most of their guts ripped out, leading Enrique to wonder what the Porfiriato (or the Church) were so desperate to hide. So rather than ponder those questions, Enrique buried his head in his math and science texts. Amidst all the political turmoil and chaos of a country in the crafting, where religion was at odds with the government and the masses grew increasingly frustrated with the Europhile regime of General Porfirio Díaz, he preferred to ask questions to which he could ascertain solid answers.

His search for solace in structure intensified upon his mother's premature death a few years later from influenza. While his dream had been to study engineering at the university in Mexico City, he was too poor. He had only two choices: join the priesthood or the military. Both provided a roof, meals and the structure he sought.

"Join me," exhorted Padre Raúl still cloaked in his coarse brown robe with a frazzled rope for a belt, his boyish coif now withered and gray. "It is a hard life but we will savor our rewards in the afterlife."

Enrique—thrust into adulthood at the early age of sixteen, like so many in those days–took stock of his father's old friend standing precariously before him. He considered the option as genuinely as Padre Raúl offered it. But he dreamt of traveling and meeting a beautiful girl in a distant town. He imagined learning more about how to build things, and maybe actually leaving his mark on the world through some sort of permanent edifice bearing his name or, at the very least, the mark of his mind.

The priest was kind and had taught him much. In all honesty, Enrique wasn't fully convinced about God and the afterlife. He didn't share Padre Raúl's zeal for delayed gratification. Despite his doubts, he knelt in the tiny shrine before the statue of the Virgen de Guadalupe and vowed to someday build something meaningful in his mother's name. He apologized to his father's friend and made the two-block journey to the army barracks, where he enlisted.

As he rose quickly through the ranks, Enrique was racked by remorse. He knew he was benefiting from racism, as his blue eyes and lighter skin naturally set him aside from the rank and file. General Díaz favored Europe and the uninterrupted flow of foreign investment into his coffers. So his commanders filled their upper ranks with those who "would photograph pretty," as the general put it. A civilized autocracy that could dance with the great powers of the world was the general's vision. The only way Enrique could reconcile his guilt was by treating his men with dignity and respect, recommending the best of them for advancement rather than holding them back to benefit exclusively from their skills. Thus, Enrique became a well-liked leader. He wore his "Federal" uniform with pride as the medals and distinctions accumulated.

He met his bride, Anita Sanchez, at an Independence Day dance in the dusty border town of Matamoros, Mexico. She caught his eye across the well-dressed crowd. Her dark hair and caramel skin were far from the Germanic tones of his mother. Anita was a true Mexican. He yearned for her embrace and the gaze of her smoldering coffee eyes the moment he saw her, standing disinterestedly amidst a circle of civilian suitors. Her eyes opened wide at the approach of his gleaming medals, his slicked back golden hair and piercing sky-blue eyes.

"Are you American?" she attempted in broken English as he approached, which surprised him.

"Soy tan Mexicano como tú," he replied, which surprised her. He reached out for her hand. "May I…?"

And they spun about the dance floor, waltzing, as was the style of the day.

It was the dawn of the twentieth century, and American, British and French investors financed the expansion of the railroads throughout Mexico. As the tracks stretched into previously unsettled territories, they came under increasing attack by bandits and Indians. So General Díaz assigned military units to protect the industrialists, their construction crews, and the shiny new railroads destined to deliver modernity to the far reaches of the nation.

The foreign bankers and corporate executives took a liking to Enrique, who looked much like them. He was tall and fit, and he carried himself with the distinction of an accomplished military man. Though he was but a captain, they jokingly called him "the colonel," impressed by his rigorous discipline. No one worked harder or with more focus, not only deflecting the assaults of the desperate bands of impoverished *campesinos* and Indians but also offering up designs for new structures to sustain the growing weight of the locomotives and railcars as they traversed valleys and rivers.

As Enrique moved about the country, his young and growing family followed. They would set up house in the largest city near the region in which Enrique was deployed. And he would visit every chance he got, receiving free train tickets from his patrons at the rail company. First it was just Enrique and his Anita, who would quickly pack their meager belongings in burlap sacks and happily clasp his hand while venturing into new lands. Then they were joined by their first daughter, Magdalena, brought into the world with the help of a Huastec Indian midwife named Manuela in the tiny bedroom of the apartment they rented in Ciudad Victoria. A year later came Esperanza, again birthed with the help of Manuela, who had followed them to Monterrey. If Anita was his earthly dream, his girls were surely the equivalent of the glory of the afterlife Padre Raúl had rhapsodized about. Enrique was startled by the depth of emotion he felt for Magdalena and Esperanza. His love drove him to dream more than ever of achieving great things, so that they could enjoy the rewards of a life different from the one of orphaned deprivation and hardship he had always known.

In those days leading up to the Mexican Revolution, Enrique once again tasted the frustration of his dream to build monuments that might stand the test of time or defy the dynamics of nature. But this time the structure was not as tangible as a sandcastle.

Stationed in Chihuahua, Enrique's unit was dedicated to protecting the railway projects as they expanded towards the west coast through the Sonoran Desert. The tours of duty in the dry, scorching heat stretched mercilessly for months at a time. Communication was sparse and intermittent, usually by couriers on horseback bringing telegrams from the nearest train depot or military outpost. With his family safe back in the city of Chihuahua, Enrique faced a daunting task. He was ordered to grapple with the greatest enemies in the sprawling, untamed region, at least to the railway company, wealthy *hacendados*, and the *Federales* sworn to protect them: the Yaqui Indians.

"The Yaqui are fierce savages," read the terse missive from Enrique's direct commander. "You must eliminate them at all costs."

Enrique burned the paper in the candlelight within his solitary tent. Nobody but Anita knew that his father had been half Indian. He had led his troops into battle before against various bandits and smaller Indian tribes, but it had always been in defensive maneuvers to protect the railways against attacks. Clearly, this time his commander's orders were to preemptively seek out and eliminate the Yaqui. Everyone in the military and government considered them the greatest threat to control over the western provinces. General Díaz clung to his vision of promoting foreign investment and settlement of the northwestern regions of Mexico, but in order to achieve this goal, the Yaqui had to be quelled. Fighting with the Yaqui Indians had raged on and off for centuries, but time and again, they had proven as resilient as the cactus plants that thrived in the desert.

"This is suicide," Enrique muttered to Sergeant Cruz, his right hand man.

Sergeant Cruz was a squat dark-skinned man with a bushy, drooping moustache and a potbelly. He reminded Enrique of Pancho Villa, the northern border bandit who was rising in popularity among the people, displeased with the government's foreign compliance as well as the widespread poverty, and the widening gulf between the rich and the poor.

Sergeant Cruz was twenty years older than Enrique. He had seen many more battles, but he respected Enrique's benevolence and his obvious preference for building rather than destroying. Because of this affinity, he had passed up Enrique's commendations to head his own unit on four different occasions, choosing instead to remain at Enrique's side.

"What is suicide?" he asked, shifting back and forth uncomfortably in his worn boots. He was not accustomed to being summoned in the middle of the night into the captain's tent.

"They want us to wipe out the Yaqui altogether," Enrique motioned for the sergeant to sit at the small table across from him. In the middle of the table sat a crude chess set carved from wood. Enrique always carried it with him. It was a gift from Anita who, despite his protests, portrayed him as a great strategist to their children. He never played, but he found it strangely comforting to stare at the pieces and move them around into different formations, imagining how a game might unfold.

Enrique rarely drank, but it seemed apropos. Silently, he poured two small tin cups of tequila in the flickering light.

After a healthy sip, the two men stared at each other resolutely across the idle chessboard.

"It's been attempted before," Sergeant Cruz stated plainly. "Back in '68, the army set fire to a church where hundreds of

Yaqui had been locked up for the night. More than a hundred and fifty were burned alive. Of course, that was before my time. Just a few years ago, I think it was in January of 1900, nearly a thousand were massacred at Mazocoba in the Bacatete Mountains. Each time we lost quite a few men, and the Yaqui, they never give up. It's not in their blood to quit."

Enrique listened, picturing families of Yaqui Indians burning alive within the confines of their small village church. Had they been tricked in there, and then been barricaded behind the cold funereal stone? He knew them to be a religious people that had blended their own mythology with that of the Catholic Church, introduced by the same Jesuits who had taught him. Perhaps there had been a call for a prayer vigil and then...

"What if we talk them into leaving?" He shuffled some pieces around on the board

"Trick or talk?" The sergeant smiled, flashing broken teeth.

Enrique separated all of the dark brown pieces into one corner before looking Sergeant Cruz straight in the eyes. "You know how I feel about trickery. It's no way to build a lasting solution."

"Yes, you're right about that," The sergeant took another gulp of his tequila, savoring the burn in his throat.

"I hear there is a need for workers down in the plantations in the Yucatán and Oaxaca," Enrique continued. "What if we offered to move them there and get them jobs?"

Sergeant Cruz removed his broad sombrero, which he wore out of habit even after sundown, and scratched his head. "*Híjole, capitán.* How are we going to do that? We're not *políticos*. We're *guerreros*."

"What's a politician, but a warrior whose weapons are words?" Enrique realigned the chess pieces into their original spots.

The next day, Enrique sent a telegram to his commander, requesting a month to organize the mass exodus of Yaqui in collaboration with the railway companies.

"If that doesn't work," his telegram read, "then I will need more troops, about five thousand."

The army would be short on men; it would take at least a month to gather that many, so Enrique expected that his superiors would see no harm in giving him the time to build a diplomatic solution. Besides, if they could avoid redeploying troops from the more sensitive urban areas, this arrangement might be seen as a watershed victory by General Díaz.

After receiving approval on his plan, Enrique worked tirelessly, galloping over the arid desert lands from one Yaqui village to another. He traveled with a small contingent of his most trusted men, minus the sergeant, who stayed behind to manage Enrique's unit of five hundred soldiers. With every Yaqui chief he met, Enrique's hopes grew: perhaps he could save their families from suffering. He watched the Yaqui men interact with their wives and children and, to him, they seemed different only in appearance and dress from other families he'd encountered throughout the country. He found them strangely…human. In fact, being around the Yaqui families, huddled in their small villages, irrigating small patches of land to grow their crops, he found himself missing his own wife and daughters more than ever. He hoped that maybe, if he could pull this off, he'd receive another promotion and finally be able to settle down in one of the big cities, where he could go home at the end of each work day to Anita's embrace and the laughter of little Magdalena and Esperanza.

He spurred himself on with more fervor than he did his steed. After three weeks, he convinced all but one of the important Yaqui chiefs to gather their remote settlements and prepare for directions to move their people towards the railroad tracks in order to board trains upon his notice. He assured them they would move towards the promise of peace and prosperity in the south of Mexico, to more fertile lands and hospitable climates.

"I'm becoming more of a salesman than a military man," Enrique smiled at Sergeant Cruz over a celebratory tequila back at their camp. "I only have one more call to make before I can close the deal completely."

"How are you so sure when they get down south, they'll be fine?" the sergeant inquired, swirling his tequila around in his tin cup.

"The railway investors have guaranteed me," Enrique replied confidently, his eyes dancing exuberantly. "They have camps and jobs ready for them down there."

But the final Yaqui chief's approval was perhaps the most difficult one to attain, and many of the other agreements hinged on his assent. His name was Stone of Silver, one of the eldest and most respected of all Yaqui chiefs. Enrique knew his delicate house of cards would come tumbling down if he could not secure the legendary chief's support. So he loaded two pack mules with tequila, cured Jamón Serrano, and other pickled delicacies imported from Spain, in the hopes that these exotic gifts would soften the ground for his critical diplomatic overture. He even accepted two bilingual Yaqui guides from one of the villages, so that his entourage could better understand the chief's needs and gain his trust. Finally, at the suggestion of the Yaqui guides, he allowed them to bring a young Yaqui orphan girl along as part of the package of gifts. According to the guide, it was an honor in their culture to be given the opportunity to rescue such a child from the horrors of a life without the protection of a parent. And for the Yaqui chief, additions to his family would only serve to burnish his prestige.

Stopping to make camp on a barren rocky plateau, Enrique and his men gathered around a fire prepared by the guides while the temperatures plummeted in the ink of night.

In the light of the dancing flames, Enrique watched how the deep black eyes of the Yaqui glowed like coals. Their russet skin reflected the fire softly, rendering the broad planes of their smooth faces into sculpted masks of baked clay. One of the Indians was tall and gaunt, another short and squat, neither more than twenty years old. The young girl must have been about Magdalena's age, eight years old at the most, Enrique thought. And he felt good about finding her a home. Finally, he was doing something that felt satisfying. He was building something, perhaps not with metal beams and wooden supports, but rather with people and commitments. Instead of raising walls, he was tearing them down and placing something infinitely more beautiful and meaningful in their place. Enrique wondered if this was how the Jesuits felt when they accomplished their goals. Maybe they did have a divine destiny after all. Maybe so did he.

He asked the shortest guide, who was the most talkative of the two, what the young girl's name was, to which he responded: "Bo'obicha."

"What does it mean, 'Bo...obicha'?" Enrique repeated haltingly.

"It means...how do you say it...*esperanza*," the guide replied.

"*Esperanza*," Enrique whispered, as if it were the first time he had heard of it. The concept of "hope" was a notion as rare as a spring of water in the midst of the Sonoran Desert. But it was shock that drove his response not a lack of familiarity with the concept.

"You look like you've seen a spirit," the Yaqui Indian said.

"No, I am simply surprised," Enrique said. "I know someone with the same name back where I live."

Enrique knew better than to reveal any hint of what he had to lose, or to live for, to anyone in the field but his closest confidant, Sergeant Cruz. Yet he was moved by the fact that the young girl shared his own daughter's name, at least in meaning. He had never believed in signs, and he found it quite odd that he would have to make a journey into the desert to find signs of faith, but surely, this had to be more than a coincidence. The idea that he was meant to save this young girl took root in his heart.

The Yaqui guide stirred the fire with a long stick and smiled sourly back through the dancing sparks that flew between them. "Hope is something that lives in both our worlds, captain."

Enrique couldn't help but wonder what hidden meaning lay beneath the guide's words. Certainly, the hopes of their peoples were at constant odds. Was it destiny that in order for the hope of one culture to prevail, the hopes of the other would have to be crushed? Or could that gap somehow be bridged? Could both hopes survive? Could a common ground be built? That night Enrique tossed and turned in his tent, the questions haunting him. He wished for the answer to be affirmative, for his entire scheme of peacefully removing the Yaqui from their territory depended on it.

The next day, as their horses neared the Yaqui village of the great chief, Enrique instructed one of his fastest horsemen to stay behind in a small oasis, beneath a cluster of soaring saguaro cactus trees.

"Stay here," Enrique instructed the young soldier. "If we are not back by the middle of the night, ride back to the encampment and bring reinforcements."

The Yaqui village was a cluster of adobe huts at the crest of a brush-covered hill It was a highly defensible position, Enrique noted as they approached across the scorching desert, travelling at a respectfully slow pace. The two Yaqui guides rode in the front, with Enrique directly between them several horse lengths back. The other five men followed with the two mules and the girl bringing up the rear.

Only then did it dawn on Enrique exactly how outlandish his scheme was. He was entering the village of one of the most obstinate Yaqui chiefs, to face several hundred fierce warriors with a small contingent that was one-third Yaqui itself.

"What was I thinking?" he muttered beneath his breath as their horses climbed up the hill, following a well-worn path through the waist-high brush and cactus. What if the Yaqui chief simply killed them all, without warning? Surely the network of alliances that Enrique had carefully crafted, the trust he had gained of the Yaqui chief's friends and relatives in other villages, would grant him a measure of protection. He could feel his pulse quicken as Yaqui scouts yelped out from positions high above them.

"Tell them we mean no harm," Enrique quickly urged the guides, who in turn called back sharply to the guards.

As the party reached the top of the hill, the two guards surveyed Enrique suspiciously, keeping their distance. The guides exchanged a few sparse phrases with the guards, who appeared to ease and escorted the group to a small clearing in the middle of the village. As the captain's horse paraded past the tiny adobe huts, children gathered around him, staring up in a mixture of fear and awe.

The guards came to a stop before an assemblage of elders who stood on a small rocky ledge elevated a few feet above the ground by boulders. Enrique surmised that this might be a stage for their ceremonial dances or an altar for religious ceremonies. He knew the Yaqui practiced a fascinating blend of their own ancient mythology and the Catholic religion brought to them by the Jesuits centuries before. However, today it might just as easily serve as a sacrificial site for six "Federal" soldiers.

Enrique stroked his moustache lightly as he surveyed the group of nearly two dozen elders standing before him. At the center was a broad-shouldered man in a dark cloak, with a dark face sculpted from onyx. Crowned with a long silver mane, he wore a necklace of oversized pearls and carried a long wooden staff in his weathered hands. Enrique could easily surmise he was either the leader or the high priest, or both. Usually the Yaqui were not so dark-skinned, but clearly this man was not one to hide in the shade.

When the silver-haired man spoke, every Yaqui in the village seemed to hang intently on each of his words. He spoke sparingly and haltingly, and then nodded to the guides, allowing them to translate.

"He is Stone of Silver," the shorter guide translated nervously. "I have heard of him. He is much feared," he editorialized. "He welcomes you to his village and asks what business brings you here."

"Tell him I have brought him gifts and come with a message of peace," Enrique replied fluidly, his blue eyes unwavering as they aimed to penetrate Stone of Silver's dark visage.

Enrique listened carefully to the tone of the guide's translation to ensure he was capturing the spirit of his message. He could hear the fear in the tenor of the guide's voice and saw tiny droplets of perspiration beading on his forehead. He could only hope that his own perfectly upright stance and steady gaze would convey to the chief that he was not a man filled with fear but, rather, one worthy of the leader's respect and ear.

Again the chief spoke and the guide translated, "'Let him present his gifts,' Stone of Silver says."

Parting for the captain, the group of elders watched as Enrique's men unloaded the mules, their eyes settling curiously on the young girl sitting atop the one in the back.

Enrique did not dismount, but maintained his gaze on the chief as his lieutenants displayed on the boulder the bounty they had hauled over the desert: hunks of cured ham, jars of pickled delicacies and bottles of tequila were laid out before the crowd. Enrique felt a hidden shame that this material bounty seemed pitiful compared with the request he came to make. But still his eyes did not waver from their target. And neither did the chief's. Perhaps the girl, Bo'obicha, would provide a sliver of her namesake to his fortunes in this bold endeavor. At last, when the guides helped her down from the mule and presented her with a scant few murmured words, the lead guide's voice now quivering in anticipation of the chief's response, the chief's eyes finally broke away from the captain's.

Stone of Silver's voice softened as he issued a gentle stream of words in the direction of the girl. Enrique watched as her eyes searched the sand beneath her feet, either for answers or for a stone beneath which to hide. Enrique could not decipher the exchange, so he looked to the guides, who shifted nervously back and forth on the balls of their feet, as if the ground was growing way too hot for them to stand upon in their tattered moccasins.

The shorter guide looked towards Enrique but failed to meet his eyes. "Stone of Silver thanks you for your tribute and accepts it. His guards will escort you to a house he keeps for guests such as yourselves. And tonight he will dine with you to listen to your business."

Enrique heard his contingent of soldiers exhale collectively in relief. The guides exchanged a nervous smile. And Enrique nodded slightly in deference and gratitude to the chief, as he and his men were led to a large adobe hut bordering the clearing. The hut was simple but ample enough for them to sleep on the burlap sacks, which were neatly stacked in the corner. He did not intend to stay past dinner, for his sentry would be waiting back at the oasis. Enrique and his men drank water heartily and cleaned up as best they could. Outside the hut, Enrique noticed a bustle of activity and preparations for the dinner. This seemed to be going better than he had expected. Flowers were strewn about in decoration. How the Yaqui could produce flowers within this vast desert was beyond his comprehension. Yet, in his experience, the arid terrain yielded more than met the eye.

As they waited for the sun to set, Enrique directed his men to take a siesta so they would be fresh for the night's ride back through the desert. He himself straddled the only chair in the hut and sat in the doorway, observing the preparations outside studiously, stroking his moustache as he watched.

Dusk settling, torches punctuated the circumference of the clearing in the center of the village. Flowers dangled from poles high above the rocky altar. Their guides and the two guards that had first greeted them brought Enrique and his men out to a row of chairs at the foot of the stage to view a series of dances such as Enrique had never witnessed before. Then an elder was introduced as the "*pascola.*"

Speaking in broken Spanish, Chief Stone of Silver himself explained to his guests of honor: "The *pascola* will perform for you our most treasured dance of the deer."

For a man easily twice his age, the dancer astonished Enrique with his fluidity and energy. It was captivating to watch the *pascola* emulate the grace and power of the deer, a most sought-after and cherished prey for the Yaqui. He wore strings of seashells around his ankles and calves, shaking rhythmically with his disciplined footwork. In his hands, he shook two large maracas in cadence to his footsteps. A kilt-like piece of fabric covered his groin area. But the most unique feature of his costume was a white turban wrapped around his head and crowned by the mounted head of a young deer, horns and all. The village chanted in unison with the beat of the tribal drums and the chords of roughly hewn flutes. Enrique fought back the urge to tap his foot as if he were listening to one of the marching bands that had blared dissonantly back at the military academy during his training days.

After the dance concluded, the crowd broke into merriment, eating and drinking. Young Yaqui women served Enrique and his men samplings of the very bounty they had brought earlier in the day, along with other Yaqui specialties. Chief Stone of Silver sat across from Enrique and at last spoke to him in Spanish, "So, *capitan*, what can I do for you on this special evening?"

Curious at the level of festivity, Enrique raised an eyebrow slowly, "Well to begin with, chief, I would appreciate it if you would enlighten me on the nature of this lovely night we are so fortunate to share with you, for I doubt that it is merely my presence which you celebrate."

Stone of Silver smiled wanly, "Yes. Well, young *capitan*, I am honored to have the official presence of one of the general's finest thinkers at my wedding."

"Your wedding!" Enrique struggled to shrug off the surprise. Why had the guides not informed him? It seemed like a critical detail for them to have simply forgotten to mention. His eyes searched for the two Yaqui scouts who had brought him here. But they were nowhere in sight. His pulse quickened at once.

"Yes," Stone of Silver confirmed. "It is thanks to you that I have a lovely new bride to add to my family." His arm glided out as smoothly as the deer's motions that had so mesmerized the audience, pointing straight at Bo'obicha, who stood amidst a flock of women that included a raven-haired dark-skinned princess of about fifteen and a blind matron with wiry silver hair, who looked about sixty-five. Bo'obicha was clad in a simple white frock embroidered with bright pink flowers across the chest, and her hair had been brushed, rendering her a vision of innocent beauty beneath the flickering torchlight.

Enrique's eyes widened in horror. At once he realized he had been tricked by the guides, not only in bringing the girl, but also in who the girl was and why she had truly been brought here. Recalling the chess moves he played against unseen opponents in the solitude of his tent, night after night, Enrique guessed at the meaning of the chief's words even as he spoke them in his native tongue, without the help of his "translators," who now appeared comfortably at his sides. As the chief spoke, the tall, lanky guide—who had never talked before in Enrique's presence—at last translated smugly the words of the chief:

"Do not be surprised, my young friend. News of the alliances you have brokered for your general's benefit reached me even before you completed the truce in the first village you visited. Remember how long that one took? But then it got easier as you went along. I have been with you, guiding the responses to your moves like an unseen spirit every step of the way. At the last village, where my loyal spies convinced you to offer this young girl a home, you aided me unwittingly in attaining a treasure I have long sought. For you see, five years ago I defeated her father, my blood-sworn enemy in battle. I had loved his wife once but he stole her from me. Now I steal back from his own blood. And at last you will serve me as a messenger to your general."

At this point, Stone of Silver switched into Spanish and brushed his translators aside, stepping forward with his ornately carved staff in his hand, his silver hair flowing in the moonlight. Resolutely, he used the tip of the staff to sketch a line in the sand between himself and Enrique's tightly positioned crew of men.

"Tell him this land is *Hiakim*, the ancient ground of my people. And just as my direct ancestor drew a holy dividing line in the sand the Spaniards were never able to cross, I now draw that line again. Our people will never willingly go with you. We will not abandon our deserts and our valleys, our pueblos and our rivers. Your alliances are an illusion allowed to you by my hand. It is as if you had smoked our legendary peyote and seen a vision of what could be, only to watch it sift through your hands like sand in the desert wind."

Enrique's eyes landed on Bo'ochiba, who seemed incapable of understanding the betrayal at hand—the fact she was now possessed by her father's killer, thanks to his unwitting complicity. He now realized that the chief had played him thoroughly, buying precious time to prepare his own plans throughout the Yaqui pueblos, to fight the oncoming war that would be waged to meet the needs of the investors.

Then Enrique heard a breathless whisper: "They stole our weapons."

It was his lieutenant. Enrique did not flinch. But how, when? He mentally retraced his moves during the afternoon's long wait. Only once, while the men had slept, had his position wavered, when he made the long trip to the outhouse at the fringe of the settlement reserved for guests with European preferences. It must have been then, Enrique mused, his chapped lips almost breaking into a painful smile at the chief's meticulous plan. He wondered in which way the chief would choose to kill them. And whether he would send the captain back in pieces to Chihuahua with the message pinned on the remnants of his uniform as a gift back to the *Federales*.

"I can see you are wondering if I am going to kill you, *capitan*," Stone of Silver assessed. "But no, that would be too easy and I would not enjoy the benefit of you personally informing your superior of the strength of my people's ways and the weakness of your own. I hear many call you the 'colonel' throughout this land even though you have not earned that distinction. I suspect they will now more likely call you a fool."

Enrique's former guides snickered but were quickly silenced by the chief's piercing glare.

"Hang his men," Stone of Silver commanded sharply, motioning to his own soldiers, who quickly overwhelmed the defenseless *Federales*. Enrique stood motionless in the center of the tumult, his eyes now staring down at the line in the sand. He felt like a castrated bull. Impotent. Suicide crossed his mind. Perhaps if Stone of Silver sent him out into the desert, he could simply take his own life with his pistol. But then he thought of Anita, Magdalena and his own Esperanza, hope. His eyes flickered to Bo'obicha, whose hair was lightly stroked and admired by the chief's older wives. The little girl seemed completely unaware of the violation that was soon to take place.

Enrique tasted bile in his throat and a foreign stinging in his eyes.

"Your eyes melt, young *capitan*," Stone of Silver ascertained. "Imagine how many tears your people have caused to be spilled on my land with your hostilities and your impunity and your thirst for conquest. If they were drops of blood from Jesus himself, these lands would be covered in flowers rather than thorns."

Enrique grimaced as he heard the cracking of necks in the background and the cheering of the bloodthirsty throng gathered around the hanging trees, soaring saguaro cacti reaching into the starry sky.

"Go. Run. Tell the others what you have learned, and who they must face. Fly like a hawk…but never, my young friend, never cross this line," the chief's eyes followed Enrique's to the line he had inscribed upon the sand. "Meet me here. Fight me. Claw at my soul with your very last breath as we stand at that line, but I vow to you, as long as I live and as long as my children's hearts beat, you will not cross it. You will not blur it. You will not make it disappear."

Enrique looked straight into the chief's black eyes, swirling with a laughter all their own, like deep black wells taunting him to dive in and try to survive. Then he met the young girl's eyes. She smiled at him shyly and looked down at her pretty new sandals. And then he slowly backed away. One of the guards who had met them upon their arrival brought him his horse.

Silently, slowly, Enrique straightened his uniform jacket, dusted it off, and mounted his horse. Sullenly, he rode down the hillside.

He could hear cackles of unrestrained laughter and jubilant celebration as he retreated east, to the base of the hill. Every few minutes, Enrique would pause and listen for followers, but there was no one. Surely, they would not think him so stupid or bold as to return. Whispering to himself, Enrique calmed his nerves and his swelling rage by spouting a series of numbers that would have seemed like gibberish to anyone eavesdropping. After heading into the deep brush, following the path back to the oasis, Enrique dismounted and led his horse off the path slightly, tying it to a solid saguaro. He surveyed the stars to confirm his bearings. Then he circled back through the thick and prickly brush towards the hill, ascending on the southern flank. Counting still, beneath his breath, he climbed with deft precision, not minding the gashes that sliced across his hands and fingers. The pain calmed him, providing an outlet for his anger. He had heard the stories of the Yaqui wedding tradition, just as he had also heard the tales of the deer dance. If his understanding of the former was as accurate as it had been with regards to the latter, then he had about two hours to sneak back into the village and infiltrate Chief Stone of Silver's family home. He would wait for the chief and his young bride to be escorted to his bedroom, to consummate the unholy marriage. Before that, the dancers would play the roles of bride and groom, in the center of the village. Then, the family of the bride, in this case, perhaps played by the brood of affectionate wives, would bring a basket of food and gifts to the patio of the groom's home. Then the young wife would be shown the areas she would sweep, where she would wash clothes and grind corn with the *metate*. And, at long last, Stone of Silver and Bo'obicha would be walked to the door of his private chamber and left alone.

During his hours of watching the activities in the village that afternoon, Enrique had discerned who lived where, how many warriors there were, what kinds of weapons they possessed, and, most importantly, where the chief resided. The last of these facts had not been difficult to ascertain: it was the largest home, as he had the largest family.

Enrique emerged from the brush behind an adobe structure used for grain storage. He withdrew a gleaming silver dagger with a gold handle from a hidden pocket in his khaki field jacket. Small, yes, but quietly effective. The desert night sky shed ample light on the village, and the flames from the torches still danced in the clearing. Enrique worked his way to the back of the chief's house, managing to avoid any human contact, as most of the villagers were still involved in the rituals. From behind the corner of the building, he spied the throng parading slowly towards the house. A *pascola* bearing a flamboyant pink scarf represented the bride, as the wives and bride trailed behind, giggling. The musicians accompanied them, wearing white scarves. He glimpsed the back of the chief's flowing black robe and silver mane as he waited patiently in his patio near a stone cross rising from the ground.

As Enrique crept towards a high window in the back wall, he heard footsteps approaching from the other corner. Quickly, he backed up around the corner and waited. As the sentry walked nearer, Enrique clutched his dagger so tightly his knuckles glowed a skeletal white in the moonlight. As the guard was about to turn the corner, Enrique pounced. Having judged the man's stature by the weight of his steps and the length of his gait, he knew exactly where to place the blade in order to swiftly slice his neck. His hand clamped over the guard's mouth to muffle his dying cry as the body crumpled in a geyser of blood upon the sand. Enrique looked down at the mask of shock on his victim's face. It was the short, stout guide that had betrayed him.

"Serves you right, you infidel," Enrique muttered, spitting on the dead Yaqui, then stepping on him to reach up to the window overhead. Blood spurted with the increased pressure, spraying his dusty khaki pants and boots. Grabbing the edge of the window with his bare hands, Enrique lifted himself up and wriggled through the opening.

Inside, the house was cool, dark and musty. An alien fragrance permeated the air. Perhaps it was the incense, a blend of the peyote the Yaqui chiefs favored, the flowers and spices they so adored. It was not a comforting smell for Enrique, but it was not unpleasant. It merely served to remind Enrique that he was a trespasser, destined to die if discovered.

Moving stealthily, he found the chief's sleeping chamber. There was a large bed made of roughly carved posts, fresh flowers adorning a colorful serape draped over the mattress. Candles flickered in the breeze from an open window. Peering outside, he could tell the window would give him a quick exit into a side alley, from where he could dart back into the brush for his escape.

He envisioned that flight clearly in his mind, sliding beneath the bed frame with ease. He inhaled deeply to slow his heart. And he waited.

After what seemed like an eternity, he heard cheering and clapping outside, then footsteps and the clicking shut of the door. They were in the room.

Stone of Silver spoke in a dark, gravelly voice, giving directions. Enrique watched the young girl's white frock fall to the cold stone floor, inches from where he was laying in wait. Then the bed creaked as she crawled backwards onto it, her breath agitated and fearful.

Enrique could not understand her feeble words, but to him they sounded like meek pleas for mercy. The dream celebration was transforming into a nightmare. The petals scattered onto the floor as the chief crawled onto the bed, the frame buckling slightly under his weight. Bo'obicha whimpered as he reached out to touch her, his calloused hands surely like sandpaper against her tender skin.

In a move so fluid he might have learned it from the deer dancer, Enrique swooped up from under the bed and found himself astride the chief's back, smashing the blade of his still bloody dagger deep into the hulking man's jugular.

With his other hand, Enrique covered the young girl's mouth to prevent her from screaming and alerting the guards. The family was still celebrating in the front patio around the flower-strewn cross. Stone of Silver reared back like a stunned stallion, his eyes round with terror, a gasping, gurgling, guttural sound escaping slowly from his throat, as blood bubbled out of his mouth onto his lips and chin.

Enrique looked him in the eyes for a moment and sneered, "How is that for crossing the line?"

He tossed the chief aside, and slung the naked girl over his shoulder as he leapt through the window. Barely breathing, he took long strides at a gallop. He could feel Bo'obicha's hot breath against his cheek, her heart pounding at his shoulder as he neared the brush. And then a simple sound stopped him. It was a sweet, discrete zing, a hiss of air and a gentle thud. The girl gasped in pain, her nails clawing into his arms. Flanked by saguaros that arched on either side, Enrique turned. Standing at the bedroom window was Stone of Silver, his bow steady in his hand, Enrique's dagger still firmly planted beneath his chin, his eyes glowering, and his jaw set defiantly. For a moment, their eyes met and the line disappeared entirely. Then the chief crumpled to the floor. Enrique vanished into the forest, dashing through the cactus in search of a small clearing where he might examine the girl's wound. Finding one, he ripped his jacket off and spread it on the ground. Atop it, he gently placed Bo'obicha on her side. She was so small; he was able to wrap her in it like a tiny taco, working the fabric around the arrow stuck in her spine.

"Don't worry, little Bo'obicha, little *Esperanzita*, you'll be fine," Enrique whispered, clasping the arrow and then letting it go, unsure which course of action might spare her the most pain.

The little girl smiled feebly up at him, her black eyes reflecting the cool starlight, her lips a bluish purple, her skin ashen as the life faded from her.

"*Gracias*," she said. "My *papá* will be proud. You did him a favor. You saved my honor."

Enrique wondered how many lines could be crossed, erased and redrawn out here in the brush-mottled sands of the Sonoran Desert, a monotonous chessboard of some demon's cruel imagination.

He held her quietly, and did not resist the sobs that welled up inside and shook his body. He had not cried for his mother. He had not shed a tear for any of his men. But here, in the desert, beneath the moon, with this empty shell of a Yaqui girl clasped in his trembling arms, he wept inconsolably. He felt at one with her, dead with her, stone like her, and he rebelled at the knowledge that somehow he breathed on.

After the tide of his emotions subsided, he pulled the arrow free and carried her back to his horse, counting his steps and steering by the stars. As he placed her delicately behind the saddle and tied her to the horse, he remembered how he'd felt as a child, that morning at the beach, when he'd found no trace of his glorious sandcastle with all of its fortifications and ditches and drainage canals. As he mounted his steed and spurred it on over the desert at lightning speed, he realized that he was that sandcastle. The chief's line drawn with the staff was that sandcastle. His dream of building a peaceful alliance with the Yaqui for their relocation was that sandcastle. And it was all being washed away by a tide he simply could not control.

After several days of meandering in the desert, Enrique realized he was hopelessly lost. It was unlike him, as he was a good navigator and knew the stars, as well as the Indian trails. But he was staying off the trails to avoid capture, given the events at the last Yaqui village. He figured his only hope might be that, by now, the sentry had alerted Sergeant Cruz of the failed mission and his henchman would have sent out search parties. When he realized that buzzards were beginning to follow him due to the presence of his cargo, he decided to make a straight line for the coast and bury her at sea. Surely he could travel west until he hit the Gulf of California. A couple of days later, he set the girl off on a crudely made raft into the waters. Then he turned around. If he headed east he would eventually find some semblance of civilization, or die trying. He lost track of the days, running out of food and water. Attacked by a small party of Yaqui travelers, he managed to kill all three with his sword and pistol. He mused that they must have been the worst Yaqui fighters ever, as he doubted that he was ever in his right mind any more. And only after he ate their food, drank their water and rode away, did he wonder what precise seed of darkness had blossomed from him into the uncharacteristic act of malice he'd committed by stringing them up on saguaro trees at the side of the road for all who might pass by to see. Then, a day later, dying of thirst and wandering yet again, he marveled at the lack of dignity in his base human instincts when he found himself circling back to their decaying corpses still swinging from the trees, eyes pecked out by vultures, in order to drink from the pools of their bodily fluids collected on the gravelly ground beneath their feet. But somehow in those puddles he found the strength to carry on another day. And it was just enough for Sergeant Cruz to find him, lying next to his dead horse, still one day's full ride from the nearest town.

The colonel awoke in a cot at the fort in the coastal town of Guaymas, in Sonora. He heard the waves crashing against the rocks outside his window and the incessant lament of the seagulls.

"*Mamá*?" he asked, rubbing his eyes. "Did the tide come in?"

"No, colonel," he heard a gruff but familiar voice respond. "But your orders have."

The colonel snapped straight up from his repose, his vision focusing on Sergeant Cruz at last.

"Jesus Christ, I thought I'd died and gone to heaven," the colonel exhaled.

"Well hopefully I won't be the first one you see when you get there, sir," The sergeant flashed his wry but comforting broken-tooth grin. "But before you chart a course for the afterlife, I've heard via telegram that your wife and daughters are eager to see you first…alive and well, preferably."

"How long since we last saw each other?" the colonel asked.

"Oh, I'd say a little over a month," the sergeant answered, sitting down on a rustic stool next to the bed and handing Enrique a newspaper. "You're a hero."

"Far from it," Enrique muttered, opening the paper.

The bold headline read: "*¡Ataque contra el Yaqui!*" Beneath that, in large type, "Colonel Shulz slays legendary Yaqui chief, hangs traitors in the streets, and arranges largest deportation in history."

"What?" Enrique winced, feeling a stab in his rib cage.

"Don't move too much," the sergeant urged. "The buzzards took a piece of you there."

Enrique noticed the bandages wrapped around his torso for the first time.

"Like I said, you're a hero," the sergeant smiled. "You've been promoted. You're a colonel for real now."

"Rumors of my heroism are greatly exaggerated," Enrique retorted. "But I'll live with them if it means I'll finally get to go home and be stationed near the family. You can come with me. We can use a break. Our job out here is done!" Enrique's eyes flickered with new life, nourished by the prospect of afternoons with his daughters underfoot and Anita by his side, sipping lemonade and taking lazy siestas in the courtyard beneath the shade of the avocado trees.

"Quite the contrary, colonel," Sergeant Cruz shook his head. "Our orders came in. We've been assigned the five thousand men you requested, and we're to quell the rebellions. Many of the Yaqui don't want to go and the governor insists we must continue."

Enrique slumped back onto his cot, his eyes scanning the cracked stucco ceiling for some sort of meaningful pattern.

"Colonel, the war is on! *Ándele. Ánimo*," the sergeant implored.

"I thought we won the war," Enrique bleakly replied as he ruefully lay down the sensationalist newspaper.

"Oh, colonel, come on. This is México. The war never ends," the sergeant chuckled, shaking his head. Then he pulled a cigar from his pocket and followed a pretty, white-cloaked nurse out into the corridor. "I'll be back. You rest, colonel. You have many more men to lead now. And most of them were recruited from prisons, so we'll need your leadership more than ever."

Enrique listened to the sergeant flirt with the comely nurse out in the hallway, the pungent smoke from his cigar curling its way back to him and out the window in the breeze over the bay.

Exhausted but determined, he rose from the cot, washed up and donned his crisp, starched white uniform, adorned with new medals. He pulled on his black riding boots and tied his sword and scabbard to his belt. Pulling on his cap, he stared at his likeness in a cracked mirror next to the door. He met his own blue eyes but failed to recognize himself even though his face was hardly changed: the angular features, the hawk-like nose, the strong jaw he flexed as he gritted his teeth and stepped out into the passageway. Towering over the couple in the hall, he yanked the sergeant's second cigar from his mouth and ground it out under the heel of his boot.

Flustered, the young nurse let go of the sergeant's hand and dropped a roll of bandages on the floor.

"Por favor," Colonel Enrique Shulz derided his underling. "She's a nun, for Christ's sake!"

The nun blushed, her cheeks burning a deep shade of crimson.

"But, colonel, in love and war, anything goes, no?" The sergeant appealed.

The colonel paced methodically to the door at the end of the hallway and threw it open, glancing back momentarily. "You're right, my friend. Take your time. Our ingloriousness can wait."

Then he marched out into the sun as the door flapped shut behind him in the stiff Gulf breeze.

***

For years, Enrique chased the Yaqui throughout the Sonoran Desert, and up and down the western coastline. Never again did he make the mistake of opening his heart to one of them. Instead, whenever he could, he would find a way to make it back to Chihuahua to see his beloved girls, who grew up faster than he could keep pace with. During those years, close to fifteen thousand Yaqui prisoners of war were captured and sold as slaves to toil in the haciendas of southern Mexico. Most of them perished quickly because of the steamy climate and cruel working conditions. Thousands more went into hiding, sometimes with the help of Sonoran employers opposed to General Díaz's policy of genocide. Others escaped to Arizona and established new settlements there, where their cheap labor was in demand among cotton farmers and the railway companies.

Then the Revolution broke out. Chaos ensued as numerous groups attempted to redistribute land, wealth and power from the old elite to the impoverished masses. As the challenges in the cities became greater than those in the desert, Enrique was posted to command the fort in Chihuahua. He savored the rewards of a job in which he could finally enjoy family life. During the first week of his new assignment, however, Enrique was captured in a raid by Pancho Villa. He was held hostage for an entire year, during which he joined the cause. Criss-crossing the border with Villa, meeting the rightfully-elected President Francisco Madero in exile in San Antonio, witnessing the shiny promise of industrializing America, Enrique helped to defeat the very *"Federales"* he had once led against the Yaqui.

After a year, General Villa allowed him to visit his family whenever their troop was in the city of Chihuahua. Enrique recruited Cruz as his sergeant again, and fought wherever Villa sent him. The reasons no longer seemed to matter. Each day was a new battle; all he cared about in those days was winning the battle within himself, to simply keep marching.

Often, he was thankful to no longer be in the business of hunting the Yaqui. Enough was enough. When the Revolution wound down and Villa's men disbanded, Pancho saw to it that the colonel went on his way with a large chest filled with Mexican gold coins and American dollars. Enrique took his family and settled in Matamoros, Mexico, along the border with Brownsville, Texas. Undeterred by his many failures, he focused on his final quest to build an enduring monument.

One morning, soon after their new house was organized, he proudly declared at the breakfast table to Anita, Magdalena, and Esperanza, "I'm going to build a bridge to the other side of the border, to Texas."

"But why? You finally have a chance to relax and spend some time with us at home!" Anita cried, pushing towards him a plate of pan *dulce* and a pot of coffee.

"*Sí!*" cried his girls in unison. "*Por favor, Papá!* Don't leave us again!"

"I won't leave!" He stated emphatically. "I'm going to build it right here in Matamoros!"

"But we have the ferry," Anita protested. "Besides what do you have left to prove? You're a decorated hero of the Revolution."

"Hero…" the Colonel shook his head thinking back to Bo'obicha. A real hero would have saved her. "No. I have to do this. I remember when I was a child. My mother would take me to the beach. I would look out at where the Rio pours out into the ocean and I would dream of building a bridge that could span it and stand the tests of the elements. I have to build something to prove to myself that the human spirit can triumph in this world, over nature, over the forces of the unseen."

"Unseen?" Magdalena and Esperanza looked at each other, confused. Their father had always been a virtual stranger to them, absent for months at a time. They had given up on trying to understand him years ago. But was their father losing his mind?

Anita simply shook her head in consternation. For nearly twenty years, she'd been married to a man who came and went with the thundering hooves of the cavalry and cries of war in the streets. Nothing surprised her about him. Perhaps she would be more at peace if he did disappear into a new campaign of his own making. At least, it would not be nearly as dangerous.

Even though the colonel had exchanged his military uniform for an elegantly cut European suit and tie, and traded in his horse for a Model T, the townspeople still referred to him as "the colonel." With his reputation for honesty and intelligence, his connections in the government, his seed money, and his relationships with the American railway companies, in a matter of a few months the colonel formed a consortium to build the first railroad bridge over the Rio Grande in the Tamaulipas region.

Sergeant Cruz eagerly rejoined him as the foreman of his builders. The crews worked day and night, and American engineers from the railway companies came to assist.

One evening, as Enrique and his family ate dinner in their modest home off the plaza, Anita cleared her throat and declared: "Enrique, the girls have some...exciting...news." She forced a smile.

Enrique looked at her blankly. His mind had been pondering a challenging detail of his new bridge. Anita always looked undeniably beautiful when she laughed or smiled. Age had treated her well, and she had matured into a graceful *café-con-leche* beauty, with barely a wrinkle and only a handful of silver streaks through her long raven locks, which she typically wore pulled back in a tight bun. But when her smile was false, crow's feet materialized like telltale signs. And she reminded him of the cadavers he'd so often encountered during the Revolution, frozen in fear and anguish yet oddly simulating a sickly smile.

He put down his fork and turned expectantly to face the two girls, who were now eighteen and seventeen years old. Magdalena was of medium stature, thin and lovely with grey eyes, olive skin and dark hair. Younger Esperanza had always been the mischievous foil to Magdalena's serious mother hen; she was shorter and more curvaceous, tending to fill whatever room she entered with her ebullient laughter and sparkling blue eyes. Her skin was a bit darker, but it was as if in balance between shadow and light, her genes had compensated and touched her hair with golden highlights echoing the brilliant sun Enrique recalled over the Sonoran Desert.

"What is it?" he asked, a knot forming in his throat. He already knew he was losing them. His most precious pieces were being removed from the chessboard and he'd never found the time to play with them, to laugh with them, to make memories beyond the mundane dinner or the routine move from a rented house in one strange city to yet another.

"They have suitors," Anita uttered in a clipped tone.

"I see," he swallowed. "And who might these daring young men be?"

"They are Americans," Esperanza gushed, nearly spilling her water in her excitement. "Tell him, *Mamá*. They are so handsome and so smart. You will simply adore them!"

Magdalena blushed demurely, folding the linen napkin in her lap into a tiny square.

Anita pursed her lips in disapproval. "Esperanza, really! I think your father will have to determine that for himself…when he meets them."

Enrique sat quietly at the head of the table. The only sound was the murmur of the fountain in the courtyard floating in on the evening breeze, like a never-ending prayer in hushed tones, an endless *caminata*. Enrique recalled the incessant nocturnal clicking of his mother's rosary beads as she paced the corridors of their small house during his childhood.

"Gringos?" he asked, furrowing his brow. "You want my blessing to be courted by a pair of no-good thieves from north of the border? You must be out of your minds!"

The women stared at the dried meat resting gracelessly on their white plates, their appetites disintegrating along with their meager hopes.

"Actually…" Esperanza's voice wavered and stopped as Magdalena shot her a withering glance.

Anita sat up as straight as she could, summoning her courage, "Enrique," she pleaded. "Why don't you give them a chance? They've actually come here to work on your bridge project. They are engineers. They have degrees. Tell him, Magdalena."

Magdalena did not lift her eyes from her plate, out of fear, and respect. "It's true, *Papá*. They work for the American railroad company. They speak Spanish. And they're brothers too! We met them one day in the Plaza after Church…if you'd come…you would have too."

"If I'd come, they wouldn't have been so bold as to introduce themselves to you," the colonel stated bluntly. "This is an outrage. First they steal Texas and the Border States. Now they want my daughters too?"

"*Papá*," Esperanza interjected desperately. "I thought you loved America! You're building the bridge after all."

"Love? Love?" Enrique cried, rising to his feet. "What do you know about love? Love is risking your life for someone or something you care about. Love is not made of pretty words and whispered promises. Love is written in blood and remembered in scars."

"But…" Esperanza whimpered.

"No… 'buts,'" Enrique silenced her, raising a finger sternly. "No way. I'm building the bridge for commerce. Not for the denigration of my race. *No más*."

He stalked out into the courtyard, where he paced late into the night. Sitting at the fountain's edge, he thought he was seeing a phantom when Anita materialized in a light cotton frock, embroidered with pink flowers, her hair long and untethered.

She sat next to him quietly, taking his hand in hers after a few minutes. Together they stared up at the moon overhead.

"Why is it so hard?" she asked.

He searched the stars for an answer but all that came to his mind was, "It's hard to let go of something you never fully grasped."

"Give them a chance," she soothed and urged simultaneously, skillfully. "They are young. Remember how we once felt, before life took its course."

"I wanted to build a family at last. Have them here close by, grandchildren running through the halls. I'd rather they marry an

Indio than this. At least an Indio might look at us as a step up from his lot in life. These gringos will see us as nothing but dirt beneath their fingernails. They'll take our girls north and we'll never see them again. All we'll know of our descendants will be a telegram when they are born and if we're lucky an invitation to their baptisms, their weddings."

Anita knew that she was stepping over a boundary, but yearning to protect her relationship with their daughters, she said, "You've rarely had time for more…than a telegram."

He wished he could fill the fountain with his tears. He had not cried since the night he'd held the cold and silent Yaqui child in his arms in the desert.

"You have married a severely incapacitated man, Anita," he confessed at last. He smelled jasmine in the air, from the vines that climbed over the lime-green stucco walls of the house. "Some men lost their arms or legs in the Revolution. I lost my heart."

Anita had never understood him. She had often wondered if he'd fallen in love with another woman, created another family, and returned to her only out of obligation. How had he lost his heart? He rarely spoke of his days in the deserts, on the battlefields, in the jail cells. How was she to know?

As if, for once, he could hear her thoughts, he said: "If fate is a woman, then I have cheated on you with her, and her alone. Wounds of the flesh are easier to heal than those of the soul."

Cryptic as ever, she thought, as he pulled his cold hand away from hers and rose.

"I would wear my uniform every day, if people would not think me crazy," he concluded. Then his eyes met her and he smiled with pity. "I thought that life was dead to me. But I now know otherwise."

She felt tears brimming heavily at the edge of her eyelids, blurring his form in the cool blue light.

"I will fight for what is mine, as I always have," Enrique grimaced, and marched out of the moonlight into the shadows of the arched colonnade.

He did not speak of the subject again. He eavesdropped the next morning as Anita followed his instructions to the girls: eliminate all contact with the Americans at once. Clear and simple. As he had learned over the years, that was the secret to the successful execution of military strategy. People needed to know that they were doing the right thing, delivering exactly what was expected of them, nothing more and nothing less.

From that day on, he worked with determination to complete his bridge. He eyed each and every American engineer closely, wondering which pair might be intent on stealing his treasure. He knew there were even more engineers working on the other side of the river, many of whom he had never met. But he convinced himself that his family was safe from their designs. Every night, they ate dinner at the family table and, as the months slipped by and the bridge took shape, the subject failed to resurface. To Enrique's relief, polite conversation prevailed instead. And, as the inauguration of the bridge approached, Enrique began to feel confident that his family had survived a test.

Why wouldn't it? What did America have to offer that Mexico didn't? What could two lowly gringo engineers give his daughters that he couldn't? He felt puerile for having overreacted to the potential threat, but he was glad he had snuffed out the flame of rebellion quickly. Truly, it was the only way to quell an ugly and undesirable uprising.

The opening of the bridge was celebrated with fireworks, and a shiny new locomotive steamed across. The mayors and the governors from both sides of the border regaled the crowds with grandiose speeches, applauding the colonel for his vision and determination. Bulbs popped and flashed, the newspapers lauded him as well. There was talk of moving the campaign upriver, to build four more bridges in the next two years. The investors were keen and the winning team was assembled and proven.

Sitting contentedly at the dinner table the following night, Enrique waited for Anita and the girls to pull up their chairs so he could share the good news. At long last, his monument was built, and there were more on order.

But only Anita appeared, dressed in black.

"Where are the girls?" he asked.

"They have left," she answered, her tone flat and lifeless.

"What do you mean?" His smile vanished.

"They left on that train headed north, the one that crossed the bridge this evening headed for San Antonio," she explained. "They eloped with the engineers. They're moving out west to California where there's more work for the young men." She dabbed at the corners of her eyes with her napkin. Manuela, the loyal Indian woman who had once been their midwife and was still their cook and maid, shuffled restlessly in the kitchen.

Enrique sat completely stunned. Then he heard the sobs emitting from the next room.

Pushing his chair back loudly across the marble tile floor, he saw Manuela crumpled over the stove, her dark leathery skin and wiry white hair shaking vigorously. She had birthed them, had reared them alongside Anita. A short, hunched, stocky woman, she looked at Enrique with fear, awaiting her ultimate punishment from the *patrón* who had never even noticed her presence, never even set foot in the kitchen. She had heard the tales on the streets and in the markets about the colonel. She knew he had been an Indian killer. Why not her? Why not now? Having borne no children of her own, she would gladly take it. She'd go retrieve his sword from the study if he wished to use it. Anita hovered anxiously behind him in the arched doorway, wishing he would bring her to a final justice as well. What was the point of living now that all the life was gone from their home in one instant?

Enrique stepped forward and wrapped his arms around Manuela, holding her tightly while she cried. Anita delicately placed her hand on his back to share in their communal grieving.

Then, after a few minutes, he walked out without a word. The two women stood awkwardly on the black and white checkered floor of the foyer, listening to his footsteps. Anita immediately recognized the rap of his boot heels traversing the stone in the courtyard. And she almost fell in love with him again, as he appeared in the entry wearing his white uniform and shiny black boots, sword by his side, silver hair combed back and moustache twisted up at the ends. She fought back a smile that could only arise from being swept back in time, rushing over a bridge that impossibly spanned not space but years.

"What are you doing?" Anita gasped as Manuela held the door open for him.

He set his jaw and his eyes glimmered with one final hint of fight as he replied, "I have a bridge to blow up."

The two women watched him disappear, his glowing ivory uniform fading slowly into the shadows of the night.

Fighting Words

"You are no longer allowed to speak Spanish. *Ya. Basta. Punto final!*" Olivia Saenz bitterly admonished her flustered five-year-old daughter Laura, who proceeded to pout and cry.

It was 1955, and Olivia agreed with Mrs. Collins, the kindergarten teacher, that fluency should be forced to ensure Laura's assimilation into society.

"Otherwise, she'll never belong," Mrs. Collins alarmed Olivia. "She'll never make it to college, never pass her high school classes."

"*Mamá, pasa los frijoles, por favor,*" little Laura requested one night at the dinner table.

Her mother snapped back, in her thick Spanish accent, "No. I'm not passing you the beans or any other food, until you speak in English. The only kind of 'passing' I'm interested in is you 'passing' in school."

"*Mamá!*" Laura whined, her thick black curls bobbing up and down around her small, round face, the color of milk chocolate.

"*Pero, Olivia, estás exagerando, ¿no?*" interjected Luis, Laura's father, a bespectacled and trembling leaf of a man. He worked as an assistant manager at the Sears in downtown Phoenix.

As he reached for the bowl to hand it to their daughter, Olivia slapped his wrist deftly away. "No. No more Spanish. If she's going to learn, and do better than we have, she's going to have to do good in her English."

Laura wilted like the lettuce on a day-old chalupa. "*Mamá,* pass the beans…" she mumbled reluctantly.

"*Por fa*…please," her mother nagged.

"Please," Laura surrendered.

English was hard. It was new. And sometimes Laura's tongue got all twisted and tied up.

"Mom," she complained one day after school, when she was in the sixth grade. "When we go visit, let me speak Spanish for a little while with *Abuelita* and *Abuelito*. How else am I supposed to talk to them?"

"You let me do the talking then. I'll be your translator," Olivia insisted, spraying her bouffant hairdo into place and straightening her colorful starched dress for the walk to her parents' house. "How do I look?"

Laura knew what her mom wanted to hear, "You look like a Mexican Marilyn Monroe, but classy."

Her mom smiled coquettishly into the mirror. "I've taught you well. Now, how do I really look?"

"I liked you better with your hair dark, not blonde," Laura shrugged, playing with her own shoulder length black curls. Somehow their kind of dark skin just didn't look right next to golden hair, Laura deemed, pursing her lips. It wasn't natural.

Her mom's smile evaporated like a drop of water in the scalding Arizona sun.

"You're a very rude little girl, you know that?" Olivia chastised. "If you have nothing nice to say, you shouldn't say anything at all."

Even at the age of eleven, Laura found her mother predictable. Still, she was brave enough to weather her blistering glare. "Sorry. Can we go now? How much time does it take to get ready to walk a few steps?"

After another reproachful glance from her Mexican Marilyn mother, they finally headed out into the crushing heat. Her grandparents lived a block away on the same street. It was a clean, decent, working-class barrio on the heavily Hispanic west side of town. Laura knew the name of every dog and child beyond the chain-link fence that bordered the sunbaked sidewalk between her home and her grandparents' house. Every house was a simple, white two-bedroom wooden structure, with tiny porches where families would rock or swing, after the scorching sun had set behind the distant mountains and the desert breeze cooled off the pavement under the mesquite and kumquat trees.

At her grandparents' house, Laura sulked in the corner of the dinette nook, doing math homework. Her mom was too upset about the hair comment to translate for her, so instead she gossiped in

Spanish with Laura's grandmother and aunts in the sitting room. The air hung heavily with the rich aroma of homemade tortillas, vanilla, and cinnamon. Just being there sparked a churning in her stomach.

After a while, her *abuelito* drifted in, clutching his cup of coffee and his Mexican newspaper. Absentmindedly, he sat down at the small table. She had never known him to talk much. He was short and rail thin, his skin dark and wrinkled from years in the sun, his hair contrasting sharply in cropped silver. He always dressed in baggy khaki pants and a white *guayabera*, hunching subtly under the accumulated weight of all his years of manual labor as a migrant farm worker.

Even though he'd lived in the United States all of his adult life, *Abuelito* barely spoke English. She couldn't remember the last time they had exchanged more than a smile, a hug and an "*hola*" or an "*adios*."

She smiled warmly at him and he patted her on the head as if she were still three years old. She didn't mind.

After a while, as she struggled over a long division problem, grimacing and groaning, her *abuelito* surprised her by reaching into a kitchen drawer and producing a clean sheet of paper and his own newly sharpened yellow pencil. With the neatest penmanship Laura had ever seen, *Abuelito* copied her division problems and set out to slowly show her each step towards solving them, pausing to make sure she understood what he was doing. He gestured with his hands to invisibly pull down the next number, showed her the links between the digits and squeezed out the correct remainders.

Laura's eyes flashed with renewed enthusiasm. After finishing the division problems, she pulled out her textbook and turned to a page about fractions that had mystified her for weeks. These numbers floating about with lines between them made no sense. It was like alphabet soup with digits instead of letters. She scratched her head and threw her hands up in the air, feeling like a mime since she didn't dare use her fading Spanish within earshot of her mother.

Abuelito nodded in comprehension. He reached for a Valencia orange from the colorful Talavera bowl in the middle of the table, and started peeling it with great precision.

Laura wondered if he'd gotten bored or if, perhaps, she'd waded into waters too deep for his rustic mind. But soon she realized he had a purpose. He began to illustrate the meaning of fractions with the wedges from the orange. After he peeled it, he pulled the orange in half, handing Laura one of the halves. He pointed at her half and raised one finger in the air. Then he wrote down the number "1." Then he held both halves, one in each hand for a second, acting as if he were a scale weighing them equally. Then he wrote out the rest of the fraction, drawing a straight line beneath the "1," and a neat "2" below the line.

Laura nodded, and he continued with more complex fractions, shuffling the orange wedges about and peeling yet another pair of them in the process.

"*Huele muy rico aquí, ¿qué están haciendo?*" Laura's *abuelita* wondered, venturing in to the aromatic fragrance of the freshly peeled citrus.

In her excitement, Laura blurted clumsily, "*Abuelito me está enseñando...*"

"Ah...ah..." Her mom barged into the kitchen, wagging her finger menacingly. "In English, *señorita!*"

Laura's smile quickly faded.

Abuelito's eyes twinkled as he patted her on the hand, his skin rough and weathered from all the years in the fields. She stuffed her papers into her bag and gave him a kiss on the cheek as she left with her mother.

"Mom, how is *Abuelito* so good at math?" Laura asked over the click of her mother's heels as they walked quickly in the dark.

"He was very smart, your *abuelito,*" Olivia admitted grudgingly. "He was the first in his family to finish high school in Mexico, but down there, only the rich go to college. And when he came here he knew no English, so he did what he could to make a living..." Her voice trailed off ruefully, as if she blamed him and lack of English for all of her woes in life.

"Why didn't he learn English instead, and then go to college?" Laura asked as they let themselves in the unlocked front door.

"Because he and your *abuelita* had your *tíos* and me very young. They had to feed us. It was the Great Depression. Times were very hard."

"Why'd they come from Mexico if it was so bad here?"

"Because it was worse down there," Olivia explained. "It's always worse down there. It still is. And it always will be. That's why you have to learn English. So you can go to college and be a successful American. ¡*Ya!* ¡*Basta!*"

"Maybe I can be a writer when I grow up," Laura said. "I've been reading this book at school that I love, and it's about this…"

"What?" Olivia stared back in horror. Any bystander might have suspected that Laura had mentioned the notion of growing up to be a trained assassin or a serial killer. "No. No. ¡*No!*" Olivia cried. "You have to be a doctor or a lawyer, a nurse or a schoolteacher, at least. Something respectable. What are you talking about… Writer? Writing doesn't pay the bills," her mother clucked, shaking off the concept like a bad dream.

Every afternoon that she had complicated math homework, Laura requested permission to visit her grandparents' house. Her mom usually tagged along, as there was little else to do in their miniscule house. "The one good thing about your father's long hours at Sears and us living in a small house," her mom would often sigh, "is that he brings home all these great appliances with his employee discount and there's almost no housework left for me to do!"

Abuelito was keenly aware that his domineering daughter did not allow Laura to speak Spanish. So during one of those visits, he devised a code for communicating with her. He wrote down the entire alphabet from A to Z on a sheet of paper and assigned a number to each letter. Then he wrote a string of Spanish words in code, using the numbers to substitute for the letters.

Laura loved these word games, and fought off the giggles when her Mom walked into the kitchen. She would pretend to muddle through an excruciating problem as she knit her eyebrows together in consternation.

After that, her *abuelito* would employ the code to ask her questions about her day, her friends, her likes and dislikes, hopes and dreams. Using the same code, Laura would giddily answer back. If Mom ever walked into the room and glanced down, she only saw the flood of numbers on the papers scattered across the table.

"*Ay*," Olivia would lament. "I don't know how you two do it. All those numbers make my eyes blur and my head hurt. It's like trying to read a foreign language."

Laura's mother abhorred math. "*Ay no.* It's why I've never been able to stay inside that pathetic budget we have to survive on from your father's puny salary!"

Laura suspected that her mother's budget problems were more the result of her affinity for new dresses and trips to the hair salon than poor arithmetic skills or her father's failings.

"Mom, Dad…" Laura asked her parents as they strolled home from her *abuelito's* house one weekend evening. "Why didn't the two of you go to college?"

Luis opened his mouth but, before he could speak, Olivia declared: "Well, I was not smart enough and your father—he was too scared."

Luis grimaced as if he'd been punched in the stomach. He'd known he should have worked that extra night shift. What was the point of being home? It was easier and less painful to be trampled on by total strangers than by your own wife.

Pursing her lips and wishing she hadn't asked, Laura decided not to pursue the subject further.

She tackled her homework diligently, with the help of her *abuelito*, who also taught her about their family's origins in Mexico, his unrequited childhood dreams of sailing the seven seas and even her *abuelita's* psychic tendencies. He also shared his pride and suffering over his sons' service in the American military. She already knew that her eldest *tío*, José, had fought in World War II and died in Europe. A black and white photo of him posing next to the American flag occupied a prominent spot in a homemade shrine in the living room, propped up against a colorful statuette of the Virgen de Guadalupe. And her other uncle, Juan Antonio, was still in the service, stationed at the naval base in San Diego. His photo also had a prime spot in the cramped, plastic-shrined living room, not quite as sacrosanct as standing shoulder-to-shoulder with the Virgencita but highly visible nonetheless. Laura had never considered what their service meant to her *abuelito* and, consequently, to her entire family.

Her heart swelled as she deciphered his words and translated them mentally into English:

I gave my firstborn to America. And my only regret is that I couldn't have sacrificed my life instead, so he could have enjoyed all the blessings of this country.

Her *abuelito's* sentiments made Laura realize how much she took for granted, being an American. How much her parents and grandparents were willing to give for this intangible dream. People dying for her freedom. Others willing to sacrifice their lives, their language, for acceptance and a piece of the promise.

As he opened up to her over the course of her visits, scribbling numbers quickly without ever losing the precision in his penmanship, she became fascinated by his memories of the countless years he'd grooved a path from state to state in synchronicity with the passing seasons. He had survived sweltering heat and swarms of mosquitoes in the Rio Grande Valley of Texas, harvesting onions in Weslaco and picking oranges in Mission. He had braved dry and biting winds while weeding sugar beets and hoeing potatoes as far north as Nebraska. And he'd slogged through incessant rains, picking blackberries in Oregon. Always, he wrote in code, it was noble, honest work. He quoted his own father, in a whisper when Mom wasn't listening:

"Quien de sudor la frente se moja, ante nadie se sonroja." It rhymed poetically but, even without the artistry of the language, it was a powerful statement: "He who drenches his brow in sweat hangs his head in shame before no one."

In the end, *Abuelito* had settled in Phoenix because the weather was good for his arthritis, and his brother owned a little market in town where he could help from time to time.

"I came to America to work for a better life," her *abuelito* wrote. "And that's something worth working for until the very end."

Abuelito's stories were spun for her in cryptic rows of neatly scripted numbers, which made the experience all the more intriguing. She saved the sheets of paper in a notebook under her bed. At night, when she tired of reading the books she checked out of the school library, she would reach under and pull out her binder, and re-read one of her *abuelito's* familiar stories, smiling as if she were reading it for the first time. It was as if she and her *abuelito* had woven from simple numbers a cozy, brightly-hued serape in which she could wrap herself to feel warm and safe, loved and accepted.

Soon after Laura began her senior year in high school, her *abuelito* died suddenly, of a brain tumor. Not once had he complained about feeling sick. One day, he was sitting next to her in the kitchen, jotting numbers and solving equations. The next, he was gone. She sat dazed through his funeral, seeing so many faces that reminded her of his, yet finding no connection in their eyes. Family members came from as far as Aguascalientes and Puebla in

Mexico, and from Chicago, Illinois. There were dozens of cousins she'd never even seen before. One after another, relatives approached to offer her their condolences and converse in Spanish, but she would just shake her head, scattering heavy tears on their black dresses and suits.

"No hablo español," she would answer with a slight English accent, her cheeks flushing with shame. It was one thing to read Spanish from her *abuelito's* coded messages; and it was quite another to speak it.

"Qué lástima," she overheard one rotund great aunt mourn. *"Tan bonita muchachita...por fuera parece pura mexicana...pero por dentro es pura gringa."*

The words haunted her. What good was it to be pretty or smart, if you didn't even know who you were, if your own flesh and blood derided you? Her *abuelito* had been the only link to her roots she'd ever truly experienced, and now... Now what? Sure, she had relatives in Mexico. Sure, there were stories to tell. But they could not speak to her in her *abuelito's* code. And her tongue got tied up in knots just thinking of speaking Spanish to her fluent, judgmental elders. She feared a part of herself was being lowered into the ground alongside him. Sobbing, she found an empty church pew in the shadows of the neighborhood church, and she wept until her coffee brown eyes were framed in fiery red.

After the relatives had left, and life had resumed a sense of hollow normalcy, Laura found herself at the kitchen table in her grandparents' house, staring at the oranges in the bowl, crying over her homework while her *abuelita* watched *telenovelas* in her bedroom. Olivia was now working as a secretary at an office downtown to supplement the family income, so there was no one around to keep her from speaking Spanish. But when she tried, she could not find the words. And her *abuelita* had never been any good at numbers.

A week after the funeral, feeling sorry for her despondent granddaughter, *Abuelita's* face lit up and she pleaded for Laura not to leave, *"Espérate, mi hijita. No te muevas."* Then she scurried into the back room of the house, where she had stored her husband's personal items.

Minutes later, she emerged with a tattered notebook, shaking her head in relief. *"Tu abuelito te dejó esto. No sé cómo se me olvidó. Lo siento, mi amor. Tú sabes que él te quería mucho."*

Her *abuelita* sat down next to her at the table. The warm proximity of her soft pear-shaped body, invariably draped in a faded flower-print housecoat, comforted Laura.

Delicately, Laura opened the notebook and smiled at once. The first page was filled with numbers. Quickly, she flipped ahead. More numbers. And more. She couldn't believe it!

Laura looked up at her *abuelita* in amazement, speechless.

"Te quería mucho tu abuelito. Me decía que tú eras la suma de todos sus sueños y todas sus esperanzas."

Laura pretty much knew what that meant: That her *abuelito* had loved her very much and that he would say that she was the sum of all of his dreams and all of his hopes. She was ecstatic—it was as if he'd returned for a surprise visit. She decided to pace her reading of the stories, saving them so that she could prolong his stay for as long as possible.

As she finished her senior year, she was accepted to the University of California at Los Angeles. It was a great honor. She would be the first in her family to attend college...and in America, no less. But how would she pay for it? Her parents wrung their hands in anguish, poring over their endless bills and budget shortfalls. There was a scholarship offer, due to her excellent grades. A recruiter even called and spoke to them on the phone.

"We are extremely hopeful that you will accept our generous offer," the recruiter said in English so perfect it made the phone feel light and airy. Then he added that their hopes were magnified because she would help them meet two goals: she was Hispanic, and a woman!

"I never thought being Hispanic and a woman could possibly be of benefit to anyone," Olivia muttered. "Now they decide it's a good thing...now when I have little more to do than wait for your father to get sick so I can change diapers again."

Luis frowned, wiping his brow and perching his glasses on the tip of his long crooked nose to peer at his calculations. "Even with the scholarship...*híjole*...I'm sorry...but..."

As usual Olivia finished his sentence for him, *"Ni modo,* Laura. Just like me and just like your *abuelito.* You won't be able to go to college because we simply can't afford it. Maybe your father can get you a job as a cashier at the Sears, since you're so good with numbers. It's the least he can do since he can't afford to send you to college. I had dreams for you. But dreams don't pay for themselves. Now it's time to grow up and face reality. Just like I do every day." She glanced distastefully at her husband, blame oozing forth from her eyes.

Laura ran to her room and shut the door, flinging herself onto her small bed and weeping into her lumpy pillow. Her throat ached and her stomach churned in acidic rebellion.

All that work and all those dreams, all the tests and good grades, just so she could count beans at her father's store? How could it be? Was this the American Dream?

Instinctively, she reached beneath the bed and extracted her *abuelito's* final notebook, yearning to escape into one of his fabulous tales, mentally deciphering the last few pages that remained unread.

Her tears began to roll down her smooth cheeks again as she reached the final page and read the words composed in his neat numbers:

My dear Laurita, for a while I've had these headaches and today I couldn't say the word "barbacoa," or even calculate the annual interest on $20,000. The doctor told me I have a brain tumor they can't take out. So I will be going soon. These last few years, you have made my days worth facing. And I can never say thank you enough. I feel blessed to leave my mark on the world through you. As you know, I love barbacoa. *And if this page turns out looking greasy, it is because I managed to explain myself in the end and your* abuelita *just handed me a* taco de lengua *with plenty of salsa picante. So while the* barbacoa *portion of my morning mystery may be no surprise, you might wonder why I would want to know the interest on that sum of money. It's because I have been a skinny squirrel all my life. And besides the house and savings I leave your* abuelita *so she can take care of herself, I am so happy to leave you a special something. Talk to Mr. Neighbors at the First State Bank downtown. He's gringo but he's a good man. He has a Certificate of Deposit with your name on it for $20,000 to be used to pay for your college. And when you graduate, he has a ticket for you to go on a cruise. I couldn't afford the whole seven seas, but at least a couple of them—I thought this might be a nice start to the rest of your journey on the adventure called life.* Te quiere mucho siempre, tu abuelito.

***

Laura Saenz Gonzales became not only one of the first Hispanics to graduate from the Engineering program at UCLA, but also one of the first women to do so. She even won a prize for Excellence in Mathematics! And she minored in Spanish, rediscovering her first language and mastering it as a young adult. It turned out her *abuelito* had helped cultivate not just berries and fruits in the fertile lands of America but also a bilingual mathematician in the middle of the most barren of deserts. Even though she worked in libraries and classrooms rather than fields and orchards, in his honor she marched with Cesar Chavez to fight for better conditions for migrant farm workers. She also became my mother.

When I was a kid, she would show me pictures of her *abuelito* and regale me with the stories of his days growing up in Mexico and traveling all over America to pick crops. I could tell that, through him, she had learned to value not just what was in her brain, but also what was in her heart. She told me that the most valuable thing she learned was the value of language in perpetuating culture; and she made sure she passed it on to me.

I still remember sitting at the dinner table, asking: "Mom, would you please pass the beans?"

Channeling an inverted fraction of her own mother, my mom politely intercepted my dad's hand to hold the bowl back, chiding me tenderly, *"En español, mi hijito...En español o te vas a poner muy flaquito."*

Bending the Laws of Motion

The shiny bicycle in the storefront window had my name written all over it. Not for real, but that's the way I saw it. Centered beneath my favorite words in the world—"Mac's Toys"—the Evel Knievel motocross bike was totally groovy. It gleamed white with blue stars, red stripes, and chrome highlights on the handlebars, wheels, and spokes. Evel Knievel was so cool. I pictured him jumping a long string of cars or the Grand Canyon, his cape fluttering behind him, his body a heroic streak of red, white, and blue.

"*Andale!*" My mom snapped, tugging at me sharply as my baby brother, Rene, screamed in her arms. "We still have to go grocery shopping and your brother's already losing it!"

"Mom," I sputtered as she towed me away reluctantly, "you think maybe for Christmas? The Evel Knievel bike?"

"We'll see. Maybe if things go better for your father," she sighed as we walked into the old downtown HEB store, the smell of raw meat and garlic searing my nostrils.

My dad was a tire man. Even though we lived on the American side of the border, he would cross over to Mexico almost every day to search for worn tractor-trailer tires and to make deliveries for his customers. He then brought the *cascos*, the shells, back to his little vulcanizing plant by the railroad tracks. From the outside it looked no different than any of the small wooden houses that flanked the rail yards and the old cemetery on the corner. The exterior paint had once been white with red trim, but now it was peeling and run down. A splintered sign dangled from a solitary chain near the front door: "Joe's Tire Shop."

Inside, it was cramped and stank of burnt rubber and sweat, but I loved it. Every day after school, I would beg him to take me to the shop rather than drop me off at home with my nagging mom and drooling brother. Usually, he didn't mind. He'd let me answer the phone and file papers while he talked to the plant engineer, Pedro. Pedro was a short, round man with spectacles. He looked like he'd been molded out of molten rubber himself. His overalls were always covered in soot, his hands and face dark with the black powder that constantly rubbed off the tires. Despite his weight, he rolled nimbly between the silver tire molds, checking gauges and adjusting levers and wheels. He reminded me of a pinball bouncing around inside an industrial-themed arcade machine. Through the hissing steam, he barked commands to his two helpers. It always seemed urgent to me, like he was maintaining a delicate balance and if he let it get out of hand, the whole place could blow.

My favorite part of the day was when the bell rang and Pedro would call for help, spinning one of the wheels that crowned the molds. A miniature crane would swing over the steaming tire as he lifted the lid. With a crowbar, he'd pry around the tire's edges, ensuring its clean separation from the steel mold inside. Then he'd attach the hook hanging from the crane and give the order to pull. Out would pop a big old tire that now looked brand spanking new, with deep patterns grooved into its once smooth and useless surface.

My father would beam as if he'd just witnessed his own child being born. "Another one hundred dollars," he'd smile and wink at me.

When times were good, my dad's wallet would be stuffed full of hundred dollar bills. But when times were bad, it would be crammed only with wrinkled little pieces of white paper. Receipts, he called them as he instructed me to file them away for the taxes.

Even though tires emerged from the molds every day, they were piling up in the warehouse behind the tire shop. Dad's big worry was always how to keep the lights turned on at home and at the shop, the men paid every Friday, and enough money to pay for the rubber he would order from Akron, Ohio. Accomplishing this always seemed like a delicate juggling act.

On the TV in our eat-in kitchen at home, President Carter had used the word "malaise" to describe our economy. When Mom asked what it meant, my dad said it sounded a lot like *malo*, which meant "bad."

Luckily for me, the nuns at St. Mary's Elementary School were merciful enough to let him run behind on the tuition. They knew eventually he would pay up, as always. I was in fifth grade and hoped to get the Evel Knievel bike for my eleventh birthday at the start of the school year but, sadly, the malaise had been contagious and turned my *cumpleaños* into more of a pity party than anything else. Christmas was my last hope for the bike.

"What if you send me back to public school instead of St. Mary's, Dad?" I asked as we rode home in his rattletrap of a pickup truck. "Could you afford to get me the bike then?"

"Son, the only and best thing I can give you," he replied somberly, his thick moustache rising and falling with his words as he kept his dark eyes on the road, "is an education. A bike can be stolen. But your education? No one can ever take that away from you. Besides, you have a bike."

I thought of the pink girl's bike that had been handed down to me from one of my female cousins. It collected dust in the backyard because I didn't dare ride it in the street. Was he serious? Riding that was sure to end up with a one-way trip to the hospital.

"How bad would public school really be? Maybe they finished building the new classrooms and I could have a desk of my own? It's less strict and it's free!" I envisioned riding my sparkly Evel Knievel bike to the public school, performing stunts for the awed kids in the parking lot, popping wheelies and jumping parked cars like the daredevil himself did on TV.

"Son," my dad replied, his eyes glowering beneath the brim of his tan Stetson hat, "you are a very smart boy. More than half of the kids that go to public school here in town don't even graduate. They drop out. Now, I know that wouldn't happen to you, but I want you with the nuns, where you get books and discipline."

I rested my chin on the open window and gazed out at the passing houses as dusk fell. We lived in Southmost, a neighborhood of tiny wooden shacks crammed behind leaning chain-link fences, smashed between the railroad tracks and the river levee. It was the southernmost neighborhood in the United States. All I had to do was walk across the street and climb the grassy hill in order to see the Rio Grande and Mexico beyond.

When I'd started at St. Mary's the year before, I'd told a kid at school what part of town I lived in, and his jaw had dropped. He'd backed away slowly and then turned and run. So, the next day, when the class bully was about to pounce on me, I decided to try it again.

Staring at his shiny penny loafers, his pressed and pleated navy blue slacks and white shirt, I had stalled, "Jimmy?"

"What is it, punk? Talk fast because I'm ready to smack you. It's your initiation," the biggest boy in our class snarled, droplets of saliva flinging down on my face.

"I live in Southmost," I stated flatly, searching his cold blue eyes for a response.

Jimmy lowered his fist. He reassessed me. I was short and scrawny, holes in my grayish white *guayabera*, patches on my second-hand faded blue pants, scuffs on my shoes.

"Southmost, huh?" Jimmy frowned.

"Yup."

"You ever get in a fight down there?" Jimmy asked.

"Sure, all the time," I lied.

Jimmy nodded.

"You carry a knife?" he asked.

I'd seen the teenagers in the barrio playing with switchblades while hanging out on the street corners, doing tricks, trying to impress the girls without slicing their fingers open. That was the closest I had ever been to owning a knife.

"Nah," I said. "My dad makes me leave it in a drawer in my room."

I could hear the gears turning in Jimmy's head.

"Okay, you follow me, kid," Jimmy said. "Don't tick me off and I won't mess with you. Understand?"

"Yeah, sure. No problem." I replied.

After that, I never had any problems at St. Mary's. I didn't always hang out with Jimmy, but the other kids knew he respected me and that was protection enough.

I liked the nuns' school better than the public school. At the public school, there were so many kids the building couldn't fit them. So they'd started bringing these portable trailers and parking them in the playground. The trailers were supposed to be temporary classrooms, but since they couldn't build fast enough to keep up with the growth in students, they never went away. Some teachers even tried landscaping around their trailers, but the kids would pick the flowers and trample on the plants just to be mean.

One day, while I was still at the public school, my dad had to come pick me up early because my mom was in the hospital with my baby brother in her tummy. The doctors were worried whether everything was going to be okay. When he found my classroom, his bushy eyebrows knit together like they did when he was about to hit somebody.

"Mrs. Ochoa?" he asked my teacher, a wispy spinster who always dressed in black.

"Yes, Mr. López?" she answered, her voice quivering in fear.

"Why is my son sitting on the floor back there?" he asked, pointing at me, sitting Indian-style on the floor in the back row between two desks.

"Well, we just can't fit enough desks in here, sir," she answered as if it was a perfectly acceptable answer.

My dad scanned the room. It was hot and muggy because the air conditioner units on the portable classrooms weren't very good. There must have been a dozen of us sitting along the aisles.

"How come some kids have books and others don't?" my dad asked Mrs. Ochoa, refusing to let her off the hook too easily. "My son is sitting down there on the floor and he doesn't have a book in his lap."

"Well..." Mrs. Ochoa gulped and coughed nervously. "We...uh...share books, Mr. López."

She forced a hopeful smile at him. Sharing was good, wasn't it? They taught us that in kindergarten.

"Mrs. Ochoa," my dad replied, "how can he 'share' if he can't even see the page of the person sitting next to him because he's three feet lower?"

Mrs. Ochoa pursed her lips.

"C'mon, Ramón," my father commanded.

I precariously climbed over my classmates, struggling to avoid stepping on anyone's fingers.

"Mrs. Ochoa, don't expect my boy back here. My orphaned father didn't come all the way from Yucatan to the United States of America for his grandson to go to school in a trailer and sit on the floor without a book. We could do that back in Mexico if we wanted to."

So I got a few days off from school. My mom felt better and was able to come home to finish carrying my little brother. And the next week, my dad took me to St. Mary's for the first time.

"Son, this is going to be a sacrifice," he had said in the parking lot. "But you're smart. You're going to take what you learn here and someday do great things with it. Maybe you'll even be the first López to go to college"

At St. Mary's, I devoured books and checked out magazines and biographies from the library. I liked reading about the American presidents, like Abe Lincoln and Teddy Roosevelt. I liked learning big words and impressing my teachers. The day after President Carter used the word "malaise," I had eagerly darted to the giant dictionary on the counter at the front of my spacious classroom to find the definition. My dad had been pretty close. It was *malo*. It said it was a general feeling of illness or sickness. Well, it had certainly infected my birthday proceedings, but I was determined to stop the malaise from killing my Christmas dream.

St. Mary's was not a very big school. There were only two fifth-grade classrooms. One was the A class, which were mostly the Anglo kids and the smartest of the Mexican kids. The other was the B class, which was mostly the rich kids that came in carpools from Mexico every day, and the really dumb white students.

At first, the nuns had put me in the B class. But after a few days, the teacher walked me to the principal's office and said something about me being too smart for her to feel right about holding me back. So I joined the A class. I would have been a little scared, but Jimmy was in that class and he made sure no one gave me any trouble. One of his best friends was a boy named Sergio Aranda. Even though we all had to wear uniforms, Sergio's somehow seemed nicer. His hair always looked sharply cut and shiny. And the girls always giggled when Sergio walked by. Even though he was a real Mexican, and I was Mexican-American, he was lighter-skinned than I was. Jimmy, Sergio and I hung out together during lunch. When the kids played games, we were always picked first. Jimmy was the strongest kid in class. He could beat anyone at arm wrestling. Sergio was the most athletic. When we played kickball, he always sent the ball sailing over the fence. And I was the fastest, the wind whipping through my long black hair as I zipped by everyone else in the races.

In the parking lot after school, the parents would circle through a half-moon driveway to pick up their children. I always hoped Sergio and Jimmy's parents would come before mine, because I didn't want them to see my dad's beat-up pickup truck.

Jimmy's mother drove a silver Mercedes-Benz. His family owned a chain of gentlemen's clothing stores. Sergio's father always picked him up in a beautiful white Cadillac Eldorado convertible. Luckily, my dad always ran late.

One day, Sergio invited me to visit his house.

"I don't know if my parents will let me go across the border with you," I replied.

"Well, we can go to my house here," he said.

"What do you mean?"

"We have two, one on each side," he explained casually, as if everyone else did too.

"Of course," I shrugged, forcing a grin.

After much haranguing, my parents granted me permission to go home one day with Sergio. I'd never ridden in a Cadillac before.

"Your seats are so nice and soft, Mr. Aranda," I swooned as the cold air from the vents blasted my face. This vehicle could double as a refrigerator, I thought.

"Those are leather, Ramoncito," he replied, smiling at me warmly.

"Of course," I replied, petting them as if they were a long-lost puppy.

I felt so comfortable around Mr. Aranda. It was like I'd known him my whole life. Unlike my dad, who was always sweaty and covered in tire dust, Mr. Aranda looked like he'd stepped out of that fancy magazine I'd seen in the library, *GQ*. He wore a gold Rolex watch, lizard-skin shoes and belt, a European-looking shirt and a gold chain around his neck. His eyes were shielded by the most perfect pair of Porsche Carrera sunglasses, which were all the rage.

Sergio's house was like a paradise. There was a swimming pool surrounded by palm trees in the back yard, overlooking a peaceful pond by flamingos, just like the ones at the zoo. And his bedroom was bigger than my parents' and mine combined. Actually, it was probably the size of my whole house.

I ran my fingers over the switches and buttons on his stereo, the lava lamp and touch-tone phone, allowing my eyes to float over the posters of beautiful women in bikinis and shiny red Ferraris that he had pinned up on his walls.

"Wanna go for a swim?" Sergio shouted, jumping up and down on his bed.

"*¡Vamos!*" I yelled.

We changed quickly and cannonballed into the pool with glee. This was the life. This was the dream. I knew exactly what I wanted to be when I grew up...Mr. Aranda!

During the ride back to my house, as Mr. Aranda drove me alone, I got up the nerve to ask the question: "Mr. Aranda, what do you do for a living?"

Seeming a bit surprised, he answered nonchalantly, "Oh, I'm in the...import-export business."

I'd heard of that. I nodded my head, smiling. Import-Export. It sounded good. In fact, I'd heard it quite often, living there on the border. Maybe I could get into that line of work!

Later, back at home, I saw everything in a different light. My dad was a savage beast compared to Mr. Aranda. My mom appeared tired and old, next to Mrs. Aranda, who always had her highlighted hair professionally coiffed and her make-up done at the Dillard's cosmetics counter. Our creaky, faded hardwood floors seemed primitive compared to the wall-to-wall carpet at the Arandas' house. And, when Christmas finally came, while Sergio was nearly swallowed whole by mounds of crumpled gift-wrapping paper, I found only a paltry red envelope beneath the plastic Christmas tree that teetered in the corner of our spartan living room.

"I'm sorry, *mi hijito*," my mom smiled, running her fingers through my hair. "It was all Santa could afford."

I opened it to find a wrinkled five-dollar bill and an American Greetings card with Rudolph the Red-Nosed Reindeer on it.

I fought off the knot growing in my throat. I knew times were tougher than ever. My dad had let Pedro's helpers at the plant go. Weeks went by with nothing to do at the tire shop but hope for the phone ring. My dad had run out of money, and credit to buy rubber. And the warehouse was still filled with tires he couldn't seem to sell. At night, I'd hear my parents argue through the paper-thin walls. My dad blamed the hard times on the peso devaluation, and the new radial tires that were flooding the market. My mom blamed him for not giving up on being self-employed and just getting a regular nine-to-five job like everybody else.

That Christmas, I cried myself to sleep, dreaming of the Evel Knievel bike in the store window at Mac's Toys, wondering if some other lucky boy had gotten it from a Santa Claus richer than mine.

I prayed as I drifted to sleep: "Help me, God. Help me figure out a way to get my bike. And help me grow up to be rich like Mr. Aranda some day, not poor like my dad. I'll study hard. I'll go to college. But help me now if you can! I don't want to wait forever and be an old man riding the Evel Knievel bike. It just wouldn't be the same."

I dreamt of riding my bicycle freely down the street, but then when I got a clear look at myself I realized that I was wrinkled and rickety in my dream, sporting thick glasses. Worst of all, my wavy black hair was completely gone, just a few scraggly white strands clinging to my shiny head.

The very next morning, driven by the sheer terror of that nightmare, I scribbled out a list of possible moneymaking ideas so that I could reach for my goal, all on my own. No longer would I rely on elves from the North Pole, or wait in vain for the peso's value to rise. Sadly, my list was short and unimaginative.

Wash cars. This was pointless because pretty high school girls always put on car washes at gas stations to raise money for their extracurricular activities. There was no way I could compete. I crossed it out.

Mow lawns But no one in my neighborhood would pay to have someone else mow their lawn. They'd either do it themselves or, more likely, allow the weeds to infest their yard and the grass to grow waist high. I put an angry slash through it.

Deliver newspapers. I'd need a bike; and I was not about to ride the pink one rusting in the backyard.

None of the options harbored any hope. In frustration, I crumpled up my piece of paper and tossed it into the wastebasket.

Hopefully, something would come to me.

"Please, Virgencita," I added to my prayers, appealing to the Virgen de Guadalupe tapestry hanging in my parents' bedroom. "Please remind God and Jesus to help me out with a great idea."

The following Sunday morning, my dad invited me to go with him to the *mercado* across the border to buy avocadoes, *calabacitas*, and *chile* peppers. For some reason, the ones at the H.E.B. could never measure up to the ones sold across the border.

The mercado bustled with activity, vendors hawking their goods loudly as crowds milled tightly amidst the dizzying array of stalls. Every fruit and vegetable imaginable could be found, displayed in angled crates within the covered, open-air marketplace. Scattered between the stalls were small counters where people could sit and order freshly made tortillas and *tacos al pastor* as a smorgasbord of appetizing fragrances stimulated the senses.

At the avocado stand, my father chatted with the vendor as if he'd known him since childhood. The wizened old man deftly split the avocadoes open with one fluid flick of his blade, removing the pit at the same time. He then inserted a single green chile Serrano in the groove, clap the two halves together and place them in a bag.

"Why does he take out the pit?" I asked in fascination.

"Because it's against the law to take the avocadoes to El Otro Lado with the seed still in them," he replied, counting out the colorful peso bills that shared his wallet with dull green dollars. El Otro Lado was what everyone on the Mexican side of the border called the United States. It literally meant "The Other Side."

"Why?"

"Well, because they're afraid that the seeds could carry diseases that might harm the crops in El Otro Lado," my dad explained.

"But they don't make you take the pits out of the peaches, or the mangoes or the plums," I observed. "And you couldn't take all the seeds out of the tomatoes or the chiles or the guayabas."

My dad smiled as he paid the avocado man. "You're right. I wonder why they pick on the avocadoes? Maybe they don't like guacamole."

"And why does he put the chile Serrano in the middle where the pit was?" I wondered out loud.

"It helps keep the avocado fresh and green until we eat it," my dad said, guiding me towards the chile stall. "Speaking of chiles, here, I need to get some."

My eyes swept across the vivid display of peppers. Red, green, crimson, orange, yellow, brown, they came from all parts of Mexico and in all shapes, textures, and colors. Long and gnarled, short and smooth. Fresh, dried, smoked, pickled. Big and small, round and oblong. As my dad picked out what he wanted, my eyes landed on my favorite treat from the mercado, the chile powder. It was a speckled orange and white blend of fine chile powder, salt, sugar, and crystallized lime, a taste bud tingling sensation with a spicy punch. It came in little plastic bags that were one inch wide and five inches long. All for only one peso, five American cents, in those days. And I loved it.

"*Papá*," I dared, tugging at his sleeve. "Could I get some chile powder?"

My dad glanced dismissively at me, "Not today, Ramón. Every peso counts right now."

I stared glumly at my tattered weekend sandals. Then I remembered the five-dollar Christmas bill smoldering in my pocket, and my face brightened.

"*¡Papá!*" I exclaimed. "I can pay for it myself. Look!" Digging through my loose jeans, I produced the wrinkled likeness of Abraham Lincoln. He was one of my favorites, after the biography I had read in the library. You could count on Honest Abe. Now he would help me in my time of need.

Reluctantly, my dad relented. "Okay, get your chile."

The five-dollar bill in my hand, I felt empowered. Why get one pack of chile, when I could buy...a hundred? Well, no, that would be crazy...but it felt good knowing I could if I wanted to. Instead, I grabbed a fistful of the soft, squishy packets and laid them on the tiny counter for the chile vendor to count.

"*Veinticinco pesos*," he mumbled.

I handed him the bill and he gave me back my change: four one-dollar bills and three quarters.

Giddily I scooped up my Christmas chile and cradled it all the way home. During lunch the following school day, I tore open the top of one of the packets, pouring a healthy heap of the powder into the palm of my hand. Then I proceeded to lick it straight from there. It was the only way to eat the chile powder. It tasted so good.

In moments, a small crowd of classmates had gathered around me, asking for a taste of the chile. Jimmy and Sergio Aranda were the first. I poured a slightly smaller heap into each of their outstretched palms. But then there were more. My whole packet of chile would be gone! Luckily I still had four more at home. I distributed a little bit to each of the kids, trying to save some for myself. But it wasn't enough. They wanted more.

"Please, Ramón," one little girl whined. "It tastes so yummy. I want some more."

"I don't have any more," I explained, throwing my hands up in the air.

"Can you bring me a pack tomorrow?" she cried. "I'll buy it from you."

Suddenly, I thought of Mr. Aranda and his import-export business. It was as if a choir of angels was singing in harmony and only I could hear it.

"Sure," I shrugged nonchalantly as I felt my pulse quicken.

At home, I sat on my bed and stared at the packets of chile I still had left. There were four of them, costing me twenty cents. I wondered for how much I could sell them to the kids at school? A dime a piece? A quarter? Tomorrow I would find out. I figured I should aim high.

"You can always come down on your price," my dad advised, based on his tire-selling experience. "It's a lot harder to go up."

At school, Jimmy and Sergio were the first at my side during recess. Then, the little blonde girl from the day before, and three of her friends. Five customers, but only four bags of chile. And what about me?

"How much are you selling it for?" Sergio asked.

"I was thinking a quarter," I replied casually. In seconds, the bags were all gone and I strolled away with a rewarding jingle in my pocket. I had spent a quarter on chile two days earlier, and today I had a dollar. And I'd gotten to eat a bag of chile for myself. Not bad.

At home I lined up my quarters and stacked my bills, pulling out my math notebook.

The Evel Knievel bike was $250, and worth every penny. How many bags of chile would I have to sell to reach my goal and cross the finish line in stars, stripes, steel and chrome? At a profit of twenty cents per bag, I calculated that I'd need to sell more than a thousand bags of chile to buy the bicycle. In math class, I would never look at a word problem the same way again.

I ran to the phone and called the tire shop.

"Dad," I panted. "Are you going to Mexico tonight?"

"Yes, I have to drop off some tires. Why?"

"Can I come with you, please...please...?" I begged.

"Sure, I'll swing by the house on the way," he replied.

As we rumbled across the bridge with a pile of recapped tires bouncing around in the truck bed, my dad asked, "So why the big interest in coming with me?"

"Well, I was hoping you would do me a big favor," I said slowly, lacing my response with suspense.

"Really? What favor is that?" he asked, raising an eyebrow in curiosity.

"Could we stop by the mercado so I can get some more chile," I blurted out quickly, my words running together. "I'm gonna sell it at school to make money for my bike."

A smile spread slowly across my dad's sun beaten face. "Sure, son. I'll take you to the mercado."

My dad joked with the chile vendor as I gambled my savings away. If I used all of my money, I could buy one hundred and fifteen bags. I decided to round it to a hundred and keep some change, just in case I needed it.

"Te vas a enfermar si te comes todo ese chile," the vendor warned from behind his stall.

My dad laughed, *"No, señor, el niño va a vender el chile en El Otro Lado, a sus amigos."*

The vendor grinned broadly, *"Ha! Es comerciante. Buena suerte, mi hijito!"*

My dad glanced at me out of the corner of his eye as we drove back home over the Rio Grande. I was running my hands through the bags the vendor had placed in a medium-sized cardboard box, which now sat between us. I inhaled the rich, tangy aroma. Mmmm. So spicy and sweet at the same time.

"I'm proud of you, son," he said. "There's a *dicho*—a saying—in Spanish that goes: '*Con paciencia y un ganchito, hasta una fortuna se alcanza.*'"

With patience and a little hook, even a fortune could be attained. I had my hook. And I knew I had patience. If I could put up with my crybaby little brother, I could surely work patiently towards my dream.

Day after day, I stuffed my backpack full of chile and headed off to school. And, every day, the lunchtime crowd that gathered around me grew larger. I would stand beneath a big mesquite tree in the schoolyard and dispense my imported treat in the shade. From there, I could see the concession stand, the only other alternative to bringing your lunch to school. It was a small grill from which the nuns sold hamburgers and hot dogs. Usually, the lunch line wound its way around the small building. But as time passed and my customer base grew, I noticed the grill line was shrinking. I couldn't help but think of Isaac Newton's Laws of Motion, which we'd been studying in class: For every action there was an equal and opposite reaction. Maybe that old British dude had been on to something, after all. And, if that was the case, I'd do everything in my power to be on the positive side of the equation.

Every weekend, I pooled my earnings and went to the mercado with my father to re-stock my inventory. At home, I kept two boxes under my bed. The smaller one overflowed with dollar bills and quarters. The larger one was stuffed with bags of chile powder. I was selling between thirty and forty bags a day, so my weekly profit was nearly forty dollars a week! In a couple of months, I'd have more than enough money to buy my Evel Knievel bike, which still gleamed like a beacon in the store window at Mac's Toys. I began a weekly pilgrimage to pay homage to it. And I took pride in buying two hundred bags of chile every Sunday at the mercado.

One Friday, at lunch, Mrs. Barrera, the elderly lady who ran the concession stand in the schoolyard, stuck her head out through her open window and looked both ways as if she was expecting a bus to run her over. Not only were there no oncoming vehicles plowing across the playground towards her, but there was also a conspicuous absence of customers for her hamburgers and hot dogs. At that moment it struck me like a *metate* crushing corn: she should expand her menu to include tacos and burritos. I watched as she waved her fist in the air, her eyes burning straight through me like an overdose of chile.

"Ramón López!" she declared bitterly. "Stop selling that chile. You're taking away all my business!"

Instinctively, I burst into laughter. I tried to cover my mouth to avoid angering her further, but it was too late. She slammed her fist onto the wooden counter top.

The crowd in line for my bags of chile jeered at her. And Sergio Aranda began a chant: "The nuns are going broke! The nuns are going broke!"

I blushed with embarrassment, somehow knowing this was going to hurt more than help. Mrs. Barrera closed her window and drew her blinds to shut out the noise.

Later that day, I was thrilled to put business aside and join Jimmy and Sergio at the Arandas' house for my first-ever sleepover.

Earlier that week, I'd battled my parents for the chance to spend the night at Sergio's house.

"Sleepover?" my dad had fumed. "What's that? Another gringo tradition we're supposed to adopt?"

"All the kids do it, Dad, come on, please…just this once?" I pleaded, looking to my mom for support.

She shrugged and pretended to wash dishes. She knew how to pick her battles and was not about to get her hands dirty on this one.

"It's not natural," my dad said. I'd heard the argument a hundred times before. "A child belongs at home with his parents. How else are we supposed to make sure you're safe? What do I know about the Arandas?"

I wondered if he was secretly jealous of Mr. Aranda, if he knew how much cooler Sergio's dad was, if he was afraid I wouldn't want to come back home after a night in the lap of luxury. I wondered if he was hiding his true sentiments behind his usual protests: "How do I know the Arandas are not child molesters? Perverts? Psycho killers?"

"They're nice people," I said. "Mr. Aranda is a businessman, like you, Dad! He's in import-export, just like us."

My dad fought back a chuckle. Luckily, he'd sold a handful of tires that day and he was in an unusually generous mood. "Import-export, eh? Okay, just this once," he relented. "But you better not 'import' any bad habits."

I nearly cried as I hugged him. "Thank you, *Papá*. It's going to be so much fun!"

At the Aranda's palatial home, Jimmy, Sergio and I splashed around in the pool while blaring "We Are The Champions" on the outdoor stereo speakers. As I lounged on an inflatable raft and watched the palms sway in the warm gusts of the Gulf's evening breeze, I couldn't help but call out to Mr. Aranda, who sat in white linen behind his thatched roof tiki bar: "Mr. Aranda…this is the life, sir!"

He smiled weakly and raised his glass in response. Afterwards, we all sprawled on giant leather couches and watched movies on the giant projection TV in their entertainment room. Venturing into the kitchen to microwave a new batch of popcorn, I ran into Mr. Aranda, who was sitting at the kitchen table poring over numbers. He punched at a calculator, and a roll of paper trailed onto the floor.

"How's your chile business going, Ramoncito?" he asked absentmindedly, never raising his eyes from the figures.

I placed a bag of kernels in the large microwave oven and swung the door shut, pressing the "popcorn" button.

"Well, it's been going well, sir," I replied, eager for advice from a successful importer-exporter, "but I am a bit worried."

He clicked away at his calculations. "Why's that?" he asked politely.

"It's the lunch lady, Mrs. Barrera. She's angry because I've taken all her business. I'm worried she and the nuns might shut me down."

"Yes, that would only be natural," he paused and finally looked up, furrowing his brow and running his hands through his hair. For the first time, I noticed the worry lines around his eyes and the streaks of silver through his wavy locks. "Success brings envy. You may need to give them a cut of your profits but, sometimes, even that's not enough. Greed is the root of all business, but it's also the root of all evil."

"The nuns aren't very easy to talk to," I said, as the microwave beeped. "But maybe Mrs. Barrera…although she is pretty scary herself. So, offer them a cut?" I asked, grabbing the popcorn and backing out of the room, eager to get back to the movie.

"I'd say so," he replied, frowning at his calculator. "And hope it's not too late."

As I headed back to the entertainment room, I felt somewhat dispirited. The Arandas' house was pretty incredible, but Mr. Aranda didn't seem to be enjoying it half as much as everybody else.

The next morning, I awoke with a jolt. I thought I'd heard a popping noise outside the window. Rubbing at my bleary eyes, I wondered if I'd been dreaming of the fancy microwave that yielded endless bags of popcorn the night before. Dawn was barely breaking and we'c stayed up so late, I thought I'd sleep till noon. I glanced over tc see Sergio and Jimmy snoring lightly in the sleeping bags spread out on the thick beige carpet in Sergio's room. I heard tires squealing on the street. My heartbeat quickened and I peered out the window, glimpsing a pair of taillights vanishing around the corner. I *had* heard something.

I knew I should ignore it and crawl back into my sleeping bag, but something compelled me to tiptoe out into the dark hallway.

"I'll get a drink of water," I whispered to myself.

I crept silently over the cool white marble floors, drifting past the shadowy shapes of the modern furniture in the living room. Entering the kitchen, I surveyed the table Mr. Aranda had worked at the night before. There was no trace of his papers and calculations. The table was wiped clean. That's when I noticed the door to the carport was ajar.

"That's weird," I muttered. Reaching for the doorknob, I peeked outside. In the rising blue light of dusk I could make out Mr. Aranda's white convertible sitting in the driveway with the engine running and the driver-side door wide open. There was no sign of Sergio's car.

My throat tightened as I walked slowly towards the idling Cadillac. Then I saw a dark trickle of crimson fluid on the cement and Mr. Aranda's Rolex-clad wrist and bejeweled hand on the ground, visible beneath the car door.

Without hesitating or daring to look any further, I scrambled back into the house, screaming out, "Mrs. Aranda! Sergio! Mrs. Aranda!"

The ambulances were there in minutes, but there was nothing the paramedics could do to put the blood back in Mr. Aranda's body, or to plug the numerous holes I overheard the sheriff attribute to a semi-automatic weapon.

Jimmy and I hovered uncomfortably near Sergio, who cried in his dazed mother's arms.

When my dad picked me up, he parked across the street, traversing a wide arc around the crime scene. He glowered at me beneath the brim of his Stetson, like somehow this was all my fault.

With a tip of his hat and a solemn nod, he acknowledged Mrs. Aranda and escorted me away.

It was my first and last sleepover.

Sergio didn't come to school the next week, nor the week after that. When I asked my teacher, Miss Oak, she replied that Sergio had moved back to Mexico, to be closer to family. Then she added that she needed to talk to me about my chile business.

With all the sadness and distraction, I'd never gotten around to implementing Mr. Aranda's final advice. The truth was, I'd been too intimidated by the wiry Mrs. Barrera, seething in her lonely concession stand. And the nuns seemed so remote and untouchable in their giant habits, waddling awkwardly about the hot, dusty campus like penguins dropped into a desert by some bizarre accident of nature.

"Ramón," Miss Oak explained, sitting with me on the curb outside the classroom. "I think it's very creative of you to try to make some money. It's…enterprising."

Miss Oak was an ample, friendly woman. Even though she was Anglo, she always wore colorful, flowing Mexican dresses. I wondered why she hadn't joined the convent, like most of the other teachers at the school. Maybe she shied away from the discomfort of the habits. Maybe cotton, embroidered dresses from the tourist shops across the border were too comfortable to sacrifice for a life as a bride of Jesus.

"But the sisters have asked me to talk to you about this chile business," she continued. "They want you to stop selling chile on school grounds."

My thoughts jumped like Evel Knievel to the box full of chile bags stashed beneath my bed, the shiny bike waiting in the window at Mac's Toys, the funds that still fell short of bridging the chasm between me and my dream. I decided to try the late Mr. Aranda's proposed gambit as a last resort.

"What if I shared the profits with the sisters? Could I keep doing it?" I looked up at Miss Oak eagerly, but I could read the answer in her cold blue eyes.

"I'm sorry, Ramón," pity tinged her voice. "It's not the profits the sisters are concerned about. It's the nutrition and health of the children. The parents have been complaining that their kids are using their lunch money to buy your chile. And then they're going home with sick stomachs. It has to stop."

She patted me on the head and walked into the classroom. "C'mon," she said. "We have to get back to our schoolwork.

Someday, if you stay in school, you'll have your chance to be a big entrepreneur."

I looked up the word in the dictionary the first chance I got. It read:

> *en·tre·pre·neur n*
> *somebody who sets up and finances new commercial enterprises to make a profit*

I thought of Mr. Aranda sprawled out next to his car, his perfectly pressed clothes soaked in blood. I envisioned my dad puttering about town in his rattling pickup, peddling recapped tires and praying the peso would stop deflating like a poorly patched spare. I thought of the earnings I'd sunk into my inventory of chile. It seemed like far too simple a definition for such a complex endeavor. What did Webster know about being an entrepreneur on the border? Maybe it should read: "somebody who risks his life and everything he owns for the chance to reach his dream." In that sense, wasn't everyone who dared cross the Rio Grande an entrepreneur in their own right?

At the dinner table, I commiserated with my dad. I waited patiently while he recounted his day's troubles, and then I heaped my own serving onto the platter, like an extra dollop of *arroz mexicano* from my mom's generous serving spoon.

After listening to my story, my dad cleared his throat, "Son, I'm proud of you. You can't break the nuns' rules, but you also can't give up on your dream. Never give up. Just remember, it's hard to tell the difference between taking a risk and taking a shortcut. You have to take risks to reach your dream, but you shouldn't take the shortcuts. It's about hard work and determination. There's a natural order and process and, when you try to speed things up too much, or take dangerous shortcuts, you're going to get hurt. Just look at Mr. Aranda."

With that, he got up and cleared his plate at the sink.

His silence spoke volumes. I understood. Dad was trying to tell me that Mr. Aranda had taken a shortcut to his dreams. His fast-found wealth was a mirage rippling in this hot desert parched for success stories. Whispers around town were that his money and death both flowed from his dubious dealings importing and exporting a powder far more treacherous than chile.

"The kind of success that lasts," my dad continued, scraping beans from his plate, "usually takes a long time to accomplish. But you can't give up. You have to stick with it. And here, unlike across the river, you have a chance to make it. That's why we're here. That's why it's called the *American* Dream, not the *Mexican* Dream."

He was right, of course. This was bigger than the glittering prize in the store window. It was bigger than the nuns shutting me down. It was about what kind of person I wanted to be in life. Would I be one that succeeded or one that failed? Would I keep my bike on the high road or be tempted by the detours? I struggled to reconcile those questions with the very understanding of what defined success and failure. Just days earlier I had seen my dad as a disappointment and Mr. Aranda as a role model. Now Mr. Aranda was dead, his fleeting achievements an illusion created by border-world sleight of hand. And the sheer will and integrity of my dad's efforts was crystallizing solidly, like the lime and salt mixed in with my powdered chile. Maybe he didn't make a fortune fast, but he kept food on the table and was putting me through private school in America. And he was his own boss. To him that was success, even if Mom disagreed.

Life was confusing. And living in a world of blurring boundaries, colliding cultures and contrasting values didn't make it any simpler.

Before going to sleep, I counted my bags of chile and my savings. If only I hadn't recently doubled my inventory, I would have nearly enough for the bike. Instead, I had four hundred bags of chile. I was stumped. Maybe I didn't need a bike. Did I have to take it so personally? Did it have to be a symbol of my failure?

I went to school the next day. My eyes opened wide when I saw kids walking away from Mrs. Barrera's concession stand at lunch time with burgers, hot dogs and packs of chile in their hands! The sisters were selling the same packets I had. And for a dollar a bag!

"It's an outrage, dude," Jimmy said, pouring some powder into the palm of his hand and taking a big lick. "But they're the only game in town now. Sorry."

My jaw dropped. The sisters had lied about their health concerns. I pulled my private chile bag out and took a tangy, tear-shedding wallop in my cheeks.

I yearned to show those sisters what I was made of. I vowed then to reach my goal, to sell every last packet of chile I possessed.

That night. when my dad got home, I scampered out to his pickup and pulled out the frayed city map he kept in the glove compartment.

"Dad," I asked as casually as possible at dinner. "Can I borrow your delivery map for school tomorrow?"

"Sure, son." he answered, cocking an eyebrow. "Are you working on your business plans?"

"As a matter of fact, I am," I replied with a restrained measure of self-satisfaction and steely determination.

At school, I polled my best customers, asking their addresses and placing a red dot on the map with a number for each of them. On the back, I copied the number, name and exact address. It didn't take long for me to confirm my suspicions. Most of my frequent customers lived in the two fanciest neighborhoods: Rio Viejo and Hidden Valley. I knew most of the Anglo kids got what they called their "allowances," a foreign concept to my parents, on Fridays after school. So Saturday would be the perfect day to strike.

"Dad," I asked that night at the dinner table. "Do you think you'd have time to help me on Saturday?"

"What do you need, son?" he asked.

"I think I can sell most of my chile if I go door to door with my best customers. It might take several weeks, but it's my best bet. My prices are much better than the nuns'."

"Sure, I'll help you. I can't believe those Irish mobsters," he shook his head. "Don't repeat that or I might end up like…"

He trailed off but I knew what he was thinking.

On Friday, I took orders from my schoolmates. After paying the astronomical price charged by the nuns, my rates seemed like a bargain. They ordered large quantities and with about thirty stops, it looked like I would sell half my inventory. In two weeks, I'd be home free.

Saturday morning, while most kids slept or watched cartoons, my dad and I drove from Southmost across town to the nicer subdivisions. I had only seen them in passing, on the way to the Aranda home in Hidden Valley. Palm tress soared and giant manicured lawns stretched beyond wrought iron fences and tall stucco walls. The lush, grassy expanses in front of pristine homes were like pampered private parks, completely alien to my weed-choked neighborhood where tiny patches of dirt were boxed in by sagging chain-link fences. My barrio's tiny public park was an asphalt jungle languishing in the shadows of a freeway overpass under constant construction.

Halfway through my list, I'd sold my entire inventory. I'd been paid in cash, and received a six-pack of Coke, a dozen freshly baked cookies, and a kiss on the cheek by the cutest girl in my class. My dad's truck could have run on my euphoria alone as we rumbled back home.

As I counted my money for a third time, my dad smiled, "You did it!"

"I can't believe it..." I mumbled in awe.

"Where there's a will, there's a way," my dad spouted, always able to deliver maxims as if he had personally coined them for the first time...again.

Glancing out the truck window, I suddenly didn't recognize the landscape. "Where are we going?"

"You have to ask?" he chuckled lightly. "Downtown."

"Mac's Toys!" we said in unison, beaming.

The white Evel Knievel bike sparkled in the window just as it had the first time I'd seen it.

"Wow," I gasped. "There it is."

I saw my dad and me, smiling in our reflections on the broad pane of glass that separated me from my dream. Suddenly, I did a double take, whipping my head around to scan the sidewalk and street behind me.

"What is it, *hijo*?" my dad asked, putting his hand on my shoulder to calm my nerves.

"I...I could have sworn I just saw...Mr. Aranda, walking by in the crowd," my voice quivered.

Saturday shoppers from both sides of the border bustled about in the midday heat. We both searched for a moment, but there was no sign of him.

"Anything's possible!" a voice boomed next to us, again startling me.

I turned to see a burly man with white hair, a matching beard, and tiny gold-rimmed glasses. He looked like Santa Claus, except he wore a light blue *guayabera* instead of the traditional red velvet suit, which would have been too warm for this environment.

"Mac!" my dad replied, his eyes brightening as the two hugged.

"You know Mac?" My eyes widened in awe. Maybe my dad was pretty cool after all. So what if he was grimy and reeking of tire rubber and sweat on most days? He knew Mac!

Mac opened the store, his copious key chain jingling against the glass like sleigh bells.

"Of course," my dad answered as if everyone should know Mac. "Macario and I grew up together in the old neighborhood on Garfield Street."

I eyed Mac. Macario? I had always envisioned "the Mac" of Mac's Toys to be an Anglo man, a pillar of the local elite. He looked the part, but his name was Macario? He was…one of us?

Macario lightly ruffled my hair as he led the way through the aisles bursting with toys.

He chortled, channeling the spirit of Old Saint Nick again, "*Mi hijo*, on the border things are rarely as they seem. Move a step and your whole perspective changes. Sometimes you don't even have to move, the world moves around you or the ground shifts beneath you, or the river takes an unexpected twist and turn." Then his eyes darted to my dad as he added, "Remember El Chato?"

"How could I forget?" my dad replied.

I'd heard of El Chato. He had been one of the mafia kings across the border. A few years back, he'd been holed up for days in his house, under siege by both cops and rival gangsters. There was a huge gunfight and the house was blown up with a rocket launcher. When the dust cleared, they carried out a bunch of charred bodies and it was declared that El Chato was dead. His wife and kids had been at their house on El Otro Lado at the time. After the siege, they all moved south, deep into Mexico. Then rumors started surfacing that El Chato was not dead at all, but alive and well with his family, still directing traffic from an old hacienda near Guanajuato. It was said he'd had his face surgically altered and adopted a whole new identity, but everyone still knew he was El Chato. I couldn't help but wonder…

"But enough of that!" celebrated Mac in a jubilant tone. "I have a feeling anything's possible when it comes to you and that Evel Knievel bike! My store clerk told me about your quest."

"He did?" I couldn't believe it. I was almost famous.

"Yes, are you ready to ride?" His eyes twinkled like silver Christmas tree ornaments.

"Am I ever!" I proudly deposited my shoebox full of neatly stacked dollar bills and shiny quarters on the counter.

Mac giddily counted the money like it was his first sale all over again. "He did this all by himself, huh?"

My dad nodded proudly.

"Well it looks like we have another *empresario* from the old barrio! Give me a call when you're old enough for a job!"

My smile stretched from ear to ear as he ambled over to the display shelf and lowered the bike, meticulously removing all of the tags, polishing it and adjusting the seat to my height.

As my dad and I carried it out to load on the truck, Mac held the door open for us.

"Ten cuidado, mi hijo," he said. "Be careful. That Evel Knievel is a real crazy loco. Only gringos can afford the luxury of doing wild stunts and taking risks just for fun. We Mexicans face more than enough risk in our daily lives!"

Mac and my dad shook hands and patted each other on the back. I watched my bike with an eagle eye to make sure it didn't tip over in the truck bed as we rode home.

As my dad gently placed the bike on the asphalt in front of our dilapidated house, my mom and baby brother came out on the porch to watch.

"I'm happy for you, Ramoncito," my mom said, carrying my brother, who giggled and cooed in a rare moment of cuteness. "But please be careful. I don't want you to end up in the hospital."

I knew she was thinking of the time Evel Knievel had crashed, trying to jump thirteen Pepsi delivery trucks. And I remembered the time I'd read one of his entries to her from the Guinness Book of World Records.

"Look, Mom," I had gawked. "It says here Evel Knievel has had four hundred and thirty-three broken bones...and he's still alive. It's a world record!"

I wished now, as my mom gulped fearfully and clung to my brother like a lifesaver, that I hadn't read that out loud.

"Ándale, enjoy!" My dad whispered as he helped me onto my new bike. "You've earned it."

I waved to them as I rode slowly down the street and around the corner, my mom and brother watching from the porch, my dad standing in his *guayabera* at the chain-link gate to our overgrown front yard.

The bike felt good. It handled worlds better than the rusty old girl's bike on which I'd learned to ride. I could feel the eyes following me as I rode towards the levee, old couples watching from their rockers on shady front porches and clusters of teenagers pointing from street corners.

One kid whistled and called out: "Jump, Evel. Jump!"

I hit the pedals harder, my thighs burning. I rode up a narrow path to the ridge of the grassy levee, skidding and kicking up a cloud of dust as I turned and headed south along the trail.

As I rode, a panoramic view unfolded around me. To my left lay the teeming shacks, broken streets and tin roofs of Southmost. To my right, the Rio Grande snaked mysteriously towards the horizon in the east. Beyond that, I could see the vast sprawl of Matamoros, the spires of its cathedral jutting up into the clear blue sky, then ranch lands stretching beyond the fringes of the city. Somewhere out there, the river opened up and poured into the ocean. My thoughts and emotions swirled like the treacherous waters of the river below, with stories, memories and conversations bubbling up like the remnants of a raft capsized and shattered on the rocks beneath the surface.

Life on the border was truly mystifying. It was hard, at times, to tell the difference between good and bad, failure and success, life and death, Mexican and American, dreams and delusions, especially when the thin dividing line often blurred and twisted in unexpected ways, and when my instincts were to constantly cross that border back and forth rather than stop at its edge. In my mind and heart, the border ran through all things, including me. It was a wavering high wire I always balanced upon, my center of gravity invariably and incessantly shifting from one side to the other in an instinctive search for equilibrium. It was an invisible line I straddled, rather than an imaginary boundary at which I felt compelled to stop. I saw it not as a constraint, but as an invitation. Not an end, but a beginning…maybe the same way Evel viewed a ramp pointed at a precipice.

I pumped hard at the pedals, yearning to leave the confusion behind and simply savor my moment. Riding hard along the crest of the levee, hugging the curves, I picked up speed in a flash, my knuckles tightening their grip on the chrome handlebars. I was just a kid riding my bike on a sunny day, trying not to notice the people wading across the waters below, in search of a better life. The Gulf breeze whipped through my hair. The sun warmed my face. And the golden light bounced off the red stripes, the white paint, and the blue stars of my dream in motion.

It's My Wall Now

Elia Salazar stormed angrily down the wooden steps onto her front lawn, pink curlers still in her gray hair, her sunflower housedress fluttering in the breeze. Halting at the edge of her lovingly designed flowerbed, she huffed as she planted her fists on her wide hips and glared at the alien barrier that soared before her eyes.

"What is this fence doing in the middle of my front yard?" she railed at no one in particular.

No one replied.

Elia inspected the wall more closely, tiptoeing through the bands of color she had so carefully selected at the nursery, peaches and pinks for her son's cheeks, red for his lips, greenery for his army collar and beret, deep purple standing in for the black of his hair, eyebrows and eyes.

He had been such a handsome young man, she sighed, doing her best not to crush his already-scarred likeness.

The wall towered above her, disappearing into the blazing South Texas sun. It was black and fashioned like a chain-link fence except the holes were tighter, smaller, and the metal looked thicker, stronger. It appeared impenetrable, even though you could see right through it, once you got close up. At the top, coils of barbed wire reflected the golden light harshly, searing her eyes.

"*Mi pobre hijito*. First the Iraqis and now this," she muttered, directing her thoughts at her son up in Heaven. "It looks like a prison fence."

"Those are meant to keep people in," a booming voice startled her from the other side as a silhouette approached the barrier. "This one's meant to keep them out."

The man was dressed in the familiar Border Patrol uniform: dark green pants and shirt. Through the gridwork of the fence, she strained to make out his features, shaded beneath the rim of his matching hat.

"Is that Hilda Garza's boy?" she guessed, her voice cracking in the dry late morning heat.

"Yes, ma'am. That's me," he replied, betraying no surprise. "I'm Ronny."

"El chiquito," she recalled. "You're her youngest. You went to school with my David."

"Yes, ma'am. I knew David. I'm sorry…about…well, you know."

"Yes," she licked her lips, frowning. Then she looked back down at the flowers. "Do you know anything about this fence, little Ronny?"

Ronny was over six feet tall and had the broad shoulders of a football player.

"Courtesy of Homeland Security, ma'am," he explained. "It's the new border fence."

"But…the river's about a mile south of here," she pointed past her house towards a long line of trees that bordered the levee. "You know that, right? You are with the *Border* Patrol."

He chuckled. "Yes, Mrs. Salazar. Didn't anyone explain this to you?"

"No, *nadie.* I just woke up, made my *chorizo con huevos* and my *cafecito.* And then I looked out my window to admire my flowerbed. *Y pues*…there it was. Here it is!" She motioned upwards, her arms flapping in the scorching breeze.

"It went up pretty fast," he nodded, his eyes admiring the fence as if it were a marvel of modern engineering. "It's supposed to make our job easier. Keep the *mojados* out. We'll see."

Elia knit her eyebrows together fastidiously. "I beg your pardon, but it appears that it might also keep me out! In case you haven't noticed, I seem to be on the wrong side of it."

Ronny gasped.

Elia recalled he had not quite been the brightest bulb on the cactus tree. For some reason the words "special ed" came to mind. She shook her head.

Pobrecito, she thought. And his mother had been such a nice woman.

"There's a gate!" Ronny exclaimed, proud of his own realization. "You can go through it. All you'll have to do is show your proof of citizenship to the guards."

"Proof of citizenship?" Elia blinked hard. "Like what proof? I've got a fence running through a flowerbed made to look like my son, who died for his country, and I need proof of my citizenship?"

She felt her breakfast chorizo burning a hole through her stomach. Her heart pounded. She could hear Doctor Lozano warning her not to get "*alebrestada*," which was an old Spanish term used to describe enraged barnyard animals. Heart attacks ran in her family. Why, even her husband Alonso had died of cardiac arrest ten years back while plowing the orange grove, widowing her prematurely.

Ronny stared down at his dusty boots, like a little boy who'd just been scolded by his mother.

Elia sighed, straightening her flowery housedress, "How far away is this gate of yours?"

He shifted uneasily, "A couple miles or so that way…"

She followed his pointing finger upriver. There was no road leading in that direction, but Alonso's old pick-up truck could manage the flat grassy terrain.

Suddenly, Ronny's eyes lit up. "Just a moment, Mrs. Salazar, wait here. Don't move." He nearly ran back to his Border Patrol SUV, painted white and mint green with police lights on top. Then he scrambled back, waving a glossy flyer with glee.

"What's this? Are you inviting me to your birthday party?" Elia chided.

"No," he replied. "But of course you're welcome to come to that too…"

She stared back, the corners of her lips turning downwards like the flowers wilting in the shadow of the fence.

"Anyway," he recovered. "It's got information about a hearing they're having in Harlingen about the border fence. You can come speak your mind. Who knows? Maybe Secretary Chertoff will move the fence off your land!" He stuffed the flyer through one of the narrow apertures in the fence.

Without reading it, she placed it in her roomy pocket. "*Gracias,* Ronny. Now run along. I hope your job gets easier because of this fence. Lord knows, mine sure hasn't."

Carefully, she stepped around her flowers, as her eyes scanned the fence northwards. She wondered exactly how far the gate was, and how much more gas money it was going to cost her every month to drive around this monstrosity to shop for groceries, make her doctor visits and meet with her friends for coffee at the IHOP in town. Which reminded her, she was running very late and she absolutely had to call her surviving children to tell them about this. Maybe they could help. They weren't as helpful as David had been. But now that he was gone, they had to suffice. *Ni modo.* As she ascended the stairs to the old two-story wooden house that had been in her family for generations, she glanced back at her son's mutilated visage.

"What a tragedy," she mumbled beneath the roar of the departing Border Patrol vehicle on the other side of the fence.

***

"'Why don't you just move the flowerbed?' Can you believe that? That's what my youngest son said!" Elia's eyes loomed wide with disbelief as she gawked at her gaggle of friends across the table at IHOP.

To the young waiter, who had crossed illegally a few weeks earlier in a spot untouched by the border fence, they vaguely resembled a flock of seagulls chattering over each other.

"*¿Más café?*" The waiter asked, hoisting a pot of regular in his right hand and a pot of decaf in his left, a light sweat breaking out on his sun-beaten forehead.

"*Sí, sí, claro,*" the ladies chanted in unison, dismissing the slight man with synchronized waves of their hands.

"Well, Junior has a point," Mrs. Naylor replied haughtily, patting her chestnut-dyed beehive with her diamond-studded hands. "Why *not* move the flowerbed?"

Elia's two other friends, the spindly Mrs. Vela and the rotund Mrs. Vega, pursed their lips and braced themselves for their lifelong companion's response.

But Elia contemplated the possibility quietly for a moment before replying.

"No, the idea was for me to design the flowerbed in the likeness of my son David and place it where I could see it out my window in the morning and admire it from the porch. If I move it somewhere else, I won't be able to do that. And it's my land, isn't it? Why should I move it?" Elia replied.

"Well," Mrs. Naylor retorted, knowing full well she was walking through a minefield, "it would be a shame for your son to sacrifice his life for his country and then have your family's patriotism questioned because you spoke up against this border fence, wouldn't it?" There, she'd said it, what they'd all been thinking since Elia had first started obsessing over this border fence, a few weeks earlier. And she wasn't about to stop now. "If you ask me…and I think you did…I say, don't go to that hearing and act like an ingrate. Move the flowerbed and be done with it. Understand, they've built the border wall to protect us against the terrorists. You know that's the real problem. It's not the Mexicans. Everyone loves the Mexicans."

"Want some of my chocolate chip pancake, Elia?" piped up Mrs. Vega. "I couldn't possibly eat another one."

But they all knew that she could.

"You've been eating another one your whole life," Elia snapped bitterly.

Mrs. Vega blushed and opened her mouth, but instead of responding she decided to take one for the team, stuffing another piece of pancake into it to silence her resentment.

"Elia, please…" Mrs. Vela soothed. "No need to take it out on us. We're your friends."

"Well, what do *you* think? You two never say anything. Just our *gringa* friend here speaks up like it's her God-given right. What about you?" Elia demanded.

But they were out of practice, and Mrs. Naylor beat them to the punch, "It *is* my God-given right, guaranteed by the Constitution, thank you very much."

Mrs. Vela raised her frail hand and almost shrank back into her seat when she felt all of their eyes fall on her. Her voice wavered as she ventured aloud "Well actually, I do have an opinion."

"Out with it then," Mrs. Naylor exhorted, swigging coffee with such zeal Elia suspected she might have spiked it with a dash of tequila.

"*Pues,* Elia has rights too. She is an American citizen. In fact, her family's been here in this land for a long time, longer than any of us." She looked pointedly for a fleeting moment at Mrs. Naylor but dared not meet her eyes. "That land was a Spanish grant from the king to your family generations ago, wasn't it, Elia?"

Elia nodded.

"My humble opinion," continued Mrs. Vela, "is that Elia should speak up. Or else we'll keep getting trampled by these people from Washington, D.C. They just don't understand our way of life here on the border. But we're American too. And we deserve a voice. We deserve to be heard."

They all sat quietly for a moment. Mrs. Vela had been eating breakfast at this table every Wednesday morning for fifteen years and, in all that time, she had probably not spoken as much as she had in the last fifteen seconds.

Clearing her throat and nodding respectfully towards Mrs. Vela, Elia added, "I can't believe my patriotism would be questioned. It's not like I support the terrorists or even want more *ilegales* crossing the river. I just want my land and my wishes respected. No one even asked me if they could build in my front yard. After all, I didn't cross the border; the border crossed me. The land was in my family when this was a Spanish colony, then when it was Mexico, then when it became Texas and finally when the United States took the land between the Nueces River and the Rio Grande in the US-Mexico War. And now the border's crossing me again, except it's leaving me in a no-man's land, between the river and this fence. What country am I in now?"

"That's precisely the problem, Elia," Mrs. Naylor declared imperiously. "People are going to think you don't want to be here. *You didn't cross the border. The border crossed you.* Does that mean you'd rather this still be part of Mexico? Is that why you want the fence down? So we can be re-invaded? I'm telling you, for your own good, just keep this to yourself. Don't go stirring up trouble. Think about your children and your grandchildren. Their future is here, not south of the border."

Elia fought back the anger. She hadn't eaten *chorizo con huevo* for days, in order to avoid the heartburn, but still the acid kicked up and scorched her innards. She stared at her plate of uneaten pancakes drowning in syrup. She wanted to speak up. In fact, she wanted to yell at Rebecca Naylor that very instant, for being so damn *gringa*. But she feared Rebecca was right. What if people saw her as a traitor for speaking up against the fence? What if, instead of seeing her as the proud American mother of a fallen hero, they saw her as a treacherous outsider who belonged back in Mexico? What if they deported her in retaliation?

The well-intentioned waiter reappeared with his swirling glass coffee pots but, before he could even open his mouth to ask, Mrs. Naylor cut him off sharply: "Not now, Frank," she said, reading his nametag.

For a moment, he looked confused, then he smiled, "*Oh, yo no me llamo Frank. Soy Julio.* Dis iz da only...¿*cómo se dice?*...tag...dey had..." He struggled in broken English.

The ladies all assessed each other sourly. Any other Wednesday they would have laughed, joked with him in Spanish, and left him a generous tip. Today was not that day.

***

"And why *don't* you just move the flowerbed?" Alonso Junior asked again, setting his Dos Equis down and wincing in preparation for the response.

Elia glared at him from her command position at the helm of the kitchen counter, where she vigorously kneaded the *masa* for the tamales, flanked by her daughter Elena, who delicately sipped a hearty Pouilly-Fuisse from her wine glass.

"Stop asking that ridiculous question!" Elena exploded, at risk of infusing the tamale dough with the flavor of French wine.

"I'm just sayin'," Alonso Junior's hands instinctively rose to cover his head, as if Elena might just hurl the wine glass at him.

In all fairness, she considered it, but it tasted too damn good to waste. And, frankly, it was the only way she would survive the holidays in the Valley before heading back up to Manhattan.

"Look," she swallowed, a perfect blend of tart and sweet. "We have to support Mom. That's what we're supposed to do. That's our job. She should go to that hearing...and she should be heard!"

Elena emphatically placed the glass down on the Formica counter and reached for the spoon to serve more Maseca corn *masa* mix from the nostalgically familiar bag with the green print and the iconic image of the corn ear emblazoned on the front.

"It's just..." Alonso Junior said. "I was thinking of running for school board next year. And...well...if Mom gets bad publicity...old man Sanderson might just beat me...again."

Elena stared at her brother. He was a well-toned man in his late twenties, tanned and muscular. Invariably, he wore his red shorts, white polo shirt and red cap with the emblem of a cougar on the front.

"Junior, you're a coach," she stated flatly.

He glared back at her assaulting New York City style, her low-slung, tattered jeans revealing a peak of her taut belly. Her lean, shapely walker's body seemed as foreign to him as that of a giraffe's at the Gladys Porter Zoo in Brownsville. Her long black hair was pulled back tightly into a ponytail, the long waves cascading down her back to the tattoo of a butterfly at the center of her hips. Not right, he thought, not ladylike.

The sculpted angles of her caramel face reflected his angry gaze as he retorted, "And you're an urban hamster."

Elia deftly stepped into the tension between her offspring, preempting her daughter's lunge at Junior's jugular.

"You're such a jerk!" Elena emphatically declared for the millionth time, as Elia mouthed the words from memory.

"Now, Junior," Elia clarified. "The day the *New York Times* called your sister an…" she paused to make sure she got it right, "'urban hipster' was a special day for our family. To get a book review like that on your first novel, well that's very special. And in the *New York Times*…well…it means we're for real. We're proud of you *m' hija.* Very proud," she reassured her daughter. "Now get back to work on the *masa* or we'll never finish the Christmas tamales."

As far back as she could remember Elena had helped her mother with the Christmas tamales. The next day, dozens of cousins, uncles and aunts would descend on them and they'd feast on the steaming cornhusk-clad morsels in every room, catching up while sharing tales from the previous year. Relatives came from as far north as Chicago, Seattle and New York, and as far south as Costa Rica, where one of their cousins was a programmer for Oracle.

It wasn't easy being an urban hipster, she thought, almost—but not quite—ruing the day the *Times* had christened her with the label. In the city, the moment you were trendy you were, by the same token, destined to become passé. You had to work very hard at looking like you weren't working at all. You had to be educated and trained, yet appear to be a natural talent. You had to be polished yet raw. You couldn't be some loaf-about coach who never left home The pressure was intensified up north, but it persisted on the border in its own way. In the Valley, it was "get out" or "die out." At least their older brother David had ventured beyond the confines of the border. He'd gone to West Point, no less. Joined the army as an officer and gotten shot in the early days of the fight in Baghdad. He was a hero, sure. In his quest to avoid "dying out" on the border, he'd been caught in the crossfire of the Sunnis and the Shi'ites. He deserved a frickin' flowerbed, if that's how Mom wanted to honor him, a flowerbed without a scar across his face. Hadn't the scars on his body been enough? Who the hell did this little brother think he was to oppose their mother's wishes? What had he ever done to deserve anyone listening to him?

"Well, I'm just sayin'," Alonso Junior pressed. "It's easy to run away. It's a lot harder to stay here and do the work, you know."

He thought of all the times he escorted Mom to the hospital with her heart scares that turned out to be gastro-esophageal reflux disease. He wanted to bring up all the funeral arrangements he'd had to bear on his own for their dad and then for David. But it all made him feel tired so, instead, he took another long swig from his Dos Equis and stared out the darkened window into the night.

"I think you should speak up," Elena affirmed. "It's not a right. It's a responsibility."

"What do you mean by that?" Junior inquired, dumping his empty beer bottle into the trash and pulling a fresh, frosty one from the freezer.

Feeling a bit cramped, Elena nudged up against the counter. "I mean, if we don't express ourselves, then we fail America. America is all about speaking up, making things better, changing, always changing. Or else, we'll go extinct, like the dinosaurs."

She was trying to make her argument in terms her little brother could comprehend. She wondered if it might just work.

"Dude, the dinosaurs got extinct by an asteroid," Junior replied in his wisest of tones, the one he reserved for the history and science classes he taught at the high school between Phys. Ed. and extracurriculars.

Elena reached for her wine glass again, resigned to crossing the border into alcohol-induced oblivion, if it would make the pain more bearable.

"It's not un-American to voice our opinions…it's un-American not to," she concluded before draining the glass completely.

"What are you going to do, Mom?" Junior reached for a raw tamale.

"Don't you dare," Elia slapped his hand away. "You'll get sick, like that time when you were five and you ate a dozen raw tamales and ended up in the hospital."

"That sucked," Elena agreed.

"I don't even remember it," Junior stuck his tongue out at her.

"Jerk."

"Urban hamster."

Elia normally would have smiled at the diversity of her two children. Life was a wonder to her, how a simple border girl could end up enjoying such a full experience: the perfect husband, a war hero son, a published intellectual feminist daughter, and a loyal youngest by her side. But rather than revel in her blessings, she quietly kneaded the *masa* for the tamales. She didn't know what to do. She wanted to express herself, but she was afraid of the consequences. And her children were absolutely no help at all.

***

The civic hall bustled with activity, the walls lined with reporters, photographers and armed security guards from the Sheriff's office. Beneath the fluorescent lights overhead, they all appeared lifeless to Elia, despite their animated movements. She sat still in one of the middle rows, listening quietly. At the front of the hall, on a small platform flanked on either side by the American and Texan flags, a long table was presided over by local politicians and officials from the Department of Homeland Security. One after another, they droned on about the terrorists and 9/11 and the need to "secure our borders."

She couldn't help but frown as she thought of the border fence marring her flowerbed likeness of David, her war hero, who'd died in the very War against Terror.

Junior sat to her left, fidgeting and flashing a forced apologetic grin at anyone who looked his way. Elena sat to her right, having flown in again, just for the event. Elia had begged her not to waste her money, but Elena had said *The New Yorker*, a fancy east coast magazine, had fronted her some travel money to write a feature story about the border fence's impact on her family. So, in her own way, Elena had convinced her mom that this was helping her career.

After the politicos made their speeches and presentations, using flashy images projected on giant screens, the floor was turned over to the somber public. A bureaucratic-looking middle-aged man, dressed in grey pants and a white shirt, called out, "Would anyone like to provide testimony?"

A hushed ripple ran through the sea of brown faces in the audience.

Elia blushed. She felt like she should say something, talk about her son, try to convince everyone that she was a proud American despite her heritage, despite her opposition to the fence splicing her lawn. But she knew then, as the flashbulbs popped, that she simply didn't have it in her. Not to speak up. Not to make waves. That wasn't in her upbringing. It was embarrassing. Her daughter could make her own mark, and so could her youngest son. She, well, she would have to find her own way, a different way…maybe not a flowerbed, maybe something else…

Alonso Junior squeezed her arm, whispering, "Thank you," into her ear.

Then just as the gavel was about to pound on the table and the hearing was about to close, a lone voice rose and a wiry woman stood amidst the gathered crowd. Her name, which she was asked to speak slowly and clearly into the microphone, was Eloisa Garcia Tamez. She described how she had lived on her Spanish land grant her whole life, how she was also a descendant of Apache Indians, and that she had a right to say what crossed her land. She concluded with a short statement about the lawsuit she would be filing against the Department of Homeland Security to protect her rights.

"It's so sad," Elena whispered into her mom's ear.

"Yeah," Junior agreed, eavesdropping. "The lady's crazy."

"Homeland Security has suspended the laws of the land in favor of their own agenda," Elena continued in hushed tones, her train of thought diverging from her brother's, momentarily making Elia feel like she was caught in a distorted stereo field where the two sides were not in sync.

Elena had conducted research as background for her article. "Did you know that a law was passed giving the Secretary of Homeland Security authority to waive all legal requirements, in order to build barriers and roads? Right away, Chertoff used his new power to waive the Endangered Species Act, the Clean Water Act, the Clean Air Act, and the National Historic Preservation Act to extend triple fencing through the Tijuana River National Estuarine Research Reserve near San Diego. Only the Supreme Court can change this now…maybe…"

Elena rambled on but her mother was no longer listening. Instead, Elia watched the Lipan Apache woman who spoke, a strange mixture of feelings swirling through her heart and body. For some reason she could not put her finger on, she was angry at the woman. But then she realized it was not because she disagreed with her, but rather because she was envious of her courage.

After Eloisa Garcia Tamez sat down, a professor from the local university followed with a presentation about the environmental dangers posed by a barrier, which would arbitrarily dismember ecosystems. But Elia's eyes remained fixed on the scraggly silver hair of the Lipan Apache woman.

As the hearing concluded, a familiar young man in a Border Patrol uniform approached Elia nervously, his hat in his hands.

"Good evening, Mrs. Salazar," Ronny said, his eyes darting nervously towards Elena, who was dressed all in black, a silver cross encrusted with red gemstones hanging from her neck.

To Ronny's discomfort, it took Elia a few seconds to recognize him. When she finally did, he sighed with relief.

"Oh, hola, mi hijo," Elia said, stretching her flabby arms to give him a welcoming hug.

"Hey, Ronny," Junior quipped.

"Hey there, Junior." Ronny answered, fixing his eyes on Elena's raven locks.

Completely ignoring Ronny, Elena kept whispering into Elia's ear, "I think you should…"

But her mother was gone, disappearing into the crowd and leaving her awkwardly caught between her brother and the Border Patrol agent.

Doctor Lozano's words of warning rang in Elia's ears as she limped towards the wiry woman standing amidst the reporters and photographers. Somehow, people made way for her until she found herself toe-to-toe, sandal-to-sandal with her spitting image.

"Sign me up," Elia heard the words spring forth from her dry, nervously quivering lips.

The lady who was filing the lawsuit smiled, her thousands of wrinkles unfurling like a banner of hope before Elia's eyes. They shook hands, bone against bone pressed through flagging skin, cataract-shrouded eyes shimmering with rediscovered exuberance.

"I saw you back there," Elena told her mom as they drove home down Highway 77.

"Yeah," Alonso Junior said with regret from the back seat of his father's battered pick-up truck. "Me too." He was picturing his chances at a school board seat vanishing as quickly as the endangered species threatened by the border fence. The professor had yammered at length about the ocelot and the jaguarondi, local wild cats whose movements were now restricted by the barrier.

"I'm proud of you," Elena said. "This is going to make a great story in the magazine. I might even teach a class on it at NYU next year."

"Elena, you only think about yourself," Junior accused, gazing grimly out the window at the indiscernible shadows flitting by. Both sides of the highway looked the same to him, yet he knew they were completely different. He wondered if, somewhere out there, an ocelot was dying because it couldn't reach its prey, or a litter of jaguarondi kittens was starving because their mother was trapped on the wrong side of the fence. Hmm, maybe he could teach a class about that.

Elia sat quietly in the driver's seat, navigating her way home around the long barrier, through the gate and over the grooves she'd been treading the last few months on her grassy acres of land.

***

The next morning, while the children slept in the old family home as they once had years before, Elia rose with the sun. Out in the barn, where Alonso had kept the tractors, she rummaged through a bin of spray paint canisters.

Peaches and pinks for his cheeks. Red for his lips. Olive green for his collar and his beret. Ah, and last but not least, black for his hair and eyes. That would surely be better than purple, she mused. *Qué* funny, how things worked out, she smiled.

Placing the cans gently into her wheelbarrow with her gardening tools, she headed out to the flowerbed. A few rearrangements in the soil, and then she began to meticulously spray the fence, the fumes fueling her euphoria.

Her heart beat strongly but there was no acid churning in her stomach or scorching her throat. This was not dying. This was living, she imagined herself explaining to Doctor Lozano. This was not anger or rebellion. This was joy and patriotism.

Close to noon, Elena and Alonso bumped into each other over mugs of coffee left brewing for them by their mother. Together, they looked out through the broad kitchen window. Rubbing their eyes in disbelief, they marched out onto the porch.

The sun shone directly down on the border fence. Spray painted on the black barrier—only visible from the southern side—glistened an uncanny portrait of their martyred brother, green beret and all, smiling with the exhilaration he had borne to the training grounds of West Point, and to the killing fields in the Persian Gulf. For as long as Homeland Security would allow, that image would greet the *mojados* advancing in search of their own American dream.

As Elena and Alonso Junior's eyes descended reluctantly to the flowerbed below, they slowly realized it had been rearranged into an image of the American flag. At first, they didn't see her, camouflaged discreetly in her flowery housedress. But then they both dropped their coffee mugs onto the worn planks beneath their feet as they recognized her.

Smack in the middle of the flowerbed, lay their motionless mother, her arms outstretched, a smile forever emblazoned on her face, a gardening shovel in one hand, and a can of spray paint in the other.

Each had the same instinct: to run to the phone and call David. But they knew all too well the line wouldn't reach across that great divide.

Pierce the Sky

Victor packed his Andean flute gingerly into his backpack, wondering whether he'd ever play it again.

At the crooked door to the shanty, he kissed his wizened grandmother goodbye on her dark leathery cheek and headed out into the muddy streets before sunrise.

The bus wound through the mountains, stopping at every village along the way, until people and chicken crates filled every corner of it. The rusted rack on the roof creaked beneath a teetering tower of tattered luggage, colorful bags and woven baskets. The engine strained to push the sagging tires out of the ruts in the pothole-riddled muddy roads.

Victor dozed on and off, in the far rear corner of the bus, as the sun traversed the sky, dreaming of the City of Angels his cousin Miguel had described to him.

"There's a city that shines like the diamonds you've never seen in Ecuador," Miguel had written in one letter. "The towers graze the sky. The ocean kisses its shores. There is more work than people. And you can make more in one day than you would in an entire month back home…enough for you, for your own wife and children when you settle down, and for our whole family back in the village."

Victor believed Miguel, because Miguel was his older cousin. Miguel played the guitar and wrote poems. As children, they had entertained the grown-ups at family fiestas and later, as teenagers, they'd played in the gazebo at the center of the plaza in the city nearest their village. Together they dreamed of going to America, where their work and their talents might help them escape the fate of so many they'd known. It was the place that would enable them to become more than frightened, poor villagers who simply waited for the soldiers, the paramilitaries or the drug runners to trample them in the streets, kill them in their homes and violate their wives.

Miguel had headed out first and always sent money back home, along with his poems and drawings. While the stream of poetry and images had dwindled over time, the flow of money had remained a constant, beckoning Victor with hopes of prosperity, which had long ago perished in his homeland.

At the bus terminal in Quito, Victor scanned for the man he was to meet. He would be wearing a blue sweatshirt imprinted with "Cruz Azul." Victor knew Cruz Azul was a popular soccer team in Mexico, but it would definitely stand out in Ecuador. It was easy for him to search through the crowd, because he was of a rare height for people from his country. He was dark-skinned like the rest of his family, his eyes black, his onyx hair straight and long, braided down to the middle of his back. But he was a foot taller than everyone else, thin and athletic, virtues that his cousin Miguel had cautioned him could be both helpful and dangerous once in the City of Angels.

"You'll be the first one people hire for construction or anything involving hard manual labor, but you'll also be easy to spot by the *Migra*. So, once you're here, hunch over and never look the gringos straight in the eye," Miguel had advised.

The journey was to be just as Miguel's had been, years earlier. Victor had been saving up for it since Miguel's departure. He was going through the same middlemen: the man at the bus station, the woman who would house and feed him overnight, the van driver that would take him and the others to the port, the sailor on the freight ship that would ferry them to Guatemala, the truck driver who crossed them into Chiapas and handed them off to another who would take them on the long haul to the border near Tijuana, the coyote who would take him across inside a secret compartment hollowed out beneath the seat in his van. It cost five years of hard work and playing the flute for extra money, plus helpful wire transfers sent by Miguel.

Along the journey, Victor yearned to play his flute, but he didn't dare draw attention to himself. Each guide instructed him to blend in, to lay low and keep quiet. Victor did as he was told. He paid the agreed-upon amount to every person along the way, plus a small tip. He tried not to speak to anyone unless he was spoken to first, and he concentrated on his dreams.

One night, in Tijuana, waiting for the right time to be crossed over, a small, older man with broken teeth asked him, "What are you dreaming of? I've been around you for a week and you never talk. You just have this far away look in your eyes."

The two sat on dusty, paint-peeling floorboards, near a clumsily boarded-up window through which pale moonlight filtered. Outside, a light, steady rain patted the slick, deserted streets of the abandoned midnight slum.

"I dream of freedom," Victor replied in a hushed tone.

"What is freedom?" the older man asked, pensively, slowly stroking the frayed edges of the straw cowboy hat he held in his hands.

"I don't know because I've never had it," Victor answered, noticing the image of the Virgen de Guadalupe stamped in blue ink on the side of the man's sombrero. "But I'll know when I find it. I'll know when I feel it."

"What do you think it will feel like?" the man pressed.

"I imagine it might be as simple as being able to look a man in the eye if I want to, someday. It might be having the money to send my children to school, so they can grow up and be somebody, like a doctor or a professor. It might be having papers to visit my family back in Ecuador and fly back and forth to America. It might be playing my flute in the middle of a park or in my very own backyard."

"It might be…not going to sleep hungry?" the older man interjected, an inquisitive look in his eyes. "Or not having the butt of a rifle shoved into your mouth because someone doesn't like the color of your skin or the native tongue you speak?"

"Sure, why not?" Victor smiled gently for the first time since leaving his village. He realized he'd never thought of freedom in terms of what it would *not* be. Just as freedom was the abundance of opportunity, it too was the absence of constraints.

"I am from Chiapas," the elder said. "My name is Tohil."

The two shook hands.

"I'm going to Los Angeles," Tohil added. "You?"

"*También*," Victor replied, missing the silence he had grown accustomed to over the course of his journey.

"Are you afraid?" Tohil asked, searching Victor's eyes for a clue.

Victor did not want to answer any more questions. He wasn't sure if he was afraid. He had been afraid before, when the rebels had torched his village, setting fire to his house. When he'd seen his father's skin and face melted by burns, too crippled to work again, destined to die of infections, when his mother had taken her own life because she was too sad and tired to carry on without a husband, without her eyesight, the only way of possibly earning a cent being the sale of her body to the soldiers when they invaded the village. He had been afraid then, for the fragile minds and souls of his loved ones, fearful of seeing the gently flickering light of their lives snuffed out by the cruel gusts of the world around them. He was afraid when his grandmother—the last one standing—had taken him in, afraid she'd be next to go. His cousin Miguel was still there, and Victor had clung to him. He'd been afraid to watch Miguel leave for America, afraid he'd never see him again, afraid he wouldn't make it out alive.

How could he answer the man's question honestly? If he was afraid, did that make him a coward? And if he was not afraid, was he lying…to Tohil…to himself?

Victor winced and peered through the cracks between the boards nailed over the small window of the apartment. There were about twenty of them. Some slept on piles of rags on the floor, others sat rocking back and forth, their knees gathered up to their chins, waiting endlessly, whispering prayers and remembrances in the dark.

"You have family waiting for you?" Tohil asked, concern lacing his weathered voice.

"Yes," Victor acknowledged, reaching inside his bag and extracting a photo of Miguel, his wife, and children. "My *primo*, Miguel."

"He looks happy, full of life," Tohil assessed, the picture trembling almost imperceptibly in his gnarled hand.

"You should see him when he plays the guitar," Victor smiled as Tohil delicately returned the image.

"I would like that," Tohil nodded. "I do not know many people where I'm going. I have my daughter there, but she'll be busy and I don't want to burden her. I'll make my own way, and help her as much as I can with her children. But friends are good to have. Let us exchange numbers and call each other when we are settled."

Victor copied his cousin's phone number and the two traded scraps of paper. Then they settled back into their spots on the floor, using their sacks as pillows. The older man's rhythmic snoring soothed Victor, reminding him of his grandmother's noisy nighttime breathing, back in the one-room hut they had shared in the village. And for a moment he felt comforted, slipping into sleep.

In the middle of the night, a hand on his shoulder shook him from his slumber. The coyote motioned for him to follow. Glancing back as he ducked out of the room, Victor scanned the far corner for Tohil, but there was no sign of him.

The coyote shepherded him into a battered white Suburban with ripped blue vinyl seats. The man detached one of the seats and popped open a secret compartment, pointing at a space that stretched beneath the row of seats. Victor feared his tall frame would not fit, but somehow he managed it. The coyote closed the compartment and repositioned the seat overhead.

Inside, Victor coiled up like a threatened serpent. He held his breath every time the vehicle stopped, his heart pounding in his ears. He strained to hear the murmurs of conversation up above, wondering if his presence would be revealed, dooming him back to his village and years of laboring and saving to try again. He prayed to God for a smooth passage. And, an eternity later, he squinted in broad daylight outside a bus terminal, allowing his lungs to expand with fresh, cool air.

"San Diego," he read on a wall. "Los Angeles," he mouthed as he saw the sign over the bus' windshield. A smile spread across his face. He wanted to leap into the air and wave his hands towards the sun in gratitude, but he remembered everyone's warnings and hunched over, shuffling onto the bus. The angels were calling. There was a God, Victor thought, and if he had a city on this earth surely he would call it Los Angeles. And surely, there, he could find what he was searching for: freedom, freedom from the fear, the suffering, the having to be everything but himself, freedom from stifling every dream and desire that might spring within him. For, surely, God planted those seeds of hope for a reason, surely He wished to see them sprout and take root. Surely America was the fertile soil where a person could grow and stretch his arms like the limbs of a giant tree reaching for the clouds, bending towards the sun, casting shade on those seeking refuge, yielding fruit for those who might nurture and depend on him.

***

"You made it without being robbed or nearly killed, being caught or sent back at least once! You're truly one of the lucky ones!" Miguel exclaimed, reaching up to wrap his arms around his towering cousin. "I forgot how tall you were. You grew a lot since I left! Maybe they were afraid of crossing you, the bad ones out there."

Victor smiled sheepishly, hunching over a bit more so his cousin would feel more comfortable. Behind Miguel, a woman stood tentatively. Two children's faces popped out from the shadows of her flowery skirt, their eyes wide, hungry to know their own blood.

"Victor," Miguel beamed. "This is my wife, Imelda. And our two little ones: Rosario and Jesús."

"Wow!" Victor crouched down and beckoned the children. "*Vengan.* Come here. I have something for you."

They scurried giddily, giggling and hugging him as he extracted a collection of miniature carved wooden toys, brightly painted by Indian craftsmen from their village.

"It's a dragon, *Mamá*!" cried Jesús excitedly in English.

"And a mermaid, *Mamá*!" exalted Rosario. "And there's more."

"You shouldn't have," Imelda smiled demurely and embraced Victor. "Your journey was so long. You didn't need to burden yourself with gifts."

"It is nothing," Victor said. "I am the burden to you all, but I promise I will not weigh you down for long. I will work hard and I will contribute. And I will help you in every way that I can."

They sat around the kitchen table in the cramped apartment, eating a simple meal of rice and beans.

Miguel explained between mouthfuls of food: "In the mornings, the children go to school early. Then Imelda goes to her jobs. She cleans three houses a day. I go to the construction. I lay tile. It's hard on the back, but I can teach you to help me. Then you can look for another job, if it suits you better. You are tall, strong and fast, so there may be other kinds of jobs for you. There's not as much work here as there used to be, and what you want to avoid is having to stand, waiting for jobs at the Home Depot. There's more raids all the time and it's too easy to be spotted that way. You might be good in the fields with your long legs. Or mowing yards. I'll introduce you to everyone I know, and something will come.

Ya verás. Then maybe you can find yourself a nice girl with papers, get married and become legal."

"You have my whole life planned out for me," Victor grinned, shoveling food in his mouth.

Imelda patted Miguel on the arm. "He works as hard as he plans. And so far, so good. We almost have enough saved up to make a down payment on our own house."

Victor's eyes sparkled. "Really? I am so happy for you. I can't wait for the day your children have a birthday party in your own yard and I can play the flute for them."

"We want to hear you play the flute, *Tío* Victor!" The children chanted.

"Not tonight, *niños*," Miguel chided them, yawning. "It is late and tomorrow your uncle must look for work. There's no time for fun and games, like when we were children." His eyes locked with Victor's wistfully for an instant, and then shifted over to the guitar hanging on a peg in the tiny living room.

"Algún día," Miguel said.

"Sí," Victor agreed. And he believed it. He had been right to believe his cousin all these years.

That night, he slept on the couch, covered in a striped Ecuadorian blanket from his grandmother's house. It summoned the smell of the village, of the jasmine flowers that grew on the vine outside his grandmother's door. He thought of her, alone back there, waiting to die, and felt a strange, alien pain in the middle of his chest. He was surprised by the tears streaming down his cheeks. Then he dreamt of Rosario and Jesús dancing around a colorful piñata in a lush, green backyard bordered by birds of paradise. Imelda watched happily from a tidy back porch, as he and Miguel played the flute and the guitar, the ancient songs of their ancestors floating on the ocean breeze for all the angels to hear.

***

"Why don't you write poems anymore?" Victor asked Miguel, adjusting the chain on his bicycle as they prepared to ride to work.

"Who says I don't?" Miguel grumbled.

"Pues, I haven't heard any."

"You haven't been here that long," Miguel replied as they trotted down the steps to the sidewalk, Victor easily hoisting the scratched ten-speed.

"Six months?" Victor asked, cocking a bushy eyebrow in response, as he swung a leg over the bike.

Miguel grinned. "Already?"

"*Sí...de veras,*" Victor replied, adjusting his pack on a small rack behind the seat.

"I'm glad you found this courier job," Miguel said. "I knew your talents would come in handy."

"Not my music," Victor observed, as he accompanied Miguel to the bus stop, walking his bike to one side.

"No, your long legs," Miguel said. "You always were the fastest boy in the village. That could help with the *Migra* too. The raids are getting worse."

"You can't outrun your *destino, primo*," Victor recited.

"That's the truth," Miguel spit onto the sidewalk. "*Pinches gringos*, they only want us for our bodies, not our brains or our hearts or our souls. And definitely not our music. If we sat out and played in public, we'd be asking *la Migra* to beat us with our instruments and send us back to the mother country faster than you can hum your favorite tune. There was once a time, we could have played for money at the park or the shopping mall. But those days are nothing but a memory now. That's how I met Imelda, while I was playing at a street fair in Baldwin Park. She was still in her maid's uniform...black and white. *Chula...*" For a moment his eyes shifted out of focus and he smiled faintly. Then his expression turned to Incan stone. "Too bad neither of us had our papers in order...now even the kids are in danger. And the lawyers, all they do is suck your money dry...*para nada*...more paper and more paper and still...*no papeles*."

Bitterly, Miguel glanced into the street as a bus wheezed to a halt, street litter floating in the fumes like tumbleweeds.

"*Bueno,* enough of that, *primo,*" Miguel shook his head ruefully. "*A trabajar.*"

"*No hay otra,*" Victor conceded, smiling faintly.

With a quick hug, the two cousins parted ways in diverging directions, as they did every morning, Monday through Saturday. As Miguel's bus pulled out into the street, Victor swung his leg over the bike and turned the corner to his right.

It saddened him to see Miguel grow bitter. He was not the same hopeful, idealistic poet who had had left Ecuador in search of a better life.

The wind whipped Victor's long ponytail as the rising sun warmed his face. He pedaled faster, imagining the clean air of the mountain range where he'd been born. There, the air was pure but you could barely afford to breathe it for fear someone would crush your lungs under the weight of their army boots. Here, the air was filthy, but it was free. He flew down Western Avenue towards downtown, peripherally glancing at the Korean shopkeepers as they rolled up the corrugated metal gates to their businesses. Arriving at the heart of the bustling commercial center of the city, he turned a corner, chained his bike to a rack and strode into a tower of granite and glass for his first pick-up of the day.

Inside the soaring lobby, a small crowd gathered around an expansive, flat TV monitor on the wall. The air crackled with energy as a reporter's voice spoke: "The fate of an estimated fifteen million undocumented immigrants hangs in the balance, Anderson. Rallies and marches are planned in cities throughout the nation over the next few days as Congress deliberates. The sense on the street is that this clearly will impact not only these people toiling in the shadows, but the people and companies that depend on them for their very survival."

The morning coffee churned in Victor's stomach, burning a hole in its lining. He'd been taking evening ESL classes at the Belmont Adult Education School. And, while he couldn't fully grasp the meaning of every word, he was now able to gather the gist. He tried not to worry about these things, politics and the like, for what could he do about them? He was a silent laborer, a wanderer in a foreign land clinging to a dream, not a lawyer or a leader. He wished to share in the promise of America, but what if America changed her mind? What if the promise had expired? What if it was not meant for him?

As he stepped onto the elevator, his preoccupations disappeared when he noticed a petite blonde. She was dressed too warm for the weather, her hair pulled up in a bun and clunky black horn-rimmed glasses on her otherwise attractive face. She was thin, a foot shorter than him, wearing gray stockings, a rainbow scarf on a faded military green jacket, earbuds and an iPod that cocooned her from her surroundings.

Victor struggled to fight back a smile as his eyes playfully searched the ceiling. *Qué chula estás muchacha*, he thought, sighing audibly. *Las güeritas* were so beautiful, and yet so immune to his equatorial charms. He watched the lights dance across the rising numbers lining the metal plate above the elevator door. Twelve…fifteen…doors opened and closed, people came and went, but the girl remained in the opposite corner. He studied her face. Her skin was soft and pure as a porcelain doll's. He could tell she wore no makeup, her skin clear and ivory. Her lips were the color of a faded rose, full but timid and her amber eyes were framed by curving lashes beneath the lenses. Sensing his gaze, she glanced up and he bashfully flicked his eyes to the floor.

On the twenty-second floor, a portly man in a pinstriped suit boarded, sending a shudder through the elevator shaft. Victor surmised he was a successful banker. Maybe he owned the tower, Victor mused. The man had thinning copper hair, slicked back, a pronounced hooknose, and a protruding belly. He was perhaps in his early fifties, and smelled of cigar smoke mingled with expensive cologne. His blue eyes appraised his reflection in the aluminum elevator doors.

Victor's eyes landed fleetingly—like a bee in search of nectar—on the nape of the young woman's neck and then back down on the paper in his hands, instructing him to reach the forty-third floor.

He fought back another sigh, glancing briefly back at the deep blue peace symbol tattooed to the freckled crest of her spine.

If it weren't for his years in the mountains outside of Quito, he might have needed more getting used to these unnatural ascensions, but somehow he found them remarkably pacifying, as if the elevator was simply returning him to his natural habitat, the natural altitude for which his metabolism was designed.

He watched the numbers light up as the elevator passed floor after floor. Twenty-five, thirty, thirty-five, and then…a sudden tremor, preceded an abrupt halt. The lights flickered as the elevator stopped. The shock rippled through the passengers, knocking them off balance. Victor absorbed the movement with ease. The girl, close to the front right corner of the cube, steadied herself as well. But the large man reached out futilely as he stumbled backwards to the floor.

Instinctively, Victor bent down to help the flustered man to his feet.

Muttering obscenities as he rose, his skin beet red, the man neither thanked nor met Victor's eyes. He retreated to the back right corner and fastidiously straightened his tie, looking over his shoulder as if there were video cameras trained on him.

Victor looked up, sensing the girl's eyes on him, and smiled nervously at her angular beauty. Then the lights were extinguished, plunging the elevator into absolute darkness.

Victor observed how quiet it was. In the movies, when elevators malfunctioned, people typically screamed and cried in panic. He assessed that his companions were very calm, confident Americans, and he was grateful. Surely, this would pass quickly and they could all be on their way.

He had not noticed the distorted music emitting from the woman's iPod until she shut it off, in the dark. Then, it suddenly seemed too quiet for comfort. Their clothes rustled between the groans of the cables suspending them nearly forty stories above the ground.

The large man swallowed audibly.

"There's probably an emergency phone here somewhere," the girl's angelic voice shattered the awkward silence. Her fingers grazed the polished metal surface of the control panel buttons. She sounded not overly concerned as she touched her iPod screen to illuminate the panel, flipped open a small door and reached for the phone.

Victor smiled hopefully, nodding towards the man in the corner, who evaded his gaze, staring straight ahead in the dim blue light.

"Hello? Hello?" she said. "Is anyone there?" Victor detected a slight increase in her anxiety level as her voice hung in the chilly air.

The light shut off, and he heard her slump against her corner. Reaching for his cell phone, he pressed a button to illuminate its screen. He saw her standing, with the red emergency phone against her ear, staring at him through the bleak light.

They waited. She relaxed her grip on the phone slightly, looked at the two men and said, "Nothing. No one's picking up."

Victor looked at his cell phone screen: "No signal."

He frowned.

"They don't usually work in the elevator," the girl said.

Victor smiled demurely and nodded. "Yes, that's true."

He wondered if he might lose his job as a result of this turn of events. Miguel had warned him there was rarely room for error or excuses. What if his manager didn't believe him, when he explained why his pick-up had taken ten minutes longer than usual? The manager was always punching times into his computer and talking about averages. Usually, the boss praised Victor for having the fastest average time for deliveries. How would this delay affect him? He could not afford to lose the manager's trust. Without a job, he couldn't contribute to the rent or the food. And now that the raids had increased and the deportation debate was raging across the radio stations, the TV channels and even the streets of LA, his best bet was to hold his job and his head down and hope for the best.

He startled when the woman spoke to him. "What's your name?"

He pressed the button on his cell phone so he could see how pretty she was and how the muscles in her face reacted when he responded, "Victor."

"I'm Fern."

They both looked at the man in the corner.

Victor noticed the light sheen of a cold sweat across the man's ruddy face.

He said nothing. The woman frowned, but Victor shrugged. He was used to people ignoring him. Why should the owner of the tower be any different?

She placed the red phone back in its cradle, and then picked it up again. "Hello?" she called. "Still nothing."

"At least it's not an earthquake," Victor said reassuringly, flinching at his own thick accent.

"You know, you're totally right about that," Fern said enthusiastically, sounding relaxed, as if being trapped in elevators a mile above ground happened on a regular basis.

A few moments passed in dark silence. The man in the corner breathed raggedly. Then Fern clicked her iPod and took a good long look at Victor, from toe to head, her full lips unfurling into a red banner of a smile.

Darkness again. Then a loud thump as something large fell to the floor. Victor and Fern fumbled for their digital accessories, casting twin beacons over the man splayed between them on the marble floor.

Crouching down, Victor turned him over.

"He's famous, you know." Fern whispered, hovering over the man suspiciously. "He's…on TV…and radio."

Victor had been trained in CPR, in case one of the couriers or their customers suffered a heart attack. He could hear the trainer in the back of his mind as he loosened the man's tie and put an ear to his chest, listening for a heartbeat, grasping his wrist and counting out a pulse.

"I've heard he's in bad health," Fern added. "He's got a problem with pills, alcohol, smoking…but he's Mr. Morality…"

"I think…he needs…mouth-to-mouth…" Victor ventured.

"Hmmm," she grimaced.

Victor pinched the man's nose without further thought. He pulled his chin down, opening his mouth, and breathed into it, pumping down rhythmically onto his chest.

"He…doesn't really like…immigrants," Fern ventured, her eyes surveying the bulky man disapprovingly and then lighting up when Victor glanced at her between labored exhalations.

"I think he's breathing again," Victor huffed, slapping the man lightly on the cheeks, praying for his return to consciousness.

"I'm a liberal," she spouted incongruously.

Victor smiled at her, the way he did when the Korean shopkeepers hawked their wares and waved their fists at him on his way home. He didn't know what in the world she was talking about but he didn't care, because he liked her, just as he liked the Korean shopkeepers. He liked them because he empathized with their effort and faith to reach their dream. He liked Fern because she was pretty, and he'd believe he'd died and been catapulted flesh and bones into Heaven if only she'd kiss him with those pale rose gringo lips of hers.

Then the man coughed and spit up tiny globules of saliva, struggling to sit up with Victor's aid.

"You're okay." the girl patted the man timidly on the shoulder. "You just passed out."

He choked some more, loosening his collar.

Victor wore down his cell phone battery so that the man could benefit from the light in his effort to calm down.

Fern messed with the red phone. "Hello? Yeah, finally! Hey we're stuck here, thank you! What's going on? We need some help..."

"Okay...well...just so you know, Mr. Rushmore is up here with us," she said, throwing a grim glance the man's way. "And he's not doing too hot. So you should hurry."

She sighed and rolled her eyes. "They want to talk to you, Mr. Rushmore."

She held out the phone to the man, but he shook his head, clearing his throat.

"Yeah, right. He's not in the mood. Just call EMS and get us out of here okay? Do you know how much longer?"

Victor could hear a crackle and ramble on the other end but he couldn't make out any of the words.

"I see..." she hesitated, her eyes finding Victor's. He sensed them melting slightly as they met. "Blackouts...okay. So we'll wait."

She placed the phone delicately back in its place.

Victor's cell announced the impending demise of its battery with a series of beeps, a flash of light and a final plunge into darkness.

In pitch black, Gavin Rushmore cleared his throat and finally spoke in his distinctive baritone voice. "What's wrong?"

"Nothing," she said. "At least not for you."

"What's going on?" he pressed

"Some riots, some power outages," she said. "That vote has been postponed another two weeks."

Victor gasped. He knew what they were talking about...his fate. The vote everyone was talking about, in Washington. Would the immigrants all be rounded up and deported? What kind of limits would they impose? Would there be some chance for those that had been here working for months like him, or years, like his cousin Miguel? What about the children, like Rosario and Jesús? What did their future hold?

Fern licked her lips. "Two more weeks for you to sway the public to your side, Rushmore."

The bulky man sighed, betraying his exhaustion. "I'm on the floor here, sister. You wanna give me a break?" He tried to get up but crumpled quickly back down.

"Damn college kids," Rushmore muttered beneath his labored breath.

"Excuse me, I could help you, but I can't see anything" Victor said. "Do you have some light?"

Fern illuminated her iPod again so Victor could help the man to his feet. "And I'm not some damn college kid, FYI," she said to the man. "I graduated from Berkeley two years ago, thank you very much. Summa cum laude, in case you think women don't have brains too."

"I never said that," he shook his head, smoothing out his Armani suit and running his hands through his hair in a vain attempt to put every strand back into place. "But it figures…Berkeley "

Victor picked up a shiny silver cigarette case off the floor and handed it to the man. "Yours?"

"Yes," He placed it back inside his suit pocket. His lips parted momentarily, as if he were about to thank Victor, but then pursed back shut.

"So, Mr. Big Time Tough Guy, you think you've got everyone all figured out, don't you? Just stick a label on them and be done with them," Fern quipped, tapping her foot, her bangs flopping around the edges of her glasses.

Victor envisioned removing those glasses and thrusting her backwards onto a mattress placed carelessly on a floor.

Gavin Rushmore reached into his pocket and extracted his Blackberry, then he huffed in frustration and thrust it back into the folds of his suit.

"Can't reach your agent, or your bodyguards?" Fern asked.

"Did you plan this?" he asked Fern. "Are you one of those militant types who picket in front of my house?"

"You mean in front of the sidewalk beyond the barricades around the gates to the grounds that surround your mansion?"

"Are you?"

"No," she answered. "I've got better things to do than stalk the likes of you."

Rushmore reached for a cigarette.

"Don't you even think of it," Fern shot out.

"Jesus, you're worse than my daughter."

"God bless her soul," Fern condescended. "Victor, you know who this man is, right?"

She pressed the buttons on her iPod again for more light.

Victor shook his head, apprehensive about the tension between the woman he felt drawn to and the man he had just saved.

"He rants and raves on TV and radio every day, about how we must send all the immigrants home. Don't you, Mr. Big Time Tough Guy?"

"Is this really necessary? Do we have to embarrass ourselves?" Rushmore answered.

"What, why not? You already practically soiled your pants. Why not continue the trend?" Fern answered ruthlessly.

Victor shifted uncomfortably. In his country, it was not appropriate to speak in such tones to an older man of obvious prominence, much less for a woman to do so. Yet, this was the brazen, outlandish quality of American women that was so intoxicating and foreign, not only to him but to all men from other nations. These women were fearless. And in that absence of fear, they wielded power...and freedom. Again, the notion of freedom defined for what it was *not,* rather than for what it *was*...and it was *not* fear.

Victor wanted that freedom more than ever, now, trapped in the confining walls of an elevator suspended halfway to heaven, halfway to hell. And if he could not have it in the abstract, perhaps he could, for a moment, taste it in the supple curves and yielding flesh of this mysterious and obstinate Fern.

"Okay, little one," Rushmore said, resorting to his typically televised tendency to dissect his opposition. "You want at it? Bring it on. You want to sit in the Challenge Chair? What's your challenge?"

Fern looked at Victor, explaining. "That's what he does on his show. He has people sit in the Challenge Chair and try to argue with him. And then he either tears them up, or cuts them off and goes to commercial. But here there's no commercial, Mr. Rushmore. Is there?"

The large man swallowed uncomfortably and said nothing.

"Okay, then. Mr. Rushmore, this immigrant young man with his whole life ahead of him and obviously good manners and genes, just saved your life.... Would you have him deported if his papers don't check out?"

Victor's dark eyes darted to Mr. Rushmore.

Rushmore frowned and finally looked at Victor.

"Are you legal?" he asked.

Victor raised an eyebrow.

"You expect him to answer that, Rushmore?" Fern cried. "You're not much of an interviewer anymore, are you? What happened to that young guy who once competed for a Pulitzer?"

Rushmore chewed on the inside of his cheek.

"Listen," Rushmore blurted out, reciting one of his on-air talking points, "America is a nation of laws. The rule of law is supreme. If someone comes here illegally and breaks the law in doing so, they should not be allowed to remain here. That's the bottom line. How do you challenge that?"

Rushmore exhaled through his nostrils and crossed his arms, looking to Victor and then allowing his blue eyes to waver for a moment before diverting his gaze to the dark floor.

Undeterred. Fern raised her chin, gazed up at the man and said, "Some would say the law is the law, and man must abide by it. But others would say that the law is made to *serve* man and not the other way around. If a law is broken from within, then perhaps we should change it, rather than punish those who are actually innocent."

She looked at Victor for approval, only to find his smile confused and his eyes drifting down to her breasts.

She was surprised, but smiled naughtily at Victor. Turning to Rushmore, she continued. "How about you take this challenge, and think about it while Congress deliberates? How about you think about the fact this probably undocumented immigrant saved your life in a cold, dark elevator thirty floors above the ground? How about you reconsider your position on immigration in that light? Could immigrants actually be good for America? And then, how about you tell this story, and announce your verdict on your show for the whole world to hear before Congress decides on immigration reform? How about that, Mr. Big Time Tough Guy?"

"That's a good idea. Are you in programming?" Rushmore asked.

"No."

"Okay, then. Give me your number, in case I ever need to bring an easy target on the show...but don't expect any money out of this," Rushmore said.

"Whatever," Fern said, handing him a business card.

The elevator shook suddenly and descended several floors, lurching and stopping, heaving the passengers about.

Rushmore collapsed again, his cigarettes scattering across the floor, the aroma of tobacco wafting through the clammy air.

"Oh, shit!" Fern blurted, finally losing her nerve as she allowed her knees to buckle and reached for Rushmore's body for the sheer comfort of a human being even if it was one she found revolting.

A gurgle issued from Rushmore's throat.

"I'm gonna die. We're all gonna die," Rushmore's voice quivered weakly, an antithesis to the boom, shock and awe of his exaltations over the airwaves on a daily basis.

In the dark, Victor reached into his backpack for the flute. He felt the familiar groove of the carved rosewood. He knew words paled next to the power of music. Putting his lips to the mouthpiece, he played gently, thinking of the waterfall that cascaded over the rocks on a mountainside near his village. He remembered standing on a footbridge across from the waterfall, feeling its cool mist on his face, smiling and laughing with his parents. It was perhaps the happiest memory of his life, and he let it guide him as it coursed through the flute and resonated through the metal chamber.

It may have been moments or hours later, but either way not another sound was made by the pacified Rushmore or the awed Fern as Victor played until the fluorescent lights flickered to life and the elevator jerked down to the ground floor. The doors opened to reveal the flashing reds and blues of paramedics and the clamor of the crowd in the lobby. Rushmore pulled himself together and smiled smugly for the cameras, as Fern slipped something into Victor's hand.

Victor took another elevator. As he ascended to the forty-third floor, he gawked at the card in his hand, unable to believe that, in America, an immigrant like him was just as likely to get a girl's phone number as was a famous, wealthy TV star.

***

"I can't believe he's doing it," Fern shook her head. The onyx earrings Victor had just given her danced as she watched Gavin Rushmore on the TV over the bar. They were in a Korean restaurant she'd picked for their first "date," as he'd called it, blushing to her endeared amusement.

The text beneath Rushmore's talking head scrolled: "Rushmore Puts Self in Challenge Chair on Immigration after Elevator Rescue by Peruvian."

"You're *not* Peruvian," she asserted. "What a dolt!"

"What's a 'dolt'?" Victor asked, always eager to expand his English vocabulary.

"That…" she jabbed her pointer finger towards the TV, accidentally flinging a noodle onto the floor, "is a dolt."

Victor bent down and picked up the noodle, placing it gently on his plate. Then he smiled into the enormous bowl of steaming, spicy soup they were sharing. American girls moved more quickly than he had expected. He had heard stories but took them for nothing more than the exaggerations or wishful thoughts of his male co-workers. But here he was in an American—no, Korean—restaurant, sharing a bowl of soup with the most beautiful woman who'd ever spoken to him in his life.

Their hands brushed against each other as they reached for their spoons at the same time.

Her long, thick eyelashes fluttered as she fought back a delicate smile.

Victor felt beads of perspiration collecting on his forehead.

She gazed into his dark eyes.

"Your eyes are so beautiful," she said. "They're so black, like the onyx…" She gently ran her fingers over her right earring.

"They're from Ecuador," his voice cracked. He wasn't sure if it was nerves, or the spices. He reached for his glass of water, thinking maybe he should order a beer.

"What?" She giggled. "The earrings…or your eyes?"

He nearly choked. "Both."

They laughed and then brushed hands again, spilling each other's spoonfuls of soup onto the table.

"Very clumsy!" the elderly Korean waitress scolded them, running a rag over the table before Victor could reach for his napkin. She sighed, smiling at the two for a fleeting moment, then said: "Very stiff. You'll spill *Jjamppong* all over floor if you no relax. I bring you beer. You feel better. You eat better. No one get hurt. On the house."

Fern and Victor's eyes both widened, their jaws dropped and they laughed.

"A beer sounds good," Fern agreed.

"Yes, you think they have Peruvian?"

"No, but I know where we can get some…Ecuadorian too!" Fern replied.

"Really?" Victor's eyebrows arched. "I am…how do you say…impressed. You seem to know many things about my culture then."

"I'd like to learn more," the corners of her lips turned up as she looked down at the bowl of soup. "If you'll teach me…"

"Is it hot in here, or is it the soup?" Victor tugged at the collar of his pressed white shirt and fanned himself with the laminated menu.

Their hands touched again, but this time she took hold of his fingers and didn't let go.

"It's the soup," she whispered as the waitress approached. "And you have nothing to be nervous about."

They watched her slowly pour two frosted glasses of Hite beer. "First one on the house. Second one cost double," she said, winking at them.

They reached for the glasses. Toasting silently, they drank, listening to Gavin Rushmore argue with himself about whether immigrants were good or bad for America.

Victor had never tasted Korean beer before. It was a day of firsts, he marveled. This is what he'd come to America for, new experiences, new opportunities, a place where his hard work could be rewarded. The beer tasted good, not that different from the beer back home, he thought. It was cold. And in it, he found the courage to reach for her hand again, as they talked into the evening.

***

Her hair had the familiar scent of fading jasmine in the morning. And that filled not only Victor's senses, but his heart. Two weeks on that mattress on her hardwood floor, scattered with papers with endless scribblings scattered, made him realize he'd found his American dream at last. It wasn't fortune. It wasn't fame. It wasn't the success of some generation yet to be born. It was this. It was a girl's soft, moist skin. Her rose petal lips. The desire to start again what had just transpired. It was their limbs intertwined, the dry crackle of her voice as he drove her to the edge of desire and beyond, as he lost himself in her, forgot where he came from, only the lovely darkness in which he swam.

The sun rose over the Santa Ana Mountains and illuminated the haze hanging over Los Angeles. He kissed her, lying there, and got ready to ride his bike to work.

Then his cell phone startled him with a series of beeps. He fumbled through his courier bag as Fern rustled in the sheets.

"*¿Bueno?*" he whispered.

"Victor!" Imelda sobbed loudly.

"*Sí*, what's wrong?" His heartbeat quickened. No one called him this early. And Imelda never called him at all.

"It's Miguel!" Imelda cried. "He didn't come home last night. I didn't want to bother you while you slept. Do you know where he is? Or *who* he's with?"

Victor's insides twisted, as he closed the door to the bedroom and tiptoed into the kitchen. "No...I—" he stammered. "I don't know anything."

Imelda wailed. "He's never been gone all night. *Nunca. ¡Dios mío*! What if something's happened to him? Or what if he's left me? Run off with another woman? He's seemed so jealous about you and your American girlfriend..."

Victor wondered if it was possible. Could his passionate romance with Fern have ignited Miguel's desire to recapture the thrill of his single days? No...Victor shook his head. Although that was better than the other possibilities. A fling could be forgiven, especially for a man. But if Miquel was injured—or worse—that would transform lives forever. Victor thought of Jesús and Rosario.

"*¿Y los niños?*" Victor whispered, leaning against the kitchen counter.

"They're fine. They don't know anything. I told them their dad had to work all night. For some reason they weren't surprised, even though he always comes home."

"He works hard."

"He's a good...man..." she muffled her cries.

"Yes, that's what you have to remember. We will find him. He'll be fine," Victor assured her.

"I'm afraid, Victor," Imelda replied. "We can't go to the police. None of us have our papers. We could all get deported. What are we going to do?"

"What's going on?" Fern stepped into the kitchen, wearing a white T-shirt and matching briefs, her hands ruffling her short hair.

"We need your help," Victor said. "My cousin Miguel is missing."

***

"I've talked to every hospital, every police precinct...." Fern said, two days later. She removed her glasses, set them on the open Yellow Pages and rubbed her bleary eyes. "I just don't know where else to turn."

"Nobody from his job knows anything," Victor added, shaking his head. "There have been no raids there."

Imelda looked like she might collapse. Her usually neat hair was tangled, and deep circles ran around her eyes. "He left me, didn't he? Maybe he met someone like...you...someone smart and young and pretty, someone who could make him legal citizen, once and for all..." She shook vigorously. She wept without tears.

He looked at Fern, raising an eyebrow. "Did you call...the...you know...?"

"Yes," she said.

"Where?" Imelda demanded, frowning.

"No es nada," Victor said quickly.

"Where? Are there brothels here? Did you call them?" Imelda's nostrils flared.

"No, no, no..." Victor said, wishing not only that Miguel would resurface but also that his honor could be restored. "If you have to know, Fern called the morgues."

"He's not dead," Imelda whimpered. "I can feel it. A woman knows these things."

Fern and Victor stared at each other uncomfortably.

"How can you keep defending him?" Imelda asked, her eyes burning into Victor's.

"I always have..." He knew no other way.

"But why would he do it?" Imelda pleaded. "Tell me. We have loved each other and made as good a life as we can for our little family. Having kids is hard. Working several jobs is hard. There is no time for us…anymore."

"I played the flute and he played the guitar, at many funerals in our village," Victor spoke, his voice cracking with emotion. "The funerals of our parents, of our cousins, of our best friends. We shared our sorrows, and our joys, with our music. It was pure. It was good. Life is hard, but a man's soul does not change. Miguel would not hurt you. He is not that kind of man."

Fern frowned and gingerly embraced Imelda, who sobbed into her shoulder.

"Men just can't understand women fully," Fern said.

"You'll see…" Victor said.

"Seeing is believing," Imelda pursed her lips, stood up and straightened her dress. "I have to go for the children."

***

The warm, stuffy apartment was quiet. The children slept soundly in their beds. Imelda and Fern were sleeping at the kitchen table, with their heads on the placemats. Victor dozed on the plaid sofa next to them. The phone rang, shattering the tranquility.

Before she opened her eyes or raised her head, Imelda's hand yanked the phone off its hook and pressed it against her ear.

"It's for you," she held the phone out towards Victor.

"¿Bueno?" Victor inquired, yawning. Who would call so late?

A vaguely familiar voice spoke so loudly that Fern and Imelda could hear it.

Fern grabbed Imelda's hand, "Is it Miguel?"

"No, it sounds like an old, deaf man," Imelda answered, squinting as she struggled to hear.

"Sí," Victor's voice rose.

"¡No!" he exclaimed.

Imelda swayed to her feet, her nails digging into Victor's arm. Fern pressed her glasses onto her nose.

Victor waved excitedly, *"Lápiz…papel…*something to write with…"

Fern's hands scrambled across the table, producing pen and paper.

Victor scrawled out an address and a phone number.

"Gracias...allí nos vemos. Sí. Sí lo es."

Both women held their breath, staring at Victor with wide, expectant eyes.

"Miguel is alive," Victor said. "A man I know has seen him...in a jail where they hold immigrants without papers."

Fern wrapped her arms around Victor in jubilant relief as Imelda made the sign of the cross and dropped to her knees.

"It's a miracle!" Imelda said.

"That's exactly what the man said," Victor remarked, as Imelda took his hand and looked up at him.

At last, tears of shame and joy streamed down her flushed cheeks.

***

In the early morning, as Imelda prepared the children for school, Victor and Fern drove south to Long Beach, to the address the caller had given Victor. The directions Fern had mapped on her computer led them into a run-down industrial area of rusting, abandoned warehouses near crumbling rail tracks. A dense fog smothered the docks and rolled though the alleyways, slick from the drizzling rain.

"Are you sure this is it?" Victor asked. "It's not what I imagined the jail would look like."

Fern nodded nervously. "Look," she pointed to a guard tower above a corrugated metal building, which was circled by high chain-link fence and coils of barbed wire.

"*Sí*...you should wait here," Victor gulped.

"No way...and let them take you too? C'mon."

As they walked arm in arm through the rain towards a small guardhouse, Victor almost bumped into a diminutive man standing motionless in the fog.

"Oh, excuse me, I did not see you," Victor held the man's frail arms. Then he recognized the blue stamp of the Virgen de Guadalupe on the side of the man's straw cowboy hat.

Their eyes locked. "Tohil?" Victor asked.

"Victor!"

They embraced, and Victor quickly introduced Fern.

"You look..." Victor started.

"Older..." Tohil said.

"Different," Victor demurred.

The three walked towards the gate, where Tohil waved at the guard. The door buzzed and swung open.

"I talked to him already," Tohil explained. "You see, my daughter, she works here. Sometimes I come to help her. That's how I saw him... your *primo* Miguel."

Inside a makeshift waiting area, they shook the rain off and followed Tohil to a window covered with mesh and bars.

"These are the relatives I told you about," Tohil said. "The ones that know Miguel."

The clerk behind the window, a middle-aged woman with too much hair and make-up, clicked away on her computer keyboard. "Yes, Miguel...Orozco...right?"

"Right," Victor nodded.

She looked back suspiciously, lowering her thick glasses and surveying him.

"And you're the relative? Are you legal?"

"Hey," Fern interjected. "That's immaterial!"

"Oh, well, I didn't see you there," the woman said, surprised. "Are you his attorney?"

"Maybe..." Fern cleared her throat, eager to change the subject. "What does it say in there about Miguel?"

"Bad news, I'm afraid. He's been moved," the woman didn't bother to feign concern.

"Moved?" Victor asked. Imelda would be crushed.

"Don't you let detainees make a phone call?" Fern asked, frowning.

"No, dearie. This ain't a regular jail. Them rules don't apply here."

"Why?" Fern pressed.

Tohil and Victor's eyes moved from one woman to the other.

"Well, this is a private facility. The ICE facilities overflow into here. Miguel was a random intercept at a bus stop. There was no room at the federal facility, so he was brought here. Here we don't give 'em no phone calls. Phones cost money."

"But it's a right..." Fern started.

"Not here it's not, honey," the woman said, twirling a pencil.

"Can you write down for us where we can find him?" Fern concentrated on the pencil, hoping to control her rage by avoiding the woman's eyes.

"Sure," she popped her bubble gum and wrote an address down on a yellow Post-It note, slipping it under the glass to Fern. "Just for you." She shot a disapproving glance at Tohil and Victor.

"You should be more careful, little man," she said to Tohil. "You don't want to get your daughter fired…or end up in a cell, instead of helping her mop 'em."

Victor wished he could pull the metal bars apart and throttle the woman. He took a deep breath to calm himself, shocked by his reaction. I don't know what this country's doing to me, but I'm not sure I like it. I am a peaceful person who plays the flute, a lover. But the anger swelled in him. He remembered the bitterness stewing in Miguel. How enraged would his cousin be now, forced to sleep apart from his family for the first time? Moved from cell to cell like a common dog?

Tohil lowered his head and limped to a far corner of the room, like a hobbled mongrel.

Victor touched his shoulder, "What happened to your leg?"

"I lost it in an accident at work. A pulley snapped on a crane, and a steel beam fell on me. I was in the hospital for months. That's why I never called you before. I don't want to be a burden, but I'm afraid I've been one to my daughter. The truth is, I'm lucky to be alive."

Fern wondered if that was true, but she admired Tohil's defiant optimism. Or was it obstinacy, she mused.

She looked at the address on the yellow Post-It, "They've moved him closer to the border."

"That means they're sending him back," Tohil said. "I hoped he'd still be here. My daughter says they never know when they're going to be moved. And they never tell anyone. Families come here broken-hearted all the time. Lawyers are stumped, because the men get moved to other states. Months of work on their cases can be lost. It's a terrible situation." Tohil's eyes watered as he spoke.

"How did you remember Miguel?" Victor asked him. "I showed you that picture for a moment, so long ago."

"I was helping my daughter mop," Tohil recalled. "They let us in here at night to clean. Often, we know someone they are holding. And we make sure their families know. We feel like messengers of doom, but it helps, sometimes. Anyway, I heard the most beautiful guitar-playing coming from the cafeteria. I went in there, and there he was. Your primo surrounded by an audience of guards and prisoners alike. All were enraptured by his music. His face looked familiar and I remembered what you had said about his playing. I didn't remember his name, but I remembered yours. When I asked him if he had a cousin named Victor, tall with long hair, he burst into tears. He said he should have played music with you for his kids and wife, but he never got around to it. I promised him someday he would."

Fern stared in disbelief. "Wait a minute. That's all great, but let's go back to the beginning. You mean to tell me that, in this prison that holds undocumented immigrants, they hire other undocumented immigrants to do the cleaning?"

Tohil shrugged, "It's strange but true. We work for less. They don't have to pay us, *¿cómo se dice?,* minimum wage, unemployment insurance, taxes, or health insurance…*nada.* They'd probably hire us to be the guards too, but they don't trust us with the guns. They might end up being the ones behind bars." He smiled wistfully, relishing the thought.

"Unbelievable! What's wrong with this country?" Fern declared, throwing her hands up in the air.

Tohil winked at Victor, "*Qué bien.* You found yourself the perfect girl. She's educated. She's *gringa.* And she's got a bit of Latina in her too."

Fern put her hands on her hips. "I wish! But I can't say that's true. What makes you say that?"

"Well, in spirit at least," Tohil explained. "You are feisty and *picosa.* You have the temper of a habanero pepper! You are a good match for this Incan."

Victor smiled bashfully and then wiped the smile off his face resolutely. "Thank you, Tohil. But we must not waste any more time. We must drive down to San Diego…. Can we, Fern?"

"Of course."

Victor bent down to hug Tohil. "Thank you, my friend. I will not forget you. Someday, our families must come together and rejoice. Miguel will play guitar. I will play flute. And you will dance once again."

"*Sí*…it is carved in stone." Tohil smiled, his ancient eyes dancing mysteriously, as if he knew something Victor didn't.

***

Fern fumbled with one hand for her buzzing cell phone in the console, keeping the other on the steering wheel.

"Hello? Hold for who? Okay." She shot a glance at Victor in the passenger seat. "Rushmore!"

Victor's eyebrows arched in surprise.

"Hello?" She continued, "Yes, Mr. Rushmore? Yes. Fine. I can put you in touch with him...faster than you think...here he is..."

She handed Victor the phone with an amused grin, "He wants to talk to you!"

"Me?" Victor took the phone delicately, as if it were a hand grenade. "Hi, Mr. Rushmore. This is Victor, from the elevator."

"Hi there, Victor from the elevator," Rushmore boomed. "Boy, that's going to sound great on the show. Listen, I'd like to invite you on the show. I promise I won't let the...what do you people call them...*Migra*...get you. I'll even pay you. What do you say? Ratings are up. People want to meet the man who saved me and made me reconsider this whole immigration debate."

Victor considered it for a second and then swallowed hard. "I'm sorry, Mr. Rushmore. I appreciate your invitation, but I can't right now. Your country stole my cousin."

"Victor, I understand a lot of people harbor mixed feelings about the effects of assimilation. Familial and cultural bonds can be severely tested and even broken. If your cousin has become too Americanized for your own tastes, you should just accept it, and try to learn from him. Is he legal? Don't push him away. Maybe he could help you. I know about these things, my daughter has a Ph.D. in Psychology and she's always schooling me."

"No," Victor scrunched his face up, trying his best to understand everything Rushmore was saying. "No, Mr. Rushmore, I don't think you understand what I'm trying to say. Your government, they really stole my cousin."

"Oohhh," Rushmore drawled as it dawned on him. "They apprehended him. Is he being deported? This would be great for the show. My producer is salivating like a pit bull over here. By the way, she's on the line. I hope you don't mind."

"I don't mind, Mr. Rushmore. I would very much like to see you again, but I cannot come on your show right now. I have to help my cousin."

"So Mexican...family first." Rushmore sighed. "They never think in terms of career..."

Victor wasn't sure if Rushmore was speaking to him or the producer.

"I should go. Mr. Rushmore. "

"Wait...I—but—" Rushmore stammered. Victor gently placed the phone back in the console and gazed out at the congested highway heading south.

"What happened?" Fern asked, resting her hand on his.

"He thinks I'm Mexican now," Victor stated flatly. "A few weeks ago, he thought I was Peruvian."

"I think he's a dolt!" Fern exclaimed. And they burst into laughter as she wove through traffic towards the border.

***

Fern furrowed her brows. Victor was coming to recognize this side of her. He braced himself for an outburst as he followed her eyes across the arid field dotted with small, round white tents.

"This is a prison?" Fern asked, although she knew the answer.

She parked her Prius in a patch of desert filled with cars.

Behind a soaring fence and flanked by cinderblock towers, the endless crop of tents offered up the fruit of immigrants, their dreams rotting in the merciless heat.

"We never learn," she sighed, leading Victor by the hand.

Victor anxiously eyed the border patrol agents as their vehicles streamed in and out of the compound.

"Uhh...maybe we should say our goodbyes, in case I end up sharing a tent with Miguel."

"Over my dead body!" Fern retorted.

Victor watched in awe as Fern confidently spoke to a clerk in the cheaply constructed metal building, which seemed to serve as the command center and meeting area for detainees, their families and attorneys.

Plasma screen televisions flashed news channels with updates about the immigrant debate.

"Look, there's Rushmore!" Victor pointed at the man from the elevator whose life he'd saved, only months ago although it seemed like years. He marveled at how time elapsed differently during periods of great stress. Every second, every minute seemed longer when it promised tragedy or triumph. It was exhausting. He longed for the mountains.

"What a pig!" Fern cried, causing several agents to turn around and look at her.

Victor pointed at the screen and smiled nervously, so the agents would think she was referring to the man on the TV.

Then Miguel was sitting across from them, shielded by glass, speaking into an old metal telephone receiver. He looked five years older and ten pounds lighter, his dark brow creased with worry.

"You found me? Was it the old man, Tohil? Did he call you?" Miguel asked.

"*Sí*. You remember Fern?" Victor nodded in Fern's direction. "She helped me."

"*Gracias*, Fern. I should not have been jealous about my cousin finding a good friend like you. I am very happy for both of you. Please forgive me."

"Please, we're just so relieved, you're okay. Imelda was worried that…"

Victor coughed, cutting in, "Worried that you might be dead." He tightened his hold on Fern's hand, hoping she'd get the message to reveal no more about Imelda's doubts.

Fern understood. "Yes, poor thing. She loves you so."

Miguel eyes lit up. "How is my Imelda, and the children?"

"They are just fine. Worried but fine. We called and told Imelda we had found you. She can't wait for you to come home," Victor said.

"Well, I'm heading home all right…but not this home," Miguel shook his head. "It's over. They ship me out in the next few days. Once you're in this place, you're as good as gone. That's what the others say. *Dicen que*—" he stopped and switched back to English, for Fern's sake. "They say they're trying to rush out all the *ilegales* they have in custody, in case the Congress decides to let us stay. That way, there will be fewer of us here."

"Well, we'll see…any day now…" Victor said. "When they vote for amnesty, you'll still be here and we will come get you. If you and I get kicked out, we'll all meet together back in the village."

Miguel put his hand on the glass. "And we'll play music again together, *primo.*"

Victor placed his hand on the glass over his cousin's. No more words were needed.

"I will get you a lawyer and we'll try to slow things down," Fern promised.

The cousins smiled with nostalgia. Fern could see that their thoughts were far from courtrooms and legal proceedings.

"I'll go call Imelda and let the two of you talk," Fern said, waving at Miguel "I'll wait in the car."

"Fern," Miguel added, "please tell Imelda that I am sorry for how I've been lately. When this is all over, things will be better. They will be as they once were. Tell her that, *por favor.*"

"Of course," Fern smiled soothingly. "She will be so happy."

The border patrol agents watched her walk out, admiring her tight jeans. Back in Ecuador, Victor might have retaliated. Back in Ecuador, they would have been more respectful of her in his presence. But this was not Ecuador.

For fifteen minutes, Victor and Miguel talked more than they had in six months.

***

Victor leaned over Fern's sleeping form and kissed her lightly as he headed out for work.

But she stopped him.

"No," Fern said. "Today's the day. Let me drive you, please."

The corners of his lips wavered as they curved up, realizing how much she really cared. A few days earlier, after a bottle of wine and torrent of lovemaking, she'd claimed that she'd follow him south of the equator, if she had to, and bear his children. He wouldn't hold her to it, but he was beginning to believe it might be true.

He held her close, breathing in the fragrance of her golden hair. He waited for her to throw on fatigue pants and a black T-shirt. She stuffed her iPod and laptop into her backpack, slung it over her shoulder and led the way outside.

Once in the car, she found Rushmore's show on the radio, and they headed for the first address on Victor's morning delivery list.

Traffic was worse than usual on the freeway.

"There's always standing room only for a revolt," Fern declared, taking a playful punch at the fuzzy dice with peace signs dangling from her rearview mirror.

Victor's cell phone rang, the special tone for Imelda, in case she or the children needed something while Miguel was away.

"Imelda? Prima?" he answered, attempting to sound cheerier than he felt.

"¿Cómo están? How are you?" Imelda trembled on the line.

"Bien. Aquí with Fern. Going to work. She called and checked. They still haven't sent Miguel back. There's still a chance then…and *los niños?* Are they at school?" Victor, asked, fighting back the guilt of not being with them on this, the day of reckoning. But he knew Miguel and Imelda would respect the reality that was understood amongst close family, the fact that the presence of a woman in his life had changed everything in an instant, and forever. Besides, they had all grown to appreciate Fern, even calling her *"La Habanera"* in honor of her fighting spirit and passion for their cause.

"No," Imelda confessed. "I kept them home, just in case. In case…we have to go back."

"Sí, pues…" Victor said. "If it happens that way, we call each other and meet up so we can be together, no?"

"Sí, claro."

"Okay."

"Victor…" Imelda, said, pausing.

"Yes?"

"Victor, eh…we'll talk to you then…*hablamos*…be careful out there, *Primito.*"

"Okay," Victor said, smiling. "We'll see…"

"Okay…if it happens…we'll see, right…the children…they were born here…maybe we can fight right? For…*como dicen aquí*…our rights, no?"

"Sí," Victor nodded, staring out the window at an eighteen-wheeler next to them. He noticed the door to the driver's cabin was ajar and the driver's seat empty.

He flipped his phone shut and turned to face Fern.

***

Gavin Rushmore eased into his oversized leather chair on the set. The Vietnamese-American make-up artist brushed his cheeks, as she did every morning. The director ran a sound check. The set manager clipped the earpiece to Rushmore's jacket and wrapped it around his ear, delicately placing the Lavalier mic into his Ralph Lauren lapel. He played with his Harvard ring, watching the lights dance across its facets, still impressed all these years later by just how perfectly the seal sporting the word "*Veritas*"—"truth"—gleamed on stage.

In the earpiece, he could hear the anchorman speaking in neutral tones about the issue of the day. No balls, thought Gavin Rushmore. No balls in this world any more. "Let the Bull Rush In!" had been his slogan, the one that propelled him to fame before his producer created the "Challenge Chair" after his ratings sagged.

"So, Gavin Rushmore, what do you think? Your words could sway the Congress in these waning moments. The vote is excruciatingly close. Will immigration reform pass, or will America crack down on the outlaws living in the shadows? What's your final word today on the immigration debate? You told us about your encounter in the elevator, your rescue at the hands of an illegal alien. How do you reconcile that with this vote?"

Gavin paused for a moment, the silence pressing in, the lights bearing down, the lens of the camera dispassionately staring at him. He knew when he'd started this story exactly where he would come down, but the tall, dark man's music rang in his ears still. He wanted to hear that music every day for the rest of his life. He wanted to sit down and ask Victor questions all day. Why had he come so far? Why did he want so badly to be an American? Why was he willing to be so generous, giving to one who would turn him away, wish him to be gone?

"You're live," the producer stated flatly through his earpiece.

"We have one principle, as humans," Gavin Rushmore decided, embracing his superficial persona. "And another as Americans…"

***

On the freeway, Fern and Victor's hearts sank as they sat in the car, a cacophony of horns around them in the smog.

They listened to Rushmore as he launched into a tirade, "As a human being, I feel for them. I feel for the man that helped me in the elevator. He is a man, a good man. But he does not belong here. He belongs in his own land. Why should his talents not be put to use there, I ask you? Why should he not put his life on the line for the future of the country where he was born? What if our own heroes had fled the challenges in America? What if they'd gone off in search of easier pastures? I ask you! Why is my friend from the elevator not seeking victory in climbing the mountains of his homeland in Peru? Why is he not risking his life, like our patriots once did…crying for liberty or death in his own country? I challenge you to convince me that we are not doing a favor, repaying him for saving my life that day, if he goes back and can do the same for his own people! It's not about America, perhaps, it's about you, Victor! That was the name of the man that helped me, my friends. Let him rise victorious against his own demons. And leave us to fight our own. America, this is our America. We must defend it against those who break our laws. They may be good people. But this is our home. And they should head back to tend to their own…homes. Thank you. This is Gavin Rushmore urging Congress to vote for America, vote to protect our homes against this invasion that threatens our nation."

***

"And the vote is in, Gavin. Amnesty has been denied. A mass deportation awaits those who would defy the laws of this great nation," the anchor declared, short of breath. "Gavin…? Gavin? It seems we've lost Gavin, so let's go to Florida, where…"

"Mr. Rushmore?" the petite Asian receptionist asked with concern as she saw him meander down the hallway towards the bathroom. "Are you all right?"

"I'm fine, dear," he mumbled. His cell phone rang. It was his daughter. He knew she was calling to chastise him for his decision. He pressed "ignore" and leaned over the sink, staring at the stranger in the mirror. Tears threatened to fall, a feeling quite foreign to him.

He reached into his pocket and considered the cigarette case. Then he opted instead for the bottle of pills. He turned on the faucet, wondering where Victor was at that moment.

***

Fern cried inconsolably, banging her fists against her Prius' steering wheel like it had wronged her.

Victor was unaccustomed to such emotional outbursts without the threat of military reaction. He looked at Fern, still marveling at the beauty of these American creatures, so free with their feelings and their thoughts. If only…

"This is so wrong!" she cried.

Victor's phone rang. Helicopters buzzed overhead. Sirens wailed. Horns blared. Smoke billowed into the sky from various parts of towns, where the radio reported riots had broken out. People streamed out into stalled traffic on the freeway. He stared at his bag of packages that would not be delivered.

Fern scanned the radio stations, hearing reports immigration raids descending strategically, preemptively, in several familiar neighborhoods.

"They knew!" Fern exclaimed. "They knew before the vote what was going to happen. They were informed! They won't let you get away. It's for real this time! Oh, my God!"

Victor stared into Fern's honey eyes.

"I love you," she said, searching the darkness of his pupils, seeing in them the pitch black of the elevator where they'd first met.

"*Te amo*," he smiled.

A minute passed as they sat silently amidst the chaos, thinking.

"Will you stay," she asked finally. "Hide? Fight for your rights? For the children?"

"Will you go…with me…south of the border…maybe back to Ecuador?" he asked hesitantly.

She ran through several visions of her future: Grad school, an inheritance, marrying an earnest community activist with a Master's degree, going to law school, doing good from the inside the system, providing for her kids. The alternative: traipsing across the mountains of Ecuador with a flute player, bearing his children in a mud hut, hoping they would not be raped and killed by paramilitary psychopaths.

His door swung open as she stared mutely at the radio, hearing but not listening any more.

When she finally looked up, Victor was sitting cross-legged on the hood of her car, unzipping his backpack.

Rolling down her window, she called out, her golden hair waving in the breeze, "What are you doing? Get back in here! You don't want to call attention to yourself. Are you crazy? We can keep you here. We can hide you. I want you. I'll take you to my parents' country house. No one will find us there...I promise. We'll be together. We'll fight to get Miguel back into the country and keep Imelda and the kids here, straighten out their papers..."

She watched as he unfolded the black velvet cloth around his Andean flute.

Border patrol trucks streamed down the freeway shoulder, green-clad officers pouring out onto the concrete and overtaking suspects left and right, pulling them from cars and trucks at random.

Throwing her door open, Fern felt the crunch of the hot asphalt beneath her combat boots. It was so strange to cruise on these roads every day yet never walk on them, she mused. She crossed her arms over her chest and fumed: "What in the world are you doing, Victor? You'll get yourself deported!"

"I don't know...it just hit me," he said. "It's just not worth it any more. They need us more than we need them."

She stared at him as the sun broke through the haze, and there, amidst the cars, the horns, and the fumes, he raised the flute to his lips.

He inhaled deeply. Then he played a song of triumph, the notes and melodies rising like a vine finding its way through a canopy of leaves towards sunlight. At long last, he feared nothing. He felt free. In his mind, the music blended with the memory of Miguel's guitar and harmonized with the chorus of angels he'd expected to find in this land. The notes reached higher, weaving their way through the clouds, towards the sun, and piercing the sky.

As Fern listened, a sense of peace washed over her. The lyrical sound was pure, crystalline fluid poured from a waterfall in the Andes, filling her, soothing, cleansing, nourishing her.

She climbed up on the hood next to Victor and lay back on the windshield, soaking in the sun, closing her eyes and humming along. They smiled. And she giggled with delight as she remembered that her passport was in her purse.

Liberty Lost

Libby watched the waves lap, a foot or so beneath the window ledge.

"It's higher again, Dad. About another three inches, maybe four," she called out in the direction of his bedroom at the end of the hall. "Pretty soon, we'll have to shut the balcony doors and the windows." And then what? she wondered silently. How long would the flimsy glass keep the encroaching water at bay?

"All right, all right," she shook herself out of the depths. "Time for your meds. I'm coming."

She shuffled into the kitchen, which she prided herself on keeping pristine, despite the circumstances. Sighing, she counted out rectangular tablets from the daily organizer. Two blue. One yellow. A pink. The window over the sink was higher than the ones in the living room, which meant she could keep that one open longer for fresh air.

She reached up and marked off a day on the calendar that hung on the wall. The year above the month was crossed out and updated from 2023 to 2024, and then to 2025. Each date was crossed out twice, with extra check marks for the days that had already passed in the current cycle. At first she'd thought it would be hard to keep track of time, but it became easier, once she'd established her routine.

From the well-stocked, color-coded pantry, she withdrew a small can of prune juice and placed it on an orange plastic tray next to the pills.

"Hold on. I'm coming, Dad."

Heading into the dark hallway, she didn't bother flipping the light switch. She knew exactly where everything was, and there was no need to waste the batteries.

Her dad was in his usual position, sitting upright in bed holding *The New York Times*. It didn't matter to him that it was dark and he couldn't make out the print. She knew his eyes were hypersensitive to light and there was no point in pulling open the heavy drapes, since he already knew every word on every page of the last issue ever delivered. If only he hadn't lost his voice with the disease. Progressive it was, the doctor had said, long ago. She still was trying to figure out how getting sicker could be considered progress, but then again, she'd never made it to medical school, so what did she know?

"Don't stop your reading, I'll just give you your pills. Here you go," She slipped them into his mouth while he swallowed them with juice. She adjusted the blankets pulled up around his chin, and patted him gently on the shoulder. "You're doing just fine today, aren't you? Reading that story about that attack on Israel? Be careful, don't give yourself another cardiac over something that was history long ago."

Pausing at the door, she said, "I'll be in to check on you later. I've got some work to do. I don't think we can stay here too much longer. Before you know, you'll be resting in a waterbed. And we both know that won't be any good for your back."

When the evacuation had come, they'd only taken people under fifty years old. There wasn't enough room for everyone, they'd said. Everything happened so fast. Unwilling to abandon her dad, Libby had hunkered down, determined to survive.

"I may not have become a doctor, like you and Mom wanted me too," she'd assured her dad. "But that engineering degree might be more valuable after all." Jobs had been scarce towards what she had jokingly called the End of Time. She called it that because the newspaper stopped coming and electricity stopped, shutting down the TV, radios and computers. But who needed a job anymore? Surviving was the priority. Money was no good either. People were looting, if they weren't bartering their way onto the transports or trampling over each other on bridges before they were swamped by the rising waters. She'd been grateful, then, for those childhood trips out to the shooting range with her dad and Grandpa. She'd loaded up both of her dad's rifles and the handgun, and sloshed her way to the nearest Duane Reade to get supplies. Then the real treasure trove had been revealed in the basement of her own building, where she'd ripped out coils of useless wires and hauled an old emergency power generator up to the small study she'd converted into her "war room." She'd rigged it with some store-bought...er...borrowed solar panels to charge the generator. Then she'd wired a makeshift electrical system for the apartment, since the original one didn't work anymore. She'd tucked the wires neatly along the molding, so visitors wouldn't trip, or even notice. Not that there was ever company any more. Once, Libby had been popular with boys, but that seemed like a lifetime ago. And Dad had been pretty good at scaring them off. She didn't know if it was the guns or his toothy grin that did it, but they tended to never come back after the first visit.

There had been that one. Roger. He had come back twice and even tried to bring an evac team to get them out. He'd been sweet, and strong. He'd made her feel whole and special in a way she didn't dare to remember any more, because it made her feel like she'd died. And she didn't want to feel dead. She'd sat on Roger's lap, even made love to him right on the leather office chair she now used to make "war." That was back when the water was still only a foot deep, thirty stories below. She smiled to herself, relishing the memory. And Dad hadn't even heard a peep, except maybe the creaking of the chair. She'd oiled it for his next visit, but that had been the last time. Every day, she cleaned and ironed the same outfit she'd worn that lucky day, in case he miraculously came back, floating through the living room windows on a raft to rescue her. Her low-slung, army-green pants, her polished black boots, her black sleeveless T-shirt, just a peek of taut stomach and belly button, her hair neatly up in a bun. She stared at herself in the mirror. No deep wrinkles yet. She was too young to die. Simply too young. So, it was time to work.

She sat down and ran through her inventory. They still had plenty of food and medicine. The generator was working well. The pump for the sewage from the toilet was still functional. But there was little she could do about the rising water. The water was a problem, wasn't it? And moving Dad was a problem. She couldn't abandon him, and he would require an escape raft and a team to help her. They had thought it impossible that the water would rise so high, but the experts had been right. It was still rising, and quickly. Soon, all of Manhattan would be under water. Who would be left to help her and Dad?

She leaned back in the chair and twisted the knobs on the large metal box on the table next to her. It was her last link to the outside world. She wouldn't quite call it civilization any more. Static crackled and a dim brown light flickered behind the gauges.

"Hello. This is Libby López in Battery Park City. Anyone still alive out there?"

Nothing. She tried every few days, but it had been exactly two weeks since anyone had responded. She marked her desk calendar, then reached to turn off the radio, to conserve power. She paused and thought, Maybe I should leave it on, just in case…I probably have more power stored up than I need.

She worked studiously on her diagram of an escape vessel. Hours passed.

She sat in the tan leather Eames chair in the living room, facing the windows, watching night fall over the waterlogged towers jutting above the rippled expanse of cool ink, steadily rising.

She nearly knocked her own chair over when a voice startled her from sleep. It was her brother. "Libby, hey, Libby, it's me. You all right?"

"What are you doing here? Where have you been?" she stammered, nearly choking. The night was so dark she couldn't even make out his silhouette, but she could tell from his voice that he was sitting on the couch.

"I was out on patrol. The hood's really emptied out, Libby. Almost nobody left. I think I'm the last one from the old precinct."

"Are you okay? Can I get you anything?"

"I'm cool. But listen, don't worry. I've finally come up with a plan to get us out of here. Remember how I used to like to play up on the roof? Well, I was thinking. There's these big metal boxes up there that house the old air-conditioning units. And there's big fans in there. What if we go up there and take it all apart and turn the boxes into boats and the fans into propellers? We'll use the generator and…you can wire it all up. You're good at that stuff. I'll help you carry Dad up there. We won't have to leave him behind. We'll be in Jersey before you know it."

"News flash, genius, Jersey's under water too."

"Then we'll take the boat all the way to dry land, wherever that is. You've got that generator rigged for solar, don't you?"

"Yeah, but I don't know how long it will power a motorboat," Libby shook her head. "I remember people saying the new East Coast might start in St. Louis, or some place in the middle of nowhere…. I don't think it would get that far. I don't think we'd have a chance of making it."

"Well, at least we'd be afloat. If we stay here, we'll all be drowning soon."

She couldn't argue with her little brother on that point. He was rarely right but, when he was, she found it particularly obvious.

"Have you talked it over with…her?"

He hesitated just half a second too long: "Yeah, she's in."

"Hmm. You sure? 'Cause last time I was counting on her, she left me hanging…literally."

"Yeah, yeah, she feels really bad about that, sis, but when are you gonna get over it? It was you or her, and all those zombie-like crazy folks sticking their hands out the windows while you tried to climb up the side of the building with the supplies, and well, you know, she just kind of lost her nerve…"

"Yeah, left me hanging there on the side of the building with zombies grabbing my legs. I'm lucky I still got my boots," Libby patted her soles. "She was supposed to pull me up on the rope so I could hang on to the supplies, and fend off those leeches trying to pull me into their caves, probably to eat me alive."

"Don't worry, they're all gone now, Libby. All gone. No one was as prepared as you."

"Well, where was she when they came knocking at the door, huh? Where was she when I had to shoot that old maintenance man, Moses, square in the chest, to keep him from coming in and taking our food and water?"

"Hiding, scared. C'mon. She's like a sister to you."

"Key word 'like,'" Libby fumed.

They sat in silence.

"I still love her, Libby. We're a package deal, messed up as she is."

Awkward. Libby wondered if life would be easier if older siblings could simply control the younger ones with telepathic powers. But they insisted on having a mind of their own.

Libby sighed. "Okay. Whatever. Safety in numbers. If we're going to do this, we're going to need all the help we can get. Now, let's get some sleep." She slipped her boots off and walked towards her bedroom. "You gonna crash on the couch?"

"Yeah, can I let her come in?"

"Whatever, just don't make a mess. And take her with you when you go on your morning patrol."

"Thanks, Libby. You're a good sister."

"Yeah, that's what I keep telling myself," Libby yawned, stretching as she raised her arms to pull off her shirt. Sometimes she got ideas in her dreams. Maybe she would dream about Sal's idea about the rooftop boats. It might actually have as much potential—if not more—than her alternate scheme, which was to fashion a vessel from the furniture in the apartment.

She lay in bed, turning the idea over in her mind as she drifted towards sleep, when another voice startled her.

"What the...?" She jumped out of bed, pulling her rifle from underneath and pumping it.

"Come in...come in...this is Virgil Five...come in...anybody home?"

As her head cleared, she realized the tinny quality of the voice signaled it was emanating from the ham radio in the den.

Scrambling, she burst into the room and punched a button with a hint of light in it. The warm, fuzzy gauges on the radio's face welcomed her like a pair of friendly eyes, beacons of humanity trapped in an ancient metal box from another era.

She reached for the microphone, pressing her full lips against it breathlessly.

"Virgil Five? This is Libby López in Battery Park City. Come in...are you there still? Come in..."

"Libby, this is Virgil Five in Murray Hill."

Libby rubbed her eyes in disbelief. "Are you really there?"

"Yup."

"It's been a couple months since we talked, Virgil Five." Libby said.

"Yup. We did...you still planning a move?" Virgil Five asked.

She was cautious about how much detail she could reveal. Someone might want to take her equipment or supplies for their own purposes.

"Maybe," Libby conceded.

"Well, listen, my buddy and I are planning something…maybe we can help each other out," Virgil Five crackled.

"What are you planning, an escape?" Libby asked.

"Sort of…an escape…with a bang…" Virgil Five stated.

"Talk to me," Libby pressed.

"I can't say too much over the airwaves. We need to meet in person and use the airwaves to recruit more people. We need at least seven."

"Need at least seven for what?" Libby's curiosity was piqued.

Virgil Five paused.

"You still there?" Libby tweaked the knobs for a better signal.

"Did you hear what they're doing to the Statue of Liberty?"

"I don't exactly have cable television here, Virgil Five. And my copy of *The New York Times* from two years ago doesn't mention it."

"The Chinese are coming to take it away," Virgil Five stated sanguinely. "They're taking it away before it goes completely under water, to repay some of our country's old debts."

"Lady Liberty?" Libby gasped, her voice cracking a bit.

"Yup. The one, they say she's up to her waist in the water right now."

"I was named for her," Libby whispered. "My dad and mom, they first saw her when they came on the boat from the Dominican Republic. They named me after her because they said it was the happiest sight they'd ever seen…until they saw me."

"Then they'd want you to help us. And we'll help you at the same time. We can help each other…" Virgil Five spoke quickly now, excited. "I've got a strategy. We need seven people."

"To do what?" Libby said.

"I can't say any more than that. I gotta go. Let's talk tomorrow…same time…see if we can think of a neutral place to meet…"

Libby pushed him some more, "Virgil Five, if you expect me to leave the safety of my home and go out into that crazy post-apocalyptic version of Venice we've got going out there…you gotta give me more than that…we need seven to do what?" Libby's voice quivered as she nearly shouted into the microphone, the meters jumping violently on the radio gauges.

"We need seven to stop them, that's what," Virgil Five replied.

Static crackled over the radio as Libby let his statement sink in. She sat in stunned silence.

"Libby, you still there? I'm not crazy...well maybe a little bit, but who isn't anymore? I used to be a professor at NYU, Libby. And I remember you told me you were an engineer. I've been talking to a couple of others with skills of their own...this is not a joke...do you want to talk tomorrow? Plan a place to meet?"

Libby clicked on the mic, "Yes."

She signed off and rushed out into the hallway headed towards the back room, yelling, "Dad! Dad! I'm sorry to wake you, but guess what?"

***

They agreed to meet at the Starbucks in the Woolworth Building across City Hall Park from the Municipal Building. There wasn't really a Starbucks anymore, of course, but Virgil had assured her that, due to their historical importance as meeting places, many of the old Starbucks signs with the mermaid's face had been plucked from the original shops and hoisted up high on their buildings. She found this both strangely comforting but amusing. Leave it to Americans to find a way to meet at Starbucks, even as the world was coming to an end.

It was hard to predict which landmarks would be fully submerged, rendering navigation difficult. But even if the golden goddess at the top the Municipal Building was now swimming with the fishes, the Woolworth would still soar defiantly, a beacon from another era, when America was just beginning to exert its might in the world. She decided it was a fitting place to plan to salvage the last shreds of America's fading dignity.

She worried about finding her way, not knowing how transformed the landscape would appear. What if she got lost, or a current swept her out to sea? No, she assured herself. Virgil had insisted navigation was possible and relatively safe, especially now that the city was mostly abandoned. And she knew the area well enough to find her way. She'd walked up Broadway to City Hall Park countless times. Virgil had assured her that the golden statue was still above water, in full view over the park. Back when she had access to the Internet, she could have done the calculations herself, but now she had no way of knowing the relative heights of the buildings downtown. All she could do was trust Virgil.

Examining a city map framed on the wall of the study, she guessed the voyage was only a mile and a half mile. So she chose the inflatable yellow raft she'd purchased way before the floods began, to go white-water rafting with Roger. They'd never made it, but the raft had already proven useful for short jaunts in the neighborhood, when she'd been forced to scavenge for supplies.

She hoisted the raft over the north-facing balcony, tying it to the black iron railings. She gazed out over the expanse of water that swirled before her. Before the flood, she would have looked down on West Street and an array of parking garages. This was the "affordable" side of the Liberty View building. She'd always found it ironic to live in a building called "Liberty View" and yet not have a view of Lady Liberty herself.

"Ah, who needs a view of the statue?" her dad used to say. "For free, you can look at yourself in the mirror! Plus, we can take the elevator down and you can wheel me around Battery Park. We can sit on a bench and stare at the Statue as long as we like!"

She wistfully recalled those breezy afternoons in the park with her Dad, and then climbed into the raft. She rowed gingerly up West Street towards Battery Park.

Arriving at the edge of where the park used to be, she held her breath as she passed the abandoned curve of the Ritz Carlton's glass tower. She looked south into the harbor to steal a glimpse of the Statue of Liberty.

"There she is," Libby whispered in awe. Just as Virgil had said, Lady Liberty was waist-deep in water. Next to her loomed a giant freighter with menacing cranes.

A charge of energy rippled through Libby's body, almost like the electrical shocks she'd endured while rigging her home energy system.

"No way you're taking her from us," she snarled, curling her fist. With a surge of determination, she swung left and plowed the oars into the waves with newfound resolve.

The venerable *beaux-arts* Customs House, later the National Museum of the American Indian, lay completely submerged beneath her as she turned onto Broadway and rowed uptown. She marveled how a landmark over a century old could be swallowed whole by this flood. It never stopped shocking her, the immensity of this tragedy.

"New York's almost gone," she steeled herself against the northern wind that sliced its way down Broadway. "We can't let anyone take our greatest symbol of freedom. Even if we have lost."

Rowing diligently, she followed Broadway's forlornly familiar path, plying the storied canyon of heroes between the truncated remnants of vacant towers looming like ghosts mourning their former glory.

She paddled close to the edges of the buildings, not wanting to be fully exposed in case a shut-in up high decided to do a swan dive, or take pot shots at her.

The water bubbled with debris and smelled of rotten meat and sewage. Flies buzzed everywhere. She'd never seen so many bugs in cold weather. The chaotic frenzy of cars and people had been replaced by insects and the bloated carcasses of bodies bobbing in the water. Completely absent were the few trees, as only the tops of buildings emerged from the water, their once-proud cornices humbled. Gone were the ornate facades that for so long lent character to this pantheon of American history, the world's financial hub, burial place of Alexander Hamilton. She gawked as she recognized the pinnacle of Trinity Church, now only a red metal ball bobbing in the water where a proud spire had once risen high overhead.

She recalled the throngs of hot dog and pretzel vendors that had clogged the ancient arteries of the financial district, the crowds of tourists, the merchants handing out flyers. To her right, Wall Street had drowned. She pictured the Brooklyn Bridge, swamped and swept away. And to her left, she saw the incomplete skeleton of the Freedom Tower, rising as a monument on the footprint of the former World Trade Center.

Shredded curtains occasionally wafted out of vacant windows, like withering hands waving farewell from sinking ships. But what struck her most vividly, beyond the water and the devastation around her, was how quiet the city had become. No taxis honking. No people shouting in the streets. No jackhammers drilling into the concrete. No dissonant chorus of sirens. Just the sound of wind and rain and waves sloshing against the sides of the raft and the buildings, the buzzing of the flies, the slow, rhythmic flapping of the buzzard's wings circling overhead.

After nearly forty minutes of methodic paddling, her biceps and shoulder muscles beginning to burn, she rowed into what appeared to be a vast lake lined by the tops of buildings. To her right, a red brick structure on the verge of being swallowed held up a cracked and faded Starbucks sign, strapped to the corner of the top floor.

"That can't be the place," Libby muttered to herself. "It's completely flooded already."

Glancing to her left she saw the stunning and singular top half of the Woolworth Building.

As her gaze turned further to the right, she was surprised to find the Municipal Building only halfway immersed in water, crowned still by the golden statue of Civic Fame, gleaming obstinately in the bleak grey as it reached into beneath the low-hanging clouds.

Her faith in Virgil was buoyed by a Starbucks sign dangling on chains from shattered windows high up in the Woolworth Building,

Across what used to be City Hall Park, makeshift signs hung at odd angles from windows in the Municipal Building. "Politicians R Completely Diluted" read one. And another called out: "Gone Fishin'…Permanently."

New Yorkers could find humor in just about anything, she thought. But she felt her sense of humor had long ago vanished, probably around the same time Roger had called her a lunatic and abandoned her, and her sick father, to die slow deaths.

A brief flash of light drew Libby's eyes towards the fifth window from the corner in the Woolworth Building. Pausing, she stared at the spot until a series of flashes repeated. It was Virgil, flashing "SOS" as they had agreed. And there it was. The green metal canoe he had described was anchored to a metal pipe running vertically on the side of the building. She angled the raft towards the opening and pressed through the cold drizzle. Her black raincoat shielded her body, but the falling droplets felt like tiny piercing ice daggers against her smooth face.

Nudging the canoe out of the way, she tethered her raft to the same pipe, clutched the windowsill, and lunged through the yawning rectangular opening into the blackness.

Glass powder ground beneath her boot heels as her eyes adjusted to the dark.

A man stepped forward out of the shadows. Tall and wiry, he was clad in black with a skullcap on his head.

Extending a bony hand, his steely eyes seemed to sparkle. "Libby, I'm Virgil."

"Virgil Five?" she smiled, shaking his hand. She liked him immediately.

"The one and only," he replied. "And let me introduce you to my associates." With a wave of his hand, two other men stepped forward.

"This is Professor Ho," he pointed at a short, thin Chinese man with silver hair, wearing khaki pants and a stained white shirt.

"And this is Brahim, my partner," Virgil explained, motioning to an equally tall, lanky middle-age man with bushy eyebrows and dark skin. Brahim smiled and unabashedly stepped forward with arms outstretched to hug Libby.

Before she had time to react, his arms wrapped around her. She was astonished at both how good he smelled, and how tense she was. She realized it had been a long time since anyone had touched her.

"You smell like cinnamon and vanilla," she fought back a smile as Brahim stepped back next to Virgil. "But you're lucky I didn't instinctively drop you to the floor for getting so close to me. I'm not as nice as I look, you know. My brother's a cop and he's taught me plenty of martial arts…so don't you boys get any ideas. It's probably been a long time since you've seen a girl in these parts."

Virgil chuckled, "I can't speak for Professor Ho, but he's old enough to be your grandfather. As for Brahim and me, well, we're not into that sort of thing."

Ahh, a smile slowly spread across her face. That's what he meant by "partner."

"Well I feel both stupid and more comfortable then," she chuckled, sitting down on a crate and motioning to the men to sit.

"So," Virgil said, "our mission is not about these things of the world. It's about something greater, a higher calling." He fiddled with something in his hands, what looked like prayer beads with a cross on the end. She'd seen one like it before. It was not a necklace but similar…a rosary, she recalled. Her mom and grandmother had both used one.

"You pray?" she asked.

"I have been known to, at times," Virgil confessed, glancing uncomfortably at Brahim.

"You don't?" she asked Brahim.

"To a different God," he replied, shaking his head at Virgil, like they'd had this discussion countless times before.

Professor Ho gazed out the window in patient silence.

"I didn't know there was more than one God," Libby said. "And the way things have been going, I wasn't even sure about that any more."

"We're on a mission to stop the Chinese from taking the last symbol of American greatness. And I believe it's a divine mission. We have been chosen to stay behind here, to protect what is ours," Virgil said, starting to sound less than sane to Libby.

Brahim shook his head again.

"He," Virgil motioned at Brahim disdainfully, "doesn't fully agree with my intentions."

"Why's that, Brahim?" Libby asked.

"Because I don't believe in vengeance and terrorism. And that's what this attack on the Chinese, this hare-brained scheme to save Lady Liberty, amounts to," Brahim answered. "Look, my people were persecuted for their acts of terror. But American vengeance only brought more pain and hardship on this great country. Look at us now! We made the whole world our enemy. We destroyed our environment. Instead of having friends to help us, we only found foes eager to speed our demise, who launched nuclear weapons into the polar ice cap and created a great flood to wipe out America. Just look how far we've sunk."

"Literally," Professor Ho said quietly.

"So then, why are you helping him?" Libby pressed.

"Because..." Brahim's dark eyes softened as he looked at Virgil. "I love him."

Libby stared down at her wet boots, shuffling them over the fine beads of glass that had once constituted windows in the abandoned office space.

"And you?" She pointed with her upturned chin at Professor Ho.

"I love him too," he replied.

"What kind of sick shit are you guys into?" Libby's eyebrows knit together.

The three men broke out into a rare chorus of laughter that echoed through the high-ceilinged building.

"No, it's not like that," Virgil soothed. "He's always been, like a father to me."

"Oh, I can appreciate that," Libby's said. "Actually, my dad is one of the people we've got on our side too. He's been getting better. And I think this mission will inspire him so much, he'll be rarin' to go. With a little extra dose of medicine, he'll be right there with us. He'd do anything for Liberty."

"And you say you have two more who can help?" Virgil asked, leaning forward on his creaky crate.

"Yes, my little brother Salvador. He's the cop." She hesitated.

"And…" Virgil prodded.

"And his girlfriend, Dahlia, who's a horrible excuse for a wannabe sister-in-law but she's another body if you're looking for numbers…and she goes where he goes…sadly."

Virgil cocked an eyebrow and traded glances with the other two men.

"Can she be trusted?" he asked.

"Depends."

"On what?"

"On what you ask her to do," Libby clarified. "If it's simple, she'll do fine. She's no rocket scientist. And don't expect her to risk her life, for you or anybody else. I'd say we give her the easiest job on the team, whatever that may be."

"Okay…" Virgil looked at Brahim.

"Beggars can't be choosers," Brahim said.

"I like your accent…what is it, Indian?" Libby asked.

"Arab."

"Oh, right."

"And yours? I like it too," Brahim smiled warmly.

"Spanish…well...Dominican, you know?"

"Yes," Brahim nodded, showing his crooked teeth in the dim light.

Professor Ho chipped in, "Ironic. Immigrants making the last stand. Fighting for Liberty when it was American xenophobia that ignited this whole apocalypse."

"He doesn't talk much, but when he does, he says a lot," Libby marveled.

"I'm not an immigrant," Virgil asserted. "I'm Irish-Catholic."

They stared at each other as the room grew darker and colder. Then they all laughed at how ridiculous that last statement had sounded, even Virgil.

"This is gonna be good. It's gonna be fun," Libby said, nodding. "So, can we do this and survive, save ourselves? Get out of this place? All of us?"

There was a long pause. "It depends," Virgil said. "We have some planning to do."

"Wanna get started?" Libby asked. "Before it gets too late, too dark to get back?"

"Yes." Virgil motioned to Brahim, who pulled out a large burlap sack, extracting two oil lanterns, which he proceeded to light. In the flickering shadows, Professor Ho unrolled large sheets of papers covered in diagrams of the Statue of Liberty, a giant ship, and a crane.

The four huddled around the charts. Libby shivered. She didn't know if it was from the cold or the excitement. And she didn't care. She felt alive for the first time since the lights had gone out.

Professor Ho turned to Virgil expectantly.

Virgil stated simply: "We have our seven...soldiers. So, by all means..." he waved his hands over the charts and motioned to Professor Ho, who began outlining their strategy in a methodical, rapid tone.

***

"Professor Ho is so smart!" Libby exclaimed, giving her dad his medicines. "He's a genius, I tell you. In all my years studying engineering, I never had a teacher as brilliant as him. And the other two are great, Dad. All so smart. Real intellectuals. Virgil was a Poli-Sci professor and Brahim, I'm not sure, but we're definitely in good company, Dad. So, whatever you do, when they come over, don't embarrass me, okay? Pretend like you don't even notice or care about the two being gay, okay? You know you've gotta put those old notions behind you. We're fighting for survival now, Dad. And honor too. Just think, saving the Statue of Liberty from Chinese invaders. Your favorite American symbol, Dad. My namesake, no less! I always knew that old ham radio would come in handy. I told you! So, get your rest. They come tomorrow and we'll stage the assault from here. It was meant to be, that we'd move down here to Battery Park City after I got that raise. You argued against it, but now look! It's not Spanish Harlem, but it's strategic, the perfect place to launch our mission into the harbor. Perfect. So get your rest. I'll run through the plan with Sal and Dahlia one more time, in the living room. And then tomorrow, we get started early. The boys, they'll be here at sun-up…" She giggled, struggling to contain herself. "I call them 'the boys' but they're old men, Dad, kind of like you…closer to your age than mine. You will get along great, you wait and see. And Virgil said if everything goes right, we'll not only save Liberty and escape from New York, but we'll become heroes. Heroes, Dad. Maybe inspire people to turn things around in whatever's left of this country after the waters stop rising. Maybe they'll build statues to us, in places like St. Louis and Las Vegas. I always wanted to go to Vegas. And since we're all immigrants, or the children or grandchildren of immigrants anyway, it might change how they see that too. Imagine a statue to me, Dad? Lady Libby! How cool would that be? They love their statues in Vegas, don't they? Okay, don't get overexcited. Chill. Sleep. And I'll see you in the morning. I gave you an extra dose so you can be up and at 'em with the boys come sun-up."

Libby delicately closed her dad's door and nearly skipped through the hallway towards the living room.

"Sal? Dahlia? Are you guys decent?" she called out. "Can I come in there?"

The entwined lovers sat exactly where she'd left them, on the couch.

"Okay, let's talk," Libby chattered, pulling up the Eames chair to the low coffee table. Night had fallen. "I'm firing up the lights some more. To Hell with it. We're almost out of here and we have enough batteries to last for weeks." She stood up and flipped a switch. "Cover your eyes 'cause it's gonna be bright. Want some coffee? Okay, I'm gonna brew some more. I don't think I'll be able to sleep tonight. I'm a bundle of energy. I've been chugging coffee all day. I even popped one of Dad's pills. No use in leaving too much of our inventory behind. Like Virgil said, we can't take it with us, where we're going. I've drank so much frickin' coffee I feel like I'm gonna crawl out of my skin. Anyway, I'll be right back with our java and we'll get started running through the plan again, all right. Good deal!"

She marched into the brightly illuminated kitchen, rummaging through the pantry for coffee beans.

"Guys, tomorrow is going to be an awesome day. You wait and see!" Libby called out enthusiastically. Then she muttered beneath her breath, "If Dahlia doesn't mess it up somehow. It's like her head's made out of wood or something. Great figure, which is all Sal cares about, but my God, I swear she's hollow upstairs."

She knocked her fist against the side of her head while she flipped the coffeemaker on and slipped her mug beneath the steaming brown liquid. Then she filled up two more mugs emblazoned with the NYPD logo on the side, sat them on a tray and headed back out for the final planning session before the big day.

***

When the sun rose over the East River and spilled into the harbor, the water engulfed her balcony and licked her windows' edge.

Libby peered over the vanishing rooftops of the city, bleary-eyed, rubbing out the swirls of stars clouding her vision.

Must be the brightest day in two years, she thought to herself.

After her eyes adjusted to the intensity of the light cutting through the unusually thin haze, and after she had assured herself that there was no sign of Virgil and the others yet, she retreated momentarily to take a quick tub bath, using purified water from her massive stock of gallon jugs. She changed into a fresh outfit of black jeans and a black turtleneck, slicked her hair back into a bun, brushed her teeth and slapped on some extra perfume to compete with Brahim's intoxicating fragrance of Eastern spices. She figured she might as well go out looking—and smelling—good.

She scanned her collection of sunglasses, meticulously arranged on the vanity in her bedroom, and selected a gossamer-like pair of sleek Dolce & Gabanna shades that molded to her visage seamlessly. Then she stood watch at the window, biting on her lower lip in expectation.

For the first hour, all she saw was a cadaver float by, way too slowly for her taste, a pelican fishing its eyes out as it glided from view.

She wondered just how high the water was now around Lady Liberty. Would she be up to her eyes and unrescuable, as

Professor Ho feared she might be if they took too much longer to get to her? No, the water levels had not risen that much in the past few days, or else the apartment would already be completely submerged. What if, instead, the Chinese had already hauled her off on their freighter? What then? Or would it be just as Virgil had predicted, waist high and perfectly manageable, if all went according to plan?

She stared impassively northward, waiting, when she heard a distant growling, growing louder by the moment. Then she spied three dark silhouettes in the distance, illuminated from behind by the sun, cruising towards her over the choppy water. They looked like three horsemen of the apocalypse come to deliver her reckoning, except, as they grew nearer, it became clear that their steeds were not horses but WaveRunners. They carried long automatic weapons slung over their backs, the tips jutting out over their shoulders. Virgil had boasted they had enough AK-47s for the whole group, a claim she had found hard to believe but, with every revelation, her faith in him increased. Maybe, just maybe, they could pull this off, after all.

"They're coming, Sal. Wake up, little brother. Go get Dad. It's a sight to behold." She couldn't take her eyes off the three men, gunning their engines, leaving three wakes behind them as they curved towards her tower. Guiding them in, she held a circular mirror to reflect the sunlight as a signal.

Moments later, they edged toward her balcony, smiling broadly and waving. After mooring their vehicles, the men climbed in through the window and accepted the clean towels Libby handed them. Normally, she would have protected the floors from their wet boots, but what was the point, now? This was her last day in the apartment and soon it would be flooded anyway.

"You made it!" Libby exclaimed.

"You can always count on Virgil," Brahim nodded, giving Libby a warm hug and air kisses on both cheeks.

He was so chic, even under this inhuman duress. That was class, Libby thought. Not the kind you can learn, but the kind you are born with, so no matter what situations or hell you find yourself in, you can't help but act that way. She'd never gone out with a guy like that. She wondered what it was like, briefly ruing the fact that the tall, dark man was gay, not to mention spoken for.

Virgil removed his skullcap, revealing silver and black bristles buzzed close to his scalp. He smiled, "So? Where's the rest of the crew? I'm eager to meet them."

"Right!" Libby clapped her hands together and motioned to the couple on the couch. Sal was decked out in full NYPD Blue dress uniform, polished handcuffs dangling from his belt, and Dahlia wore a dressy white chiffon strapless dress with high heels. They looked ready for the Annual Policeman's Ball, rather than a military operation. Libby proclaimed giddily: "This here is my brother Salvador; we call him Sal. And his fiancée," she decided to cut her nemesis some slack, since this was a big day. "Dahlia."

All the air seemed to suddenly drain out of the room. The only sound was that of their breathing and the WaveRunners rocking up against the glass outside.

Then Virgil burst out into what sounded to Libby like maniacal laughter. "Oh, you're good! You got us that time. Testing us, huh? I remember your quip the other night about New Yorkers and our sense of humor. No...no...that's fair...I've still got one. What about you guys?"

Brahim chuckled nervously, "Oh, yes. Ha...ha...bada-bing...bada-boom...right? You could take this act to Vegas with you, Libby. You're hilarious."

"You're a frickin' entertainer, my dear," Virgil sat in the Eames chair and tugged his boots off. "I hope you don't mind, but I've got to dry my feet off for a bit. They're soaked and freezing cold."

"Not at all, let me get you some more towels." She disappeared for a moment, during which Virgil and the men stared haplessly at each other. Brahim shrugged. Professor Ho hung his head in dismay, shaking it slowly.

Then she was back with the towels.

"So then, Libby, where *is* the rest of the team?" Virgil pondered nonchalantly.

"What do you mean?" Libby froze. Did he not like Sal and Dahlia, right off the bat? He couldn't be so choosy, under the circumstances. "Sal, Dahlia, introduce yourselves properly, come on. Don't be shy."

The three men gawked at her, Virgil and Brahim's mouths hanging open in shock.

"You're not kidding, are you?" Virgil's jaw tensed and the vein in his temple flared, pulsating.

Brahim edged subtly between him and Libby just in case she needed protection.

"Kidding about what?" Libby responded innocently, her eyes wide with concern.

"Libby, you're off your rocker...these two are nothing more than oversize dolls. They're not people. They're mannequins! Where did you get them, Macy's?"

Libby stared at Sal and Dahlia. She opened her mouth but no sound came out. She closed it, and then opened it again, gaping at them with a blank, confused look on her face.

"Sal? Dahlia?" Libby looked at them, her lower lip quivering. "Guys?"

Virgil clenched his fists and fought back the urge to jump on her and put her out of her misery right then and there. He scrubbed at the stubble growing around his chin. Professor Ho shook his head some more.

"They always talk so much. Why are they so quiet now?" Libby's eyes were as watery as the view out the windows.

Brahim laid his hand gently on her shoulder, and spoke soothingly, "It's okay, Libby. Anyone still alive here in the city has gone through a lot.... It's easy to become...confused..."

"We're more alive than these dolls!" Virgil exploded, lunging at the mannequins and wrestling them furiously to the floor. Sal's police hat flew off and Dahlia's pearls scattered onto the hardwood floor, rolling loudly in every direction. He punched at Sal until the cop lay hunched in defeat, over the coffee table. "I always hated cops. Bastards always gave me parking tickets. You couldn't take a crap in this town without getting a ticket."

"Sal wasn't a parking cop. He was a real patrol...man..." Libby's words trailed out as her gaze drifted slowly across the inert mannequins she'd fashioned into replicas of Sal and Dahlia long ago. The latter lay in a most unladylike position on the floor, her legs wide open revealing a pink thong.

She fought back the instinct to lower Dahlia's skirt, as memories rushed back of her brother and his reviled girlfriend drowning on the street in front of the building during the initial flood, pinned beneath debris she had futilely struggled to remove.

My brother, my poor brother, her heart broke again. It had all been Dahlia's fault, panicking and running out, them chasing after her. And then she just hadn't been strong enough. Too weak. Powerless. The story of her life.

The towels she carried dropped to the floor.

"We needed seven!" Virgil shouted, leaning into Libby's expressionless face. Brahim, wrapped his arm around Libby and delicately backed her away from Virgil.

"We don't really need seven," Professor Ho ventured timidly, as if he'd said that before, only to be ignored.

"What about your father?" Virgil remembered. "Is he a stick figure too? Where is he?"

"Dad!" Libby's face turned up again. "You'll love my dad. He's the sweetest man. C'mon, follow me." Hungry for redemption, Libby charged down the hallway to the back room, followed by the trampling men.

"It doesn't smell too good back here, Libby," Brahim cautioned, as if his permanent aroma of cinnamon and vanilla might be threatened by the stale, sickly sweet pungency emanating from the darkened chamber they entered in her wake.

"Dad! Here are the guys! You feel better today? You ready?" Libby flipped on the dim, battery powered lights. But all the men could discern was a shadowy shape propped up in bed behind a wide-open front section of the New York Times.

"Oh, this is ridiculous. Another mannequin?" Frustrated, Virgil yanked the newspaper out of the way and jolted back at the sight.

Professor Ho ripped the heavy drapes open to reveal a grisly figure rotted a deep black, still in its pajamas, a crazed maelstrom of white hair crowning the skull, pink and yellow rectangular pills stuffed in a yawning orifice marked by jagged teeth. The tiny pills spilled down its throat, which gaped open where decomposed flesh had fallen away, and fanned out across his flannel shirt.

Libby shrieked as if she were seeing her father's corpse for the first time. Hurriedly, she reached for the drapes to plunge the room back into darkness and scrambled to put the newspaper back in its place, to hide the ghastly remains.

Brahim gently put his hands on both of her shoulders and eased her out of the room, back into the hallway.

Her voice trembled, "I'll give him another dose of his pills and he'll be better. Come. Look."

They followed her to the pantry and she turned to face them with two pink containers, one topped by a cat's head and the other by a dog's.

Virgil said, "Let me see those."

She handed them to him, her hands shaking anxiously, hoping desperately to regain his trust.

He turned them over and then cocked the dog's head backwards. Like a tongue protruding faithfully to lick its master, a pink rectangular pill with rounded edges emerged. He gingerly pulled it out with his fingertips, smelled it and popped it into his mouth.

Libby gasped. "That might not be good for you. You don't have a prescription. I take them sometimes, but I've always taken a lot of pills...of course, mine ran out a long time ago..."

"Pez," Virgil quipped, heading back into the living room and standing at the open window with his back to the others.

"Excuse me?" Professor Ho asked.

"Pez," Brahim explained, "candy dispenser.... Here, have one." Brahim had found a pink one topped with the head of the Joker, white face and wild green hair mocking their insane misfortune. A yellow Pez peeked out and Professor Ho popped it into his mouth.

"Good." He grinned and nodded.

Brahim popped one too, swirling it around in his mouth.

Glumly, Libby settled on the couch, glancing suspiciously at the Sal and Dahlia mannequins scattered awkwardly on the floor. How could she have allowed herself to lose total touch with reality? Her body shuddered as she began to weep.

"I'm sorry," she cried in shame. "Being alone was so hard."

Sitting next to her, Brahim offered her a Pez, which she gladly accepted.

He patted her knee, waiting for Virgil's verdict.

Feeling their expectant gaze on him, Virgil turned around, his eyes a fiery blue.

"It doesn't matter. We're all dead anyway!" Virgil declared, laughing like the Joker himself might have in one of those old Batman movies Libby had seen years back, at the Union Square 14.

"Oh, no, here he goes again," Professor Ho frowned.

"He has a theory…that's why he's obsessed with having the seven," Brahim explained.

"Is he not going to try to kill me then?" Libby asked, brushing away the tears. "Because if he is, you need to let me know so I can get ready to defend myself. I wasn't kidding about knowing martial arts and how to use a weapon. Sal did teach me that… before…"

"I don't think he's going to kill you," Professor Ho spoke quietly. "Because he thinks you might already be dead."

"Huh?" Libby grimaced, a perplexed expression contorting her lovely face.

"Don't worry," Brahim assured paternally. "I won't let him hurt you."

Virgil cleared his throat, "I have this notion that maybe we are all dead, ghosts of the city. The city has died, but it's haunting itself. In the Bible, it says that when a soul is not ready to let go of its physical surroundings, it clings to them and calls down seven other bad spirits to help torment anything or anyone who dares inhabit its space. I believe the city has called us. And there must be seven of us. And that our mission is to save the soul of the city, Lady Liberty herself, from being taken. The spirit of the city will not rest, and neither will we, until our mission is accomplished and the invaders are repelled. Only then, will we all rest in peace."

"Why didn't you say so in the first place?" Libby asked, throwing her hands up in the air.

Nonplussed, they all stared at her as Brahim haltingly retorted: "You would have thought we were—"

"Crazy?" Libby finished his sentence, a mischievous lilt in her voice.

***

In the dark, the frigid murky water poured slowly over the step to the balcony, flooding the apartment.

They had eaten the best of Libby's stores, agreeing that, while Libby was unbalanced and prone to hallucinations, she was a good cook. Her talents had served her well for the past couple years. Virgil seemed to alternate in his worldview: One moment, they were all dead spirits clinging to the ruins of the city, and the next they were eating out of cans and planning their next move. It was hard to reconcile, but none of them wanted to get caught up on the technicalities of their conflicting metaphysical constructs. Their predicament was inexplicable. And it really didn't matter anymore. Even Professor Ho conceded that point. Nothing mattered anymore, he said, confessing he had always been somewhat of a nihilist.

Libby smiled and shrugged her shoulders a lot. It was good to be with living people, even if they were all ghosts or demon spirits or whatever Virgil wanted to believe. Her brain didn't have to work so hard to make everyone around her talk and come to life. She had been raised Catholic, forced to read the Bible regularly as a kid. She had a vague recollection of the passage from the Bible about the seven spirits being called to haunt a place until the original restless soul found its peace. Given her affinity for the city and her namesake, the Statue, she liked the idea that perhaps salvaging Lady Liberty from the Chinese could bring a final peace to this drowning place and everything, everyone, in it. Maybe freedom wasn't escaping to Vegas. Maybe freedom was simply peace, or simply death.

After recalibrating their plans under the direction of Professor Ho, who turned out to have once been a chess master, they were finishing off the last of the food when Libby said, "So, listen to this theory, Virgil. What if you do have your seven, in spirit? Spirits might manifest themselves in different ways. My father's spirit is probably with us, but we can't see him. Same goes for Sal and Dahlia. All that we can see may be a couple of mannequins and a skeleton in my father's favorite pajamas, but all along, I have felt their presence. I have heard their voices. Maybe I am crazy. Or maybe they've been here with me. Maybe they can't pull the trigger tomorrow, or wire the bombs, or any of that...but maybe they can help us in some way or another...maybe positive energy...maybe distracting the guards when they least expect it, an invisible presence, a sudden breeze whispering in their ears, freezing them into place a split second long enough for us to achieve our goal. Who knows, right? Maybe we only look like four but maybe we are more."

Virgil thought about it at length. Then at last he raised his eyes from his final Pez. Instead of popping it into his mouth, he handed it to Libby, straight from the Joker's mouth.

"You know what, Libby…you're deeper than I thought."

As the water rose, she wondered if he meant it straight or as a pun. You never could tell with New Yorkers.

***

Virgil and Brahim slept in Sal's old bedroom, Libby in hers, and Professor Ho on the couch as Sal and Dahlia bobbed about in the rising tide. It was still dark, around four in the morning according to Professor's Ho Rolex Oyster Perpetual, when they gathered their equipment and waded out to the WaveRunners, clinging to the disappearing railings on the balcony. Each carried a heavy backpack and two AK-47s.

Virgil and Professor Ho mounted first. Brahim waited by the window respectfully as Libby said her goodbyes. She prayed briefly over her dad, kissed him on the flannel pajama shoulder, then hugged the Sal mannequin and reluctantly gave the Dahlia one an awkward parting pat on the head. Brahim smiled, watching her. Then he helped her climb out and positioned her behind him on the third WaveRunner.

Virgil gunned his engine and pulled down his skullcap. He tugged at his black waterproof gloves.

"You're not leaving them behind, Libby!" He nodded, shouting over the roar of the WaveRunners. "We are seven for the revolution. Together we ride."

He pulled out, plunging forward into the cold water. Professor Ho followed, with Brahim and Libby bringing up the rear. As they departed, Libby glanced back one last time. Tightening her hold on Brahim's torso, she swore she saw Sal in his uniform and Dahlia in her glowing white chiffon, dancing slowly through the surging waves in the living room. The window shrank and disappeared into the night behind them.

***

"When the military and the merchant marine retreated inland at the end of the evacuation, things got pretty chaotic. They left a lot of equipment behind," Virgil explained. "We salvaged this old Coast Guard vessel and patched it up. Pretty nice, huh?"

"Could we use it to get away from here, to safety?" Libby asked, admiring the small cutter.

"No," Professor Ho shook his head, as he molded a ball of clay and attached it to a small battery. "It requires too much power. It can only go small distances on the charge we can generate from the solar panels. And it's slow."

"It's just our staging area," Virgil said, drinking from a water bottle and placing it on the small table around which they huddled in the galley.

The galley's interior was dim and musty. Rust on gray walls. The metal hull groaned and rocked with the motion of the waves. In the distance, through the cracked windows, they could make out what appeared to be a floating city of lights, less than a mile away.

"What if the Chinese vessel detects us?" Libby asked her companions as she worked on charging the batteries for their handheld radios.

"There's so much flotsam out here, their radar probably looks like a star-filled sky," Virgil said. "You know, we have to be careful. Between us and them is Ellis Island. The peaks of its turrets are right beneath the water so we need to steer clear or risk running into them under the surface."

Libby frowned pensively.

"What's wrong, Libby?" Brahim asked. "Is it Ellis Island? I was pretty shaken up too, when I realized it was gone."

Libby slowly shook her head. No, it wasn't that. But something was bothering her as she watched Professor Ho and Virgil mold the clay and pop the wires into it. She chewed on her lip, as she'd done since she was a little girl. She could hear her mother telling her to stop before she made herself bleed. Before the cancer had taken her. How she'd loved her, the softness of her long hair, the warmth of her embrace. She wondered if her mom could see her now, and whether she'd be proud of her. For some reason, she'd never encountered her mom since she'd died, unlike the others. She wondered if this was because her mom was disappointed in her. But now that Virgil had presented his theory of the seven spirits, she wondered hopefully if, perhaps, it was because her mom was different from the others. Perhaps her mom was simply at peace.

"What is it, Libby?" Brahim pressed. "Can I get you something to eat?"

"No, I'm just thinking about what Virgil said earlier..." Libby answered.

"Which part?" Virgil asked, never taking his eyes off the explosives he was assembling.

"Well, you said something about seven 'bad' spirits," Libby blurted out. "I'm just wondering what's so bad about us? If you're right, why are we here still? Why are we not at peace...like my *mamá*, who passed away when I was little?"

"I don't know," Virgil answered flatly. "Maybe we did something wrong in our lives, and now we have a chance to right it."

Professor Ho added, "When you are called to serve, it is best not to ask questions."

Libby's eyes looked to Brahim for an answer, but he was busy trying to create an appetizing snack out of a variety of canned foods.

"What's he making?" Libby wondered.

"It's our Last Supper," Virgil smiled wryly.

"We probably won't make it out of this alive, right...if we're alive?" Libby pondered.

All eyes landed on her.

"It's best not to ask questions..." repeated Professor Ho. "Let me tell you about Ellis Island. Most people don't know that..."

***

Outside, the WaveRunners knocked restlessly against the back of the boat.

Brahim dragged on a cigarette wistfully as he stared out at the floating city of lights that threatened to abscond to Asia with the Statue.

"When I was younger," he told Libby, puffs of smoke punctuating his words, "I spent much time in the real City of Lights, and in Morocco. It was my happiest time, except for when I came here. At first, I loved New York."

"Were you a scholar too?" she asked, looking up at him in the starlight and glow of the cigarette.

"Oh no," Brahim chuckled. "I was not much for books."

"What did you do...before?"

"I served...I love to serve people," Brahim said. "It is my instinct."

"Served?"

"I started in little bistros in Paris. There I was 'discovered' by one of the owners of La Mamounia, this amazing hotel in Marrakech. I went to Morocco and waited on tables for the rich and famous. Then I got my big chance to come here to New York. And I met Virgil when I served him dinner at his book release party twelve years ago. It was happy times, as Americans used to say."

"But you're American…no?"

"Of course. I became naturalized."

Funny word, Libby thought. "It's like they thought everything not American was unnatural…"

"And here we are," Brahim grinned, tossing his cigarette into the harbor. "I used to recycle. Even gave up smoking, but what does it matter anymore?"

The slapping of Virgil's scuba fins on the deck jolted them from quiet reflection.

"So, I'm going," Virgil affirmed with a tight smile.

Brahim admired him in the tight black wetsuit. "You look like a professional."

"Well, that will have to do," Virgil replied, shuffling clumsily to the rail as Professor Ho emerged from the galley, resembling a giant, flustered penguin more than a professional diver in his wetsuit.

Libby stifled a giggle as Professor Ho struggled to keep his balance and carry the heavy bags filled with detonators.

"Everyone clear on the plan?" Professor Ho asked one last time, huffing and puffing as he reached the rail.

"Clear," Libby clipped. "You wire the ship and, when you're ready to board, you signal and we create the distraction."

"When they're off guard, you board the ship from the far side," Brahim recited.

"We circle around with the WaveRunners," Libby continued. "At that point, we can break radio silence but should avoid it as long as possible."

"You take control of the crane and detach it from the Statue," Brahim continued. "By then, you'll be spotted, so we provide cover while you try to get off the ship."

"You get back here, we board the WaveRunners and we blow the ship to pieces," Libby exclaimed, pumping a fist into the frosty evening as her dark hair whipped against her smooth cheeks and her black eyes shimmered.

"Now remember, if anything goes wrong…" Virgil prompted.

"We blow up the ship, regardless of where you are," Brahim pursed his lips in distaste.

"And if the wiring for the bombs fails?" Professor Ho probed.

"I'll dive and make the fix," Libby nodded, chewing on her lip again.

"And I'll blow everyone to pieces," Brahim concluded, his bushy eyebrows knitting together in disapproval.

"But you've gotta mean it," Virgil admonished his partner.

"Just go already," Brahim waved them away.

They exchanged brief hugs.

"We'll pick you up," Brahim whispered to Virgil. "You be good."

The two divers boarded one WaveRunner and headed as quietly as they could into the fading darkness.

Soon, the edges of the horizon frayed with color. Brahim pressed a button on his stopwatch and he and Libby sat down and watched. A thin line materialized in the distance, two slightly different tones of midnight blue on either side, distinguishing the heavens from the sea. Against the lightening sky, the shadows of a structure suspending the city of lights shifted into silhouette.

When Brahim's watch beeped, the two donned their wetsuits, hoisted their weapons and backpacks, and boarded the two remaining WaveRunners, speeding away from the Coast Guard boat.

Slipping into position a few hundred yards south of the midpoint between the Chinese freighter and the Coast Guard ship, Brahim and Libby idled side by side. As they waited for the signal, the sky brightened, white and orange flares spreading from the horizon.

They could now clearly see the outlines of the massive Chinese freighter. Its looming crane cast a shadow over Lady Liberty to the right, and the tiny junk they'd abandoned bobbed like a forgotten toy boat to their left. The radios clipped to their black rubber belts beeped twice, followed by a pause and three more beeps.

It was the signal. Brahim nodded and they both lowered their sunglasses.

Libby extracted the detonator, flipped open the clear protective plastic cover and slammed her thumb onto the red button.

150   *Seven for the Revolution*

A flock of prescient seagulls ascended into the rich blue heavens, their lamentations skimming across the desolate harbor.

Libby held her breath, wondering if it was possible for it to be so quiet, or for her to be so alert that she could actually hear the ticking of Brahim's watch. Then, a split second before the boom reached them, the Coast Guard ship exploded into a ball of swirling yellow fire and black smoke. The sound cracked over the waves as pieces of sheet metal and debris spun through the air and skidded across the water. Sirens rose seconds later from the Chinese freighter, followed by a smattering of alarmed shouts in Mandarin, as sailors ran to the railings to peer across the waves.

No time to admire their handiwork, Libby and Brahim plowed through the noisy echoes and the piercing shrieks of the siren, opening up the throttles on their WaveRunners and racing in a wide arc around the stern of the ship.

Fire raged to the left. Lady Liberty prevailed amidst the swelling waters beyond the prow of the enormous cargo ship. Libby revved the engine and gritted her teeth. The red flag of the People's Republic of China fluttered in the wind, high above, blending with the crimson sun as it burst through the horizon in the east.

***

"We've been made!" Virgil crackled over the radio, grunting as he knocked out a Chinese sailor.

Libby and Brahim watched the tiny body as it spiraled off the ladder outside of the crane operator cabin. It tumbled head over heel, landing with a sharp crack as its head hit the deck.

The rattle of machine guns followed, in short, tense bursts as a handful of armed guards gathered at the base of the crane and shot up at the trespassers.

Libby peered through a pair of binoculars. "Professor Ho is wrestling with the crane operator!" Virgil kicked another sailor away from the entrance to the cabin, suspended high above the deck. "The hook is still attached to the Statue, but the Statue is already off its base, it's higher up in the water than it was yesterday."

"They started earlier than we expected," Brahim groaned. "That was not the plan."

"The plan was to disable the ship before they could remove the Statue, so it could stay in place. Now what?" Libby's voice trembled. "Do we start shooting to give them some time to get down? We'll have to blow the whole thing, statue and all."

"We're not blowing up anything!" Brahim emphatically declared. "We're not going to repeat the crimes of terror that started America's decline in the first place. That would make us as evil as those we stood against when it was still a beacon of hope in the world."

"Blow the joint!" Virgil barked again over the tinny speaker. "There's no way we're getting out of here alive. Save yourselves!"

"C'mon, let's get them out!" Brahim angled his WaveRunner against a metal ladder that clung to the side of the freighter. "Stay about twenty or thirty feet behind me at all times, Libby."

The steel rungs were cold and wet, but the two quickly rose to the top without being seen. By the time Libby reached the deck, Brahim turned a corner around a gray wall. As she followed, she nearly tripped over the lifeless body of a sailor lying on the floor with a broad sheet of paper wrapped around his face. A pool of blood rippled out from beneath his body. Libby immediately recognized the paper. It was her father's *New York Times*!

She reached for her radio, "Virgil, hang in there! You're not alone." My father's here, she thought. *Papá!* It must be true, we must be dead already, manifesting ourselves in different forms. As she turned the corner onto the foredeck, a flash of fuchsia caught her attention. Fluttering in the stiff breeze a hot pink pair of lace underpants arched through the sky. Every sailor in sight paused and followed its trajectory with eager eyes, faint smiles creasing their faces with thoughts of distant pleasures. A loud explosion of machine gun fire interrupted their reverie, as Brahim, wielding a gun in each arm, fired methodically across the deck, cutting them down like a string of dominoes. By the time anyone returned fire, he had mowed down well over a dozen men, then ducked behind a stack of barrels.

Dahlia, I knew your penchant for indiscretions would come in handy someday, Libby laughed giddily to herself, as she scrambled to rejoin Brahim. Her radio crackled with an admonishment from him, "Libby, twenty to thirty feet behind…remember?"

"Brahim," she answered back, "Did you see? They're here! They're helping us."

The remaining Chinese sailors scurried like rats for cover, giving Virgil and Professor Ho additional time.

"Virgil, what's your plan B?" Libby asked over the radio, hiding behind an enormous metal trunk and waiting for Brahim's next move. "What's going on up there?"

In answer to her question, the body of the crane operator blasted through a shattered cabin window and plunged to the waters below.

"He was a hard one to kill," Virgil muttered back. "Professor Ho is on it. The operator did some serious damage to the controls to sabotage us. We need you up here, to fix some of the wiring. Sorry, guys, you have to climb up. I'll cover."

Brahim went first, diving behind pallets and barrels as he weaved his way to the base of the crane. Virgil shot down from his sniper's perch at the lurking sailors that rose to attempt a shot at Brahim. Once Brahim began the dangerous climb up the side of the crane, Libby followed.

"You've got one on your tail," Virgil warned Brahim.

Libby was quite aware of the pursuer, now halfway between her and Brahim, about twenty rungs up on the ladder. But, when she tried to shoot at him, only a series of futile clicks issued forth. She needed to load a new clip. Bullets whizzed by her ears, clanging around her and showering sparks into the cold wind. She struggled to keep moving while she pulled a new clip from her belt.

"Libby, shoot!" Virgil cried urgently over the radio. "I don't have a clear line of fire; Brahim's in the way. The guy's on him."

Libby glanced up to see the sailor and Brahim locked in a tumultuous embrace on the ladder. The new clip slipped from her hands and rang against the metal below. She reached for another one as a bullet grazed her right calf, ripping open her black pants and exposing her burning flesh. The pain shot up her leg, sending a deep shudder up her spine as tears poured instinctively from her eyes. This was real. How could the dead feel such pain? Breathe. Breathe, she told herself. Clenching her teeth, she punched the clip into the gun and looked up again. But Brahim was gone. The sailor dangled awkwardly from what appeared to be a broken leg, his eyes staring off vacantly into the sea.

Libby climbed as fast as she could, favoring her leg. When she reached the dangling victim, she cringed. His grey uniform was soaked in blood from multiple stab wounds, his pant leg was ripped open and a jagged piece of bone protruded at an angle as he swung in the wind. His ankle remained connected, by a pair of gleaming silver handcuffs, to the side of the ladder.

Sal! Libby looked around, almost expecting to see her brother floating in mid air next to her. Thank you, she mouthed without a sound.

Her vigor renewed, Libby shimmied up to the cabin, dodging bullets as she reached up for Brahim's extended arm.

He pulled her in and shut the door as bullets sprayed across its surface and shards of glass tumbled in around them.

"A bit tight in here, no?" Libby grinned.

"Professor Ho, show her the wiring disaster left to us by our good Chinese friend who is now enjoying a swim in the harbor," Virgil said. "Glad you could join us!" He and Brahim crouched behind the windows in the cabin and fired off occasional bursts to keep the sailors at bay.

"Down here, look..." Professor Ho lay underneath a giant panel of equipment, which was emitting smoke and sparks, wires waving like the tentacles of an enraged sea monster.

Libby slid beneath the panel next to Professor Ho and pointed a small flashlight up into the maelstrom. "I see."

"Well, then hand me the flashlight and get to work," Professor Ho pleaded as more bullets clanged against the cabin.

Libby's hands flew, splicing wires together, rerouting currents, her eyes darting quickly back and forth.

"So what's the plan now?" Brahim asked, squeezing off a round and ducking back down into a corner as the enemy fired back.

"Well, the Statue's up, off its base, as you saw," Virgil answered. "Now, all we can do is lower it down into the harbor. I'm thinking, if we release it while in motion, it'll sink at an angle and land on its side As the water continues to rise, it'll be too low for any vessel to salvage."

"It does weigh half a million pounds," Professor Ho added.

"So, at least we will have kept Liberty here at home and fulfilled our mission, right, Virgil?" Libby called out from beneath the control panel, continuing her repairs.

"I think so. It sends a message too," Virgil agreed. "A message we can punctuate by blowing this ship to kingdom come when we're done."

"Why don't we take it over?" Brahim asked.

"That's pretty crazy," Virgil replied.

"We could sail west," Libby dreamed out loud.

"Depending on which view of reality you subscribe to," Professor Ho quipped.

"Try it, Professor. I think I've got it!" Libby blurted out excitedly.

The Professor hoisted himself up. "Give me cover, boys."

He pressed a button and pulled on a small red joystick, smiling like a little boy whose video game had just sputtered back to life after he'd given it up for dead.

The entire cabin shook from the movement of the crane's arm. Frantic yells rose up from the deck in a chorus as the shooting escalated, denting the walls around them.

"It's working! Libby, you did it!" Professor Ho gazed out over the harbor at the slow motion of the Statue gliding across the water at her knees. "Say the word, Virgil, and I shall release her."

"Move her a bit more out, a bit more out, clear of the island, clear of the ship," Virgil yelled over the storm of firepower descending on them.

Then the cabin jerked again and the crane shook to a stop as Professor Ho's hand released the lever suddenly, his eyes glazed over, and he slumped forward over the control panel.

"Professor Ho!" Virgil pulled him to the safety of the floor. As he lay him down, a trickle of blood poured out of a neat round hole in the side of his head. "Bastards!"

Virgil reloaded and fired vengefully down at the sailors. "Libby, take the lever. Just a little more to go."

Libby bit her lip, struggling to remove her eyes from Professor Ho's tranquil face. Could the dead die again? Virgil couldn't be right. They were alive. This nightmare was real. The pain in her leg was real. But what about the ghosts, what about Sal, Dahlia and her father? Her eyes fell on Brahim's open backpack, tossed on the floor. Inside it, she could make out a scrap of newspaper. He'd had enough time before they left to bring along a few props from her apartment. But why? To humor her? To please her? He said he liked to make people happy…what if?

"Now, Libby, now!" Virgil snarled as a bullet pierced his shoulder. "Damn it! Ah." Another hit his chest, knocking him backwards.

"Virgil!" Brahim cried, lunging over him. "No!" He pressed down on the wound with both hands, trying to contain the blood.

Libby pulled on the lever just as Professor Ho had, the cabin shuddering and groaning as the Statue continued its graceful glide out over the harbor. More bullets rained upon them, as Libby hunched down close to the control panel to avoid being hit.

"Virgil! Say when!" Libby cried.

"He can't see it any more. We're losing him!" Brahim cried. "C'mon, Virgil. Hang on. We're almost there. We'll be free just like you wanted. Virgil. Free spirits again. Our mission accomplished."

"Tell her to let it go...before it's too late..." Virgil gasped, his eyes rolling backwards momentarily.

"Do it!" Brahim shouted.

Libby punched the release button, but nothing happened. Quickly, she ducked back beneath the control panel, tracing a wire.

"What's happening?" Virgil whispered hoarsely. "I can't see."

"She's fixing something, Virgil." Brahim soothed. "Virgil, it's all going to be fine."

"Always the optimist," Virgil coughed up blood, fighting off a laugh. "It all stopped being fine a long time ago."

Brahim watched Libby splice two wires together, holding the flashlight in her jaws, perspiration dripping down her cheeks as she stared intently at the tangle she kneaded expertly.

"Too bad she's not a surgeon," he mused. "She could save you in a flash."

"There's nothing left to save," Virgil said, gurgling. "All that is left is peace. Peace will be our final freedom."

The door to the cabin was suddenly torn ajar, and one of the Chinese sailors fired a round into the small space before Brahim could kick him away and reach for the door handle. More bullets thudded into him, as he stood in the gaping doorway and looked wistfully back for a moment. Virgil convulsed and then laid perfectly still, his blue eyes giant crystal marbles, cold and frozen. Libby labored on, safely beneath the panel.

"Libby, they're coming," Brahim gasped, realizing he was incapable of regaining his balance. "Good luck..."

As Libby peered out from beneath the console, he slowly wavered and helplessly dove down to the deck, far below.

"No!" Libby called out, her eyes darting to her dead companions, Professor Ho and Virgil.

She reached up and pressed the button. Again, the cabin jerked as the weight was released from the arm.

A wave of anguished yelling rose up from the ship, as the crew rushed to the railing to watch the Statue tilt and then sink.

The door swung open again. Three large men burst into the small cabin, looming over the bodies, their menacing expressions softening and transforming into sickening smiles as their eyes took in Libby's feminine form.

Libby's heart sank. She'd seen the look before, when she'd been a young child left in the care of her mom's friend, before her mind had first splintered into a gallery of smoke and mirrors designed to distract her from her pain. Her mother had been sick with the cancer already and the family was distracted, making constant trips to the hospital. Maybe that's why she'd never seen her mom again like the others; maybe her mom was disappointed in her for allowing that transgression, that violation. But what could she have done differently? There had been no one to hear her shouts. And she had held no weapons in her hands, no detonators clasped between her fingers.

Exchanging hushed words in Chinese, the men advanced towards her with a mix of vengeance and lust in their eyes. Sometimes, you have to do something wrong to prevent something worse, Libby assured herself. Sorry, Brahim. I don't do this for revenge; I do this to save myself, at least in some small way, whatever piece of me is left to salvage. Shutting her eyes tightly, she pressed the red button.

The series of booms was deafening. Fire ripped through the ship as bodies fell into the water. The entire cabin soared into the air, detached from its elevated platform. The three aggressors retreated with shocked expressions, as their bodies were thrust away from Libby's. For an instant, Libby saw the crane's arm plunging down towards the deck, slicing the ship in half, as more explosions followed. Then she felt her body float free. Sky. Water. Sky. Water. Fire. Lady Liberty's head and torch still jutted out over the waves as debris floated down around them.

She hit the water hard, all the air knocked out of her. Then she felt nothing, nor could she move; only her eyes and her thoughts remained, as the water lapped over her. No sound. She bobbed for an instant and then dipped beneath, in tandem with the Statue.

And then it dawned on her, why she had always loved to take the ferry out to the Statue of Liberty whenever she'd felt blue. It was not just because it was her namesake. It was because her lovely face reminded her of her mom.

Mom, thank you for being here. Libby thought. Thank you for coming back. You're not ashamed of me. I can go in peace. I'm free after all.

Libby smiled as she descended into the deep blue water, Lady Liberty keeping pace with her as their forms blurred and faded, forever lost.

Inverted

I reluctantly drag one foot in front of the other. Rough and dirty, shuffling bare against the concrete. Exasperated by my pace, one of the uniformed guards runs up from behind and rams the butt of his machine gun hard against my flank. A jolt of pain streaks up my spine as I lose my balance and tumble to the ground. The colorless canvas jumpsuit tears at both knees, blood spreading across the tattered fabric.

He shouts something in his language and points me towards the ramp looming ahead, yanking me up by my long, tangled hair and shoving me forward. I'm far behind the others I rode with, in the paddy wagon, but I can still make out their silhouettes as they approach the arched gateway to the border crossing. An enormous flag, illuminated by a stark spotlight, ripples high above in the brisk night breeze.

As I draw nearer to the buzzing fluorescent light cast by soaring lamps overhead, I notice a towering bronze statue of a man in old-fashioned military uniform. His expression is stern and unwelcoming, his features angular and un-softened by his neatly clipped moustache. He gazes away from the bridge, his eyes fixed on a distant point to the east. A shudder runs through me, as I scan across the medals pinned to his chest, his saber hanging frozen at his side, his shiny tall riding boots. Inexplicably, I am overwhelmed by the sense that he resents the bridge as much as I do, as if it let him down and he wants nothing more to do with it.

It takes all my willpower to keep moving. And, when that's not enough, I unearth motivation in the suspicion that the next time I stop the guard won't bother to push me along, but rather cut me down with his weapon. Gritting my teeth, I trudge on, not knowing what's worse: the land I leave behind, or the one that lies ahead. I've always had this thing about bridges. Are they a tool, a dilemma, a punishment, or an opportunity? I guess it depends on the time and the place. What might have been built to reach a better place can quickly become a road to destruction. All I know is that, in my short life, bridges have brought me bad luck, little more than the illusion of choice.

My body is close to collapse, but my mind has yet to surrender. My instinct, as always, is to find a pathway to freedom, to a better life, to a place where I can simply live without fear, to do something more than struggle for survival. Just because I haven't succeeded doesn't mean I can stop trying. So I brace myself to cross once again, my bloodied feet stinging as I begin the long climb over the river.

***

"Do it, Kay! Jump!" Lenny screamed from below. "They're coming!"

Lenny was down in the water, hugging a rock. We both knew once he let go, the current would quickly sweep him away.

My shivering little feet were already up on the first rung of the cold metal railings that lined the rusted old railroad bridge. My toes were covered in mud from running through a soggy field. I was twelve years old and my mother had taught me well, before she was killed in a bombing at the vegetable market. She taught me that my life depended on avoiding capture by the self-police or the drug gangs or any man. She'd called them savages, bloodthirsty, sex-starved beasts.

They were called the self-police because they appointed themselves. They wore uniforms and carried lots of guns. They hid behind shiny badges but controlled people through fear, rewriting the law of the land to suit their shifting needs. And they fought with other self-police and the drug gangs, night and day. The gangs feared nothing, not even the self-police, because they didn't feel pain. Father said they were always so doped up they could get shot ten times before they even noticed. My parents agreed that the only men I could trust were my father, my grandpa, Little Johnny and Lenny. Little Johnny was my younger brother. He was a baby when my mother died, four years earlier. He didn't even remember her. Lenny was about my age. He was like an older brother even though he wasn't. We'd adopted him when his parents were killed in one of the slum fires. Fires were always breaking out, and there were no emergency services any more. Father said it was on account of life always being an emergency.

I looked to my right and saw the drug gang boys, coming like zombies on speed, a crazed look in their eyes, their long black hair swirling about their bony, angular faces in the cold wind. They yelled and screamed and waved bats and crowbars and machetes. Whipping my head around to the left, my long wavy strawberry hair got in my eyes, like it always did. But I could make out the shiny badges of the self-police reflecting the bright midday sun.

They wouldn't shoot because both sides wanted me alive. Mother had said my hair made me stand out, made them want me more. And she'd said when my body started changing, it would get harder and harder to hide from them. Their boots thundered onto the bridge from both sides, rattling the metal and shaking my bones.

"Jump, Kay, jump now!" Lenny repeated, waving frantically at me.

I hate this life, I thought. There has to be something better than this. Always running. Always scared. I didn't want to be scared any more. I wanted to be big and strong and fight back, but there were so many of them with their weapons and their drugs and their appetite for destruction. Everyone was so angry. Nothing was like the world I escaped into, in the books my mother had saved for me and taught me from before she died. Nothing.

I took another step up as they closed in from both sides. Searching the water below, I knew I could do it. It was a long way down, but not so long my bones would snap. It was just a matter of not hitting the rocks.

"Drop straight down, like I did!" Lenny shouted, as waves rushed over the boulder he clung to and swamped his pale face, his wet black hair slicked back.

I hated bridges. They never took you anywhere but always brought you trouble. And while you were on them, it was like you were neither here nor there. What kind of world was this, anyway? Not the one in the fairytales, where bridges took you to promised lands and riches.

I could hear panting as they approached. If I didn't jump, the gang members would reach me first. Then the self-police. Then there would be a big fight between them, and I'd probably be ripped to pieces like a piece of meat, being fought over by starving wolves. Like young Timmy Plassico. I'd seen him torn apart like that, literally, by wolves. The wild animals were almost as dangerous as the humans. But at least they didn't carry guns, and they could feel pain.

I reached the final rung and stopped. I always had perfect balance. Mother said I would have been a ballerina had I been born in a different time. Maybe I was, she'd said. She believed we lived many lives and had probably known each other before. She was cool like that, my mother, my mom. Even with the world as horrible as it was, she could find magic, she could dream, she could remember better times even though she hadn't lived them. She carried memories in the stories she recalled from her own mother, and in the pages of her sacred tomes, as she called them. They were her treasure, which she shared with me every night by the fire in our little two-room log cabin out in the wilderness. It was hard out there, even harder now that she was gone, but it was better than the city and the slums. There was always hiding and constant fear, but we were less likely to be killed by accident, caught in the crossfire.

I stretched out my arms and felt the warmth of the sun overpower the cold wind. The shouts of the men were deafening now on both sides of me as they reached out their arms and clawed at me.

I took a deep breath as my eyes fluttered shut and I slowly leaned forward, descending quietly, imagining I was a feather floating gently in the breeze, feeling the wind rip through my hair, hitting the cold water, smack, and then blacking out…hearing the screaming.

Lenny yelled. Bullets whizzed overhead. I couldn't feel anything but I knew something was terribly wrong. The water was red all around me and I could barely breathe. I had expected my breath to get knocked out of me, but this was something else altogether. Then the pain came in waves, like the water threatening to swallow me whole. Lenny was pushing and pulling at me. I was pinned to something beneath the surface.

"She's stuck on this rod!" Lenny called to the shore. More machine gun fire rattled above us. Bodies rained down around us. I prayed none of them would land on me.

Then I remember feeling it, with my hands. It was an inch thick and longer than I could guess. It was coming out of my abdomen, on my left side. Lenny held me up, trying to pull the rod and me together.

"Mama! Mama!" I cried like a baby, momentarily forgetting she was gone.

"I'm here, Kay," Lenny whispered. "It's gonna be all right. Just hang on. Just hang on!"

I swallowed a bucketful of water and coughed up blood on Lenny's face, but he kept swimming and kicking. Bullets zipped into the water around us. I could see the fight raging up on the bridge. It was chaos. They probably didn't know who to kill first, each other, us, or the men firing at them from the green armored Jeep by the riverbank.

That's when I realized why they weren't coming after us. I caught a glimpse of my dad and Grandpa, firing from the machine gun turrets on the Jeep, picking anyone off who might make a move for the railing.

Lenny wheezed and even went under a few times. But he always came back up, pulling me, metal rod and all, until we made it to the shore and Grandpa drew us in with a rope.

In the back of the Jeep, Little Johnny held my hand and whispered the "Our Father" in my ear, over and over, as Grandpa worked furiously on me. Father sped away, spewing curses I'd never heard or imagined, while Lenny fired the guns so no one would follow.

"We've gotta pull it out. There's just no other way," is the last thing I remember hearing for a long time. I thought I was going to die.

***

As I pass grudgingly beneath the arched gateway to the bridge, it's not my old injury but the painful new bump at the base of my neck that I instinctively reach for. My knees nearly buckle but then the agony passes. As I regain my footing, I see a heap of dusty rags slumped against the cinderblock wall. I'm caught off guard when a sun-scarred face pops out, covered in scabs, puss and blood.

It's an old woman, barely recognizable as human, who croaks, "It's the chip. You got one in you just like everyone else."

I nod, feeling sorry for her. She must have skin cancer from working in the fields. Or maybe she was whipped repeatedly across the face by a barbarian. I have nothing left to give but my pity. I hold out empty palms to her and force an apologetic smile.

"Don't worry," she says in a raspy voice, scratching her mangy crown of frazzled auburn hair. "I'm not here for money. Nobody leaves by choice, unless they're running drugs or guns, and if they are, they don't pass through here. No, only the deported go through here. And they got nothing but their uniform and their broken spirit."

"So then, why are you here?" I ask, grateful for any excuse to slow down. "How come they don't force you to cross?"

"They can't," she replies. "I got amnesty back in the day, when our hosts still had a heart. I'm here to remind myself there's some still got it worse than me." She chuckles.

I shake my head, smiling. "Isn't that the truth? Does everyone's chip burn when they pass through this gateway? Doesn't yours?"

"Yeah, it burns because there's a jolt of electricity when the scanners sweep over it," the scraggly, broken-tooth woman explains. "But mine is messed up. It's inverted. Whenever I'm anywhere but here under the arch it burns. But if I just sit here, I'm okay. It's the only way I can survive. Just being here, watching the deported go by. Trapped between one place and another."

I stand there for a moment, contemplating the shambles of this human being, wondering who she once was, what she did, what her story might be. Did someone once love her? Did she bear children? Did she have a dream? Tears prick my eyes but I fight them off out of habit.

"Won't they fix it for you? The chip? Since you have amnesty?" I ask, always searching for a solution. Shouldn't there be some redeeming quality in this fabled land of opportunity?

"No, I tried, stood in line till blood was coming out of my ears from the pain. They don't care. They're too busy putting chips into people to bother taking one out."

"I'm sorry. I guess they'll always know where I am now. And if I try to come back, they'll catch me."

"Oh, I reckon they could even kill you remotely straight from the chip, if they want to," she coughs. "Sometimes I wish they'd try. In my case it might give me new life."

I smile at the audacity of her imagination. "Well, in that case, I hope you do something someday deserving of such a punishment."

"Scanned personnel continue moving in a northern direction or prepare for shock," a robotic voice on the loudspeaker startles me, echoing: "Prepare for shock."

"You better move, honey," she says. "Think happy thoughts. Something that might reach somebody's heart. You know, they say the chips also record your memories. They record everything you do and everything you think from the moment they're put in. Then when they recover the dead, they use the data as part of a giant research project. The scientists, they see the same pictures you see through your eyes and conjure in your memory, hear the same words, feel the same emotions even. So someday, who knows, even when you're dead, your memories might be shared by someone, might make someone change their mind about how they're running this crazy world towards total annihilation and extinction of the human race."

I'm zapped with a powerful jolt of electricity, ripping from the top of my spine to the tips of my limbs, sending my eyes spinning and my hair standing on end. Breathless, I collapse in front of her.

"Oh, dearie, I would help you if I could, but I can't." The woman bemoans my fate. "Get up and move. I don't want another one frying in front of me, and such a pretty one to boot. The smell can get God darn awful when the flesh starts to singe."

A wave of nausea comes over me and pushes me along like flotsam away from one shore and towards another.

I wave feebly and move past her, shuffling in misery. How bad can things get, when even an old, broken-down transient feels pity for me. Not long ago, I had strength, and beauty, and I had a boatload of dreams. And now what? I dig deep inside me, searching for a way back to myself. I've got to replay my dreams and fill this memory chip with hope, rather than rage. What if—like the supernatural magic my mother used to dream of—my positive thoughts could reverse or transform the effect of the chip, in some way similar to the homeless woman's case? What if, somehow, instead of tracking me, the chip would hide me from the authorities? What if, at last, anonymous in a new land, I could find freedom, find

Little Johnny and Lenny, and make a new life? What if the doctors at the deportation center were all wrong, and somehow I could make a miracle baby and pass on my mother's teachings, plant a seed of hope from those ancient and nearly forgotten ideals she shared with me on those cold winter nights huddled in the log cabin reading by the light of the fire to bear fruit for this weary world to discover, savor, be nourished by, and enjoy? What if?

I'm down to prayers now, I realize bitterly, as my thighs burn from the ascent. A cool breeze wafts in from the east, where the river flows out to the sea. But if you believe the books, then you believe that now and then prayers can be answered, miracles may materialize, and wishes occasionally—if rarely—do come true. I clutch at the subcutaneous throbbing in my neck. I close my eyes. And I remember what drove me here in the first place. I see it in my mind, like one of those old movies my family and I used to watch together before the equipment broke down and we ran out of parts to fix it. Remembering such moments, I pray to God and hope the chip can really capture it all. I hope it gets overloaded and shorts out. I hope it fails completely. I hope, at the very least, someday someone will see it and feel it and be inspired to treat people like me differently. Most of all, I hope for change.

***

When I turned sixteen, we had a party. It was just Little Johnny, Lenny, my father, Grandpa, and me. Just like every other day and night. But it was special.

"We all thought you were gonna die," Grandpa smiled and winked as he reminisced about that day I jumped from the bridge. "But look at it this way, at least you earned yourself a great nickname. That's more than most can say."

Shish-Kay-bob, they called me since then.

"I'm too old for that," I smiled sheepishly as father walked gingerly into the room, carrying a homemade cake decorated with a miniature metal skewer. But they all knew I loved it.

"Six feet of metal rod through you and somehow you survived. Now that's a fighter for you!" My father beamed in the flickering light of the fireplace.

Grandpa, Little Johnny and Lenny smiled at me as we huddled about the rough-hewn kitchen table.

Ever since I'd been injured, I walked a little funny but otherwise I was fine. I had to cover my hair and pull a cloak up over my face, not because of any scars but because I'd inherited my mother's clear blue eyes and porcelain skin.

"Keep your beauty hidden," my father repeated, as we ate birthday cake. "It is between God and you. It is for no one else, until you decide to take a husband."

As hard as I tried, I couldn't keep my eyes from flickering to Lenny, whose lips twitched at the corners as he fought back a smile, his long black locks curving down around his angled jaw.

In the city and the slums, there were no laws, no traditions anymore. Nothing was sacred or respected, Father said. Most of the women had been turned into slaves for sex or housework and they were often traded. All sense of decency had been destroyed after the floods wiped out everything east of the Mississippi. The computer networks had been ravaged by terrorist viruses, and the country had been divided into feuding realms ruled by generals with "nukes." Washington, the Constitution, the Declaration of Independence, all those things I read about with curiosity in the dog-eared textbooks my mother had salvaged for me were ancient history.

"Keep your decency and grow your intelligence," her words echoed in my mind years later. "And someday you'll find freedom and know what do with it."

I smiled, eating my cake, and gazed at the men in my life. It made me wonder: How would we know freedom when we found it? And what if we forgot how to use it?

Nevertheless, the cake tasted good. We'd used Mom's recipe. It was almost, but not quite, as good as if she'd made it herself.

***

As far back as I can remember, I'd dreamt of escaping, not by myself, of course, but with the whole family. This was no life, any kid could tell. We lived on constant alert. After Mom was killed at the market, we did everything possible to keep to ourselves. We lived on a scrap of an old farm that had been in my father's family. We fenced it in, and defended it with video cameras and guard dogs. We grew our own vegetables and bred our own livestock. I studied from the books and lesson plans Mom left me, and I even tutored Lenny and Little Johnny. They were both smart, so it was easy. Grandpa helped too. He would tell us stories about the olden days, when times were better, so we could understand the principles our country had been built upon. He also talked to us a lot about the Promised Land to the south.

"They have order down there," Grandpa would say wistfully, stroking his neatly cropped white beard as his blue eyes twinkled like an innocent child's. "You don't have to worry about being robbed or killed at every turn. You're free to enjoy your family, the rewards of your hard work. You even have the freedom to choose your leaders, express your thoughts, practice your religion, without fearing any punishment."

"That's how it once was here, right?" I asked, even though I knew the answer by heart.

"Of course, this nation was the greatest on earth," he rued.

Night after night, there was a running debate between my father and me. I wanted to leave and he refused, saying he would be buried next to my mother, out beneath the looming oak on the hill.

"Plus," he'd often retort, "the trip south is dangerous. Few make it alive. At least, here, we have some safety. We're well protected. And our neighbors have our backs too."

I respectfully repressed a scoff. Neighbors? The men occasionally traded with the farmers down the road, and there was some communal sense of protection, but I had no doubt that, in a pinch, any of them would sell us out to save their own hides.

To silence my badgering, Papa said that when I turned eighteen I'd be an adult and could go south then, and there would be nothing he could do to stop me. I knew there was little Papa valued more than our lives, my mother's memory and his word. So I trusted that, unable to let me go by myself, he would come with me. For a few months, at least, I remained patient and Papa found peace on the home front.

When I awoke on my eighteenth birthday, Papa and Lenny were out hunting. Little Johnny slept while Grandpa toiled in the barn, struggling to repair our decrepit tractor. Finding parts was becoming nearly impossible. My chore for the day was to chop firewood, so I wrapped myself up in a parka, tucked my tangled copper hair into the hood, pulled on my boots, slung the axe over my shoulder, and trudged past the frozen pond to the receding tree line. Glancing over my shoulder, I could tell the ribbon of white smoke rising from our log cabin was sputtering out. We needed that firewood.

The snow fell in thick white sheets, as though suspended from an invisible clothesline hung far above the dense gray clouds. The harsh winter gusts cut through the layers of rags and strips of fur wrapped around me for insulation. For over a year now, I'd been forced to venture beyond our electrified fence to reach the tree line. It was hard to tell what was more dangerous: the hungry wolves or the human marauders searching for easy prey. I never went out without my rifle strapped to my back. I'd only used it twice. Once for some tasty wolf meat roasted over the fire. The other time, it scared off a couple of interlopers on horseback. Luckily, concealed by the winter clothes, there was no way they could tell I was a woman.

I opened the padlock on the shoulder-high gate, careful to touch only the rubber-coated lock and the wooden gate handle. Then I locked it again and followed my well-worn path into the woods. I chopped steadily until I heard the distant bay of wolves growing louder. Then, I hauled the wood back towards home in a rusty wheelbarrow.

As I neared the gate, I could hear the wolves closing in. Quickening my pace, I panted as I reached the fence. The one-eyed padlock stared back at me like an ominous Cyclops as I reached into my coat pocket for the key. There was nothing there. The wolves barked sharply. I could tell they were within a hundred yards or so. My eyes widened and my heartbeat accelerated. My fingers probed my pockets as I scanned the freshly fallen snow.

I must have dropped the keys, I realized. But, how? My fingers were so numb beneath the flimsy, homemade leather gloves that I must have thought they'd gone into my pocket when they'd actually fallen to the ground. I kicked the snow aside with my boots around the gate.

C'mon. C'mon. Keys. Keys!

The leader of the pack howled distinctively, piercing the crisp, still air.

Getting closer.

My eyes locked with the leader's, at the edge of the woods.

Instinctively, I dropped to one knee. With my left hand I scoured through the powdery snow, searching. With my right hand I fumbled numbly with the strap that held the rifle to my back.

The lead wolf paused for what seemed like an eternity as my pulse beat in my eardrums.

Calm down. Remember everything Papa has taught you. The cool will survive.

The gun was in my hands and I pumped it deftly. The wolf stood still. I kept one hand on the rifle and the other searching in an arc about the gate area.

Then two other wolves joined the leader, one on each side. He lunged forward, his front paws sinking deep into the snow, his back paws kicking up a white cloud as the trio ran towards me.

When you live in constant danger, moments of crisis are strangely soothing. It's like you're watching yourself perform routines you've practiced in your mind time and again while lying in bed waiting for sleep to momentarily relieve you from the conscious torments of your daily existence.

It was like that as the wolves bore down on me, saliva dripping from their jaws and freezing before it hit the ground as a drizzle of tiny icicles.

I searched for the keys as long as I could, knowing my best chance was to get myself on the other side of the electrified fence. The wolves knew better than to try to climb or jump it. And so did I.

When the wolves were fifty yards away, I fired a warning shot into the air, hoping to scare them away. They advanced, undeterred.

I dug in and aimed, firing at the lead wolf's head. The crack echoed through the trees as the shot burrowed into his skull. The wolf smashed forward into the snow, his limbs flailing and tangling awkwardly as he tumbled head over heels. The question in my mind was not whether I could shoot a wolf to save my life. But could I shoot all three before their fangs were at my throat?

I pumped again.

20 yards. Two more to go.

I squinted and fired.

The second one fell and rolled, kicking snow and blood up into the bleak afternoon sky.

Ten yards. Pump. Aim. Fire.

The wolf dodged slightly in expectation and the shot grazed its cheek, blood spouting as it plunged forward hungrily.

Five yards. Pump. No time to aim. I pulled the trigger, falling backwards as the wolf slammed into me full force, knocking us both back onto the snow and rolling. I held onto the wolf with all my strength, straining to position it between me and the fence, just in case I'd missed.

Then I let go and kicked away, reversing my momentum from the gate.

A loud crackle buzzed around me and the stench of singed fur and burning flesh seared my nostrils. As I rose to my feet, I saw a spray of blood staining the pristine snow around me and smearing my clothes.

I didn't miss that time.

But I'd made sure that wolf was dead, hadn't I? Papa would be proud. Then, in the middle of a red blotch on the ground, I spotted the keys, unearthed by the scuffle.

I reached for the keys and hoisted the final wolf onto the wheelbarrow, as it could not carry any more. After unlocking and relocking the gate, I pushed the wheelbarrow towards the cabin in the distance. The smoke had ceased to rise from the chimney. Inside, it would be frighteningly cold. Halfway back, I paused, hunched over the warm carcass of the wolf, and let out two ragged sobs that racked my body.

I almost never saw you again, Lenny…Papa…Little Johnny…Grandpa. But I was strong. Mama would be proud. Thank you, God.

Then I plowed onward as the short day drew to a dark end.

***

"No way, little missy! Absolutely not!" Papa bellowed as the smoke snaked up from the crudely fashioned birthday candles. "After what happened today? You don't need any more proof of how dangerous it is out there. No way you, or any of us, is making the trip down south."

Grandpa bit his parched lip in remorse as he stared at the hearty fire we'd made with the wood for which I'd nearly bartered my life.

Lenny gazed straight at me, sorrow filling his eyes.

I knew he loved me, but Papa was the alpha. He was the leader. We all yearned for his blessing. We seemed immobilized without it.

"But you promised!" I protested.

"You almost died today, Kay!" Papa replied, setting down his fork. "That's enough of that. The world's only getting worse. The risks are too high. This is the only place we can be safe. And if we die, we'll be buried next to your mother…beneath the oak on the hill."

I stared down at the cake. All of the sweetness was gone, as tears welled in my eyes.

Mama's recipe. Live. Love. Suffer. Die young.

Must it be the same for me?

The men sullenly shuffled off, leaving their slices of cake nearly untouched. Little Johnny helped me clean up in silence. Then we retreated to our little closet of a room. Little Johnny and I slept on two cots that barely fit in it, but we loved it nonetheless. Pictures of our mother in her youth clung to the wall of logs. A rough-hewn wooden desk and bookcase sagged under the weight of books piled high. My window, frosted over, barely managed to keep winter on the other side. But there we escaped into the pages of our favorite books, yearning for the freedom of Huckleberry Finn floating down the Mississippi. In a cramped room on the other side of the cabin, the three adult men slept on cots just like ours. Between us yawned the central space that encompassed our humble living, kitchen and dining area.

That night, we went to sleep without much talking. Worn out from the day's events, I extinguished the lantern between our cots, not even bothering to read. The house grew dark and still. The fire died out while the family slept. Little Johnny curled up in a ball under his blanket, as he always did. I slipped into a deep sleep, ruing the twisting edge of the wintery draft that penetrated the logs around my window.

In the middle of the night, I awoke to the snapping of a branch outside. My eyes opened wide as I lay in bed. For a moment all was still and silent. Suddenly, with a loud bang, the front door of our house blew open.

Papa and Lenny jumped out of bed, the floorboards thundering beneath their feet. I saw them reaching for their rifles as they came out of their room, but the intruders swarmed over them, striking them with the butts of their guns and kicking them. Lenny took a vicious blow to the head, blood gushing down his face as he fell to the floor. Seeing the blood, Papa exploded in fury, lunging at the attacker, his hands throttling the large man's throat.

A loud crack shook through the cabin as I pushed Little Johnny under my cot. Then I wriggled through the window onto the freshly fallen snow. Outside, I leaned against the frozen cabin wall, puffing mist into the night air as my heart raced.

Peering in through the living room window, I could see there were three invaders. The leader seemed to be a large, agile man, with one tall, lanky henchman and another who was short and round. As Papa scuffled with them, the tall henchman fired his weapon straight into Papa's gut.

Papa's eyes glassed over. His grip on the man loosened and he slid to the floor.

Lenny wailed mournfully from his spot on the floor, "Papa…"

Waving towards the rear of the cabin, the leader demanded, "What's in the back room, huh?"

Lenny answered, "Nothing. We've got next to nothing. Look, there's a trapdoor under the table. Down below's all we got. Take it all. Just leave us alone."

"Us, huh?" the bandit leader replied.

"Sounds like you got someone in the back room 'cause you're surely not referring to this sack of bones," The lanky henchman kicked Papa's body as Lenny winced, gritting his teeth.

Salivating, the obese henchman addressed their leader, "Sergeant, I heard he's got himself a pretty girl in here somewhere. Oughta be ripe age for mothering, if you know what I mean."

"Shut up, Butterball," the leader barked. Then he motioned to the lanky one: "Lefty, go check the other rooms."

"I told you, there's nothing back there, Sergeant," Lenny insisted, wiping blood out of his eyes. He struggled to get up but the leader's boot was firmly positioned on his chest, clamping him down to the floor.

"We'll see about that, won't we?" Sergeant replied bitterly.

Lefty reappeared with Grandpa and Little Johnny in tow. Johnny rubbed at his eyes.

Grandpa croaked, "What's going on here? Who are you people?"

"Can it old man," Sergeant instructed. "On the floor."

He smacked Grandpa across the cheek with his gun, knocking him to the floor. Little Johnny threw himself on top of him, sobbing.

"Is this it?" Sergeant taunted. "What a sorry bunch of sons of bitches. With your video cameras and electrical fence, I would have thought you had something worth protecting…. All that may have worked to keep out the local folk, but not a former soldier like me."

He stomped over the hunched figures on the floor and peered into the back room for himself, only finding empty beds.

"We'll see then…. Boys, empty out the cellar and torch this hellhole. I'll keep an eye on these fools," he commanded.

Ducking out into the windy night, Lefty answered, "I'll get the kerosene."

Butterball shoved the table aside, opening the cellar door and squealing with delight.

Outside, Lefty stomped through the snow towards a large truck silhouetted against the moonlight, oblivious to the set of barefoot tracks I had left in the snow between the cabin and a large tree near where they'd parked. He put his gun in the truck bed and lifted up two large canisters.

Lenny, Little Johnny and Grandpa lay bound, face down on the floor. Butterball emerged from the cellar and added to the bundles of food and supplies by the front door. Sergeant sat squarely in front of his hostages, tapping his fingers on the barrel of the shotgun across his legs.

Lefty burst back into the cabin, dropped the heavy fuel cans on the floor next to Sergeant, and asked, "Which you think we oughta shoot first, Boss?"

"I'll let you pick, if you use your own ammo," Sergeant replied.

"All right!" Lefty yelped. "I'm gonna do the old man first. He looks like he's lived too long. I'll be doing him a favor. Besides, I hate old people. They give me the creeps."

"Did you hear that, Butterball?" Sergeant reveled. "We've got a mercy killing on our hands. The fire'll cleanse our sins."

Butterball laughed as he heaved another sack onto the pile. "That about does it for the supplies."

Sergeant's fingers rested on the barrel of his shotgun. "Then load up the truck and let's do this thing. You ready, Lefty?"

"Aw, shoot. I left my gun outside," Lefty noticed. "Butter, let's take this stuff out. I'll get my gun and we'll torch this joint."

Lefty and Butterball hoisted the bags and walked outside. They trudged through the snow towards the truck. Suddenly, just as they passed the large tree next to their vehicle, I whirled out, slamming the butt of Lefty's rifle against his face.

As Lefty landed with a thud on the snow, Butterball dropped the bags he was carrying and reached for something at his side. Before he could pull a weapon, I struck him with a powerful head butt. As he slipped to the ground, unconscious, I pulled a gleaming dagger from the sheath at Butterball's side and crouched over my prey in the shadows.

Inside the cabin, Sergeant tapped his fingers impatiently on his gun.

"What the hell is taking those idiots so long?" he muttered, getting up and pouring the kerosene around the cabin, and onto Grandpa, Lenny, Little Johnny, and Papa's motionless body. He then turned to the front door, threw it open and shouted out into the dark.

"Hey, what's taking you so—"

That's when I smacked him in the face with Lefty's rifle butt. As he fell backward into the cabin, pouring kerosene all over himself in the process, his shotgun went off and the spark ignited the gas that he had doused on the surroundings.

Sergeant and our home shot up in flames, while I struggled to pull out my family, carrying Little Johnny over my shoulder and dragging first Lenny, then Grandpa and my father out onto the snow, where they rolled around to smother the flames licking at their pajamas.

Finally, I collapsed next to them, coughing from the smoke as the flames overtook the house.

Sometime before sunup, I used the bloody dagger to cut away the ropes around my family's arms and legs.

When morning came, we sat huddled in the snow, half-frozen, staring glumly at the charred ruins of the cabin. I scanned Little Johnny, Grandpa, and Lenny, my eyes tracing the lines of pain and hardship in their scarred, soot-streaked faces. Behind them, close to the big truck, lay the two lifeless forms of Butterball and Lefty in the bloodstained snow.

After a long time, Lenny finally spoke, "Papa's dead."

We all stared impassively at the smoldering ruins.

"Rebuilding will be hard without him," Lenny concluded sanguinely.

"We're rebuilding our lives, not just our shelter," I surprised myself as I answered, as if hearing my true voice for the first time.

The others hesitated, slowly turning their eyes towards me.

Then Lenny's expression turned sheepish. "What do you mean, Kay?"

I took a deep breath as if I was trying to gather wind in my sails, "I mean, it's long overdue that we leave this place before we're all dead. I say put it to a vote. Who agrees with me?"

Slowly, Johnny and Grandpa raised their hands, staring timidly at Papa's motionless body, and then at Lenny.

"He's at peace now," Lenny whispered, his gaze falling to the snow. "There's no reason to stay."

The shovels were out in the barn. They were cold in our hands as we dug a hole beneath the ancient oak on the hill.

The fresh mound by Mom's tombstone marked Papa's passing. I watered it with so many salty tears, I figured it would be years before grass or weeds could grow to cover it. Papa had reached his goal. Now, it was our turn.

***

Grandpa and Lenny traded the tractor and our Jeep to a man who knew a crosser. Hands were shaken and promises were exchanged. And ten days later, the four of us were wrapped from head to toe in rags and strips of fur, rattling around in the back of the crosser's pick-up truck.

The crosser had more hair on his chin than on his head. His short blonde stubble reflected the sun as brightly as his blue eyes mirrored the sky. He smoked hand-rolled cigarettes and popped pills to go to sleep, but other than that, he seemed reliable enough. He talked little, but he posted a photo of his wife and children on the dashboard, and a rosary dangled from the rearview mirror. That gave us hope we were in good hands.

"Crossing is half the challenge," Grandpa said as we tried to protect ourselves from the harsh cold and the blistering sun in the truck bed. "Having a good crosser is the key. Old Man Henderson swore to me, this man, Crosser Jackson, is one of the best. He's taking us down straight through Old Texas. He has to know the routes to avoid trouble. Old Texas is crazy now, like it was in the days of the Wild Wild West."

We'd heard and read folktales about Texas, the Alamo and cowboys and Indians. If it had been that scary and violent back then, I didn't want to imagine how bad it was now.

One night, outside the remnants of San Antonio, we gathered around a campfire by the Guadalupe River. The climate was growing warmer, so we bathed by the moonlight and dried off by the fire. As the sparks flickered and danced, we roasted venison sausage the crosser had doled out from an ice chest behind his seat.

"This whole state is run by the drug gangs now," Crosser Jackson explained. "At least up north, you've got a balance of power between the self-police and the gangs. But here, the gangs are fueled by the drug cartels down south, and they were able to wipe out all the opposition. They have a monopoly here. People wonder how the countries down south have stayed prosperous while the world to the north has fallen apart...and it's all that...the drugs. They grow them, they make them, they ship them, they sell them. And the once-civilized world is enslaved to them. Sure, they have their order and their technology, and they're working to build a colony on the moon for when we blow this whole world up, once and for all..." He blew a kiss at the picture of his kids in the truck cabin nearby. As he made the sign of the cross, he quipped bitterly, "But don't fool yourselves. Where you're going is not much better than where you're at."

"Well, it may not be morally better," Lenny said, chewing on a strip of sausage. "But if we can settle down and not worry every day about being killed, that will be a step in the right direction."

"Yeah, I guess so," the crosser replied, staring blankly into the fire.

I preferred to believe in the dreams Grandpa had taught us from childhood, about the freedom and the opportunity on The Other Side. Apart from the remaining members of my family, those dreams were all I had left in the world. I was going to cling to them until my heart stopped beating and they were stolen from me by death itself.

The next day, we were down near the border. Crosser Jackson stuffed us into a tool shed in the back of somebody's house. When it got dark, he took us down to the river, walking through fields of sorghum. We crossed over the remains of what he said was once a border fence to keep out the illegal aliens trying to come north. We didn't have much time to ponder that before we were knee deep in muck amidst towering reeds. Mosquitoes swarmed all around us, sucking blood from our sweaty skin. I held Little Johnny tightly as Lenny helped Grandpa, whose eyes twinkled with more life than I'd seen since my mom—his daughter—was still alive.

"We're almost there, little ones," Grandpa murmured excitedly. "All we've got to do is cross."

The murky waters swirled in front of us. Beyond the river, a steep bank rose menacingly into a well-lit sky reflecting city lights.

"It's different over there," Crosser Jackson warned, his voice trembling. "Listen to me good, before we go...get down..."

We crouched in the reeds as river eels slithered between our bare feet. Little Johnny clung to me like he was a baby. I could feel his heart pounding.

"Don't worry, Little Johnny. It's freedom we're fighting for...and it's just a few feet away now."

Crosser Jackson couldn't help himself, retorting, "All depends what your definition of freedom is."

Our eyes wandered south, over the river to the illuminated sky. The cacophony of traffic and revelry of people was distorted by distance, echoing off the banks of the Rio Grande.

Crosser Jackson continued: "Follow me closely. Hang on to the rope. There is a path, and there is a time. Every night at three a.m., the guards on the border change shifts. During that couple of minutes, we can cross without being watched, right in the shadow of the Gateway Bridge. They don't bother placing cameras and sensors because they don't think anyone's crazy enough to try it right beneath their noses. But if we do it right, when they change guards, we'll scramble up the other side and Francisco will be waiting on the other side of the levee in his yellow MaxiTaxi van. The door will be open and his midget wife in a pink dress and braids will be waiting on the sidewalk, okay? I get you there, you jump in, no questions asked. He takes you the rest of the way. Your next stop is deep in the country, where there's plenty of work and people willing to help you, hire you, house you...marry you..." His eyes lingered too long for comfort on my bosom, and then shifted nervously to Lenny, who cleared his throat. "But if we get found, if something goes wrong while we're crossing...every man for himself...you got it? There's no guarantees...and if you stray from the path…forget it…you're as good as drowned in one of the whirlpools."

The crosser nervously checked his wristwatch, which gleamed silver in the night. "Okay, let's go. *Vámonos.*"

He let out the rope for each of us to hold. Grandpa went first, followed by Little Johnny. Lenny and I brought up the rear, in case anyone needed help. We marched deeper into the water, until the water reached our necks and the current threatened to yank us off the boulders we stepped on. Little Johnny was held afloat only by the rope and me.

"Slow down, we're about to be swept away," I called as filthy water splashed across my face.

But it was no use; Crosser Jackson could not hear me. I could tell Grandpa was struggling to keep his balance. Overhead, the bridge loomed over us, casting a shadow that was either protective or menacing, I wasn't sure. We were nearly halfway when, suddenly, Crosser Jackson dove beneath the water and vanished.

Grandpa faltered in the lead position. We all knew one wrong step could take us to our Maker. The water swirled around us and rushed to the east, where it passed under the bridge and then twisted and turned until it emptied into the Gulf of Mexico.

"Jackson!" Lenny called out, but not so loud that he might be heard by the guards on the banks.

Grandpa's eyes flashed with fear. He threw his hands up in the air and struggled forward, swaying in the current. "We have to keep trying," he gasped. "If I go…don't stop…keep going…save yourselves."

He took one step, then another, and then his head disappeared beneath the waves. We saw him bob up, and then he was rushed south into the dark shadows of the bridge.

"Grandpa!" Little Johnny called out feebly, but it was too late. He was gone.

I hung on to Little Johnny more tightly than ever, and gritted my teeth as the tears streamed down our faces, mixing with the muddy water. We can do this, I thought, fighting back the surging waves of grief. I turned back and met Lenny's eyes. His jaw flexed. His wet hair clung to his flushed cheeks. Behind him, I made out Crosser Jackson scrambling up to safety toward his truck. Bastard.

I wondered if there truly was a Francisco with a yellow MaxiTaxi van and a midget wife waiting for us on the other side, or was that a pack of lies too? Were the guards really changing shifts, or were we simply walking into a trap? And if freedom was so close, did the risks really matter? No, they don't, I told myself.

I plunged ahead, feeling my way instinctively over the rocks, leveraging every bit of that natural ballerina my mother had always seen in me. Lenny tugged on the rope gently. There were three tugs at a time and then none. It was a game we had played for years, a secret code to let each other know what we were feeling in the presence of others that might not approve. I love you—three simple syllables. A world of meaning. I knew then what I'd felt but not spoken over the years: If we made it through this alive, he would be my husband. There was nobody left to withhold the blessing. Together, we would raise my younger brother and build a family. A surge of determination powered through me, coursing through my limbs, anchoring me against the volatile currents. Little Johnny quivered in my arms as I moved on.

About three quarters of the way, the rocks dropped down and I fought the pull of the currents, kicking, holding on to my little brother with one arm and swimming desperately with the other. The rope went slack as Lenny dove towards us. The one time we nearly went under, his arms pulled us back up. By the time we reached the muddy shores, we were spitting up dirty river water, tasting chemicals and sewage. Our eyes and lungs burned as we lay on our backs and looked up at the stars and moon. Overhead, a gigantic flag flapped in the mild Gulf breeze, with vertical stripes of green, white and red that were strangely alien to me. In the white center field, a powerful eagle poised on a cactus clutched a serpent in its menacing beak.

"We have to hurry...keep moving..." Lenny gasped as his eyes pierced mine and his calming hands held Little Johnny.

"But what about Grandpa?" Little Johnny asked.

"He's free for sure now..." Lenny said, damming his emotions. "He'd want us to carry on."

"Let's go," I said, rising but staying low in the reeds, in case the guards had finished changing shifts.

"Jackson said there's a tear in the fence right up there," Lenny pointed up at a barely visible path through the reeds to a tall metal fence topped with coils of barbed wire. "He said we'd go through, cross a little dirt path, go down the grass levee and find the van on the other side. What else can we do now?"

I grabbed Little Johnny by the hand and darted up the path under the moonlight. The reeds swayed in rhythm beneath the breeze. The rip in the fence was there. We ducked through, our eyes wide. Maybe Crosser Jackson was not so bad after all. Nervously, we looked both ways at the dirt path. Nothing. Nobody. We slid and tumbled down the levee, and when we reached the sidewalk, it seemed like we were in a different world.

Crowds milled in the street. Everyone's skin was a different, darker tone. Their hair was black like the night, and they wore brightly colored, clean clothing. The smells of freshly cooked foods wafted thickly through the air, and so did something else. It was something magical, like angels playing harps. I reached deep into my memory for one of Grandpa's stories…this was music. My eyes landed on a little square across the street—a *plaza* he had called it, in the tale he'd retold countless times. Warm lights hung from trees, couples strolled arm in arm, and in a wrought iron gazebo at the center, a group of musicians in elaborate black suits and broad-brimmed hats played violins, guitars and trumpets. A man's clear, smooth voice rose elegantly and passionately into the night. My only regret was I had not learned the tongue of this country to the south. Then I might have understood what he was singing about, for it sounded like it was about love and beauty.

"C'mon, can't stop now," Lenny tugged me eagerly towards the yellow van emblazoned with the words "MaxiTaxi" framed by a black and white checkered pattern.

The van door slid open and a diminutive woman in a pink dress descended to the sidewalk, her braids sweeping the dust aside at her feet. A man with a gold tooth smiled from the driver's seat, waving frantically for us to hurry.

Laughing, I'll never forget the smiles I saw on Lenny and Little Johnny's faces as we dove into the van and the door slid shut behind us.

"We made it!" I shouted as we held each other in the dark recesses of the van. "We made it! We're free!"

The driver and his wife chuckled gently in the front as we rode away from the border.

"I am Francisco," the driver said in a friendly voice, as he turned a corner and put some distance between the river and us. Turning back for a moment to face us, he smiled broadly in the shadows as he added: "*Bienvenidos a México.*"

***

Nothing was quite as I had expected it to be, but it was still better than the world I had left behind, I reflect as I reach the bridge's summit and gaze ahead to the towering fences at the northern end of the crossing. There, the others I was brought here with are already shuffling through the turnstiles to The Other Side. This time, The Other Side is where I originally came from. Beyond the fences, the sky is lit up by gunfire and explosions. The "music" is little more than a percussive cacophony of machine guns and screams, punctuated by occasional sirens. The border cities are the worst, they say. They are extreme places, where the most adventurous and the least fortunate collide, clinging to the fringes for survival. I see the soot-covered faces of desperate people beyond the metal fence, peering out like caged animals, their fingers clutching the chain links with tiny embers of hope.

As long as I keep moving forward, however slowly, the implant in my neck does not bother me at all. But the moment I hesitate, it begins to throb. At the top of the bridge, the brushed-aluminum railings reach up to my shoulders. A bronze plaque with a vertical line down the middle marks the spot where one country gives way to another. I stand in the middle of it, dissected by the border. The chip pulsates ominously as I stop to read the words in Spanish, using what little I learned during my days down south. It mentions something about a colonel who first built the bridge and then destroyed it. Something about him spending the rest of his days in prison for his violent act, only to be recognized as a hero years later for his vision of both the promise and the danger of our nations' relationship. I recall the statue of the soldier I'd seen at the entrance to the bridge, his sullen, solitary expression staring at the point where the river flows out to the sea. I wish he were here, right now, to blow up this bridge once and for all. What had his people learned from him? Why were they so confused about whether he was a criminal or a champion? And why had they rebuilt his bridge, if they revered him for tearing it down? I stare down into the swirling waters below, searching for an answer to no avail. This country seems to have mixed feelings about bridges, a love-hate relationship with what they stand for, and to whom they connect.

The chip sears into my flesh as I touch the cool metal railing and press my chest against the plaque, breathing in the fresh Gulf breeze. My eyes close as it dawns on me, there is only one direction I can pursue and remain true to myself.

My mud-caked feet step up on the railing, just as they did years ago. I remove the rubber band holding my hair together and let the wind rip through it, locks unfurling like a copper banner under the buzzing lights high above. I have a thing for bridges. I don't know where this one will take me, so I shut my eyes tightly to store one last memory into the burning chip.

***

In the fertile fields of Coahuila, we picked grapes, apples and potatoes beneath the sweltering sun. The three of us shared a small hut at the edge of the fields. Our employers housed us, and several hundred others, in a camp far from the main road where the *Federales* patrolled in sleek black and white armored vehicles. The *Federales* wore light armor and carried a different kind of weapon from those I'd seen up north. These fired a bluish jolt of energy, and could kill a person in an instant without leaving a trace or spilling any blood. I knew this because I'd seen them use it one day in the city. There had been a squabble in the marketplace, which had been swiftly quelled. This is how order was maintained. Of course, the authorities knew about the workers from up north and where our camps were located, but our employers made "special arrangements" for us to work unperturbed, for our lives to march on in an orderly and peaceful way while we supplied the produce for the legal citizens of the Republic. It was said, once we spent enough time here, or married and birthed a child on this soil, we could petition to be legalized. Then our fortunes could dramatically change for the better, we could afford to attend school, learn the language and get good jobs in the cities. Our hope was to do it quickly, so Little Johnny could benefit from it.

Beneath the shade of an avocado tree at the center of the camp, Lenny knelt on one knee and proposed to me. There was no money for rings or lavish ceremonies. But with a crown of jasmine blossoms one of the older female workers made for me, and wearing a white cotton frock embroidered with colorful flowers, I married Lenny beneath that avocado tree. A Mexican priest, who risked his life by marrying people like us, performed the simple ceremony.

Afterwards, we thanked him profusely as we sipped *horchata*, a delightful milky, icy beverage made from rice and cinnamon.

The priest humbly replied, "No, no thanks are necessary, my children. Something must change in this land of ours. We must begin to treat each other like human beings, not like aliens. We are all made by the same God, whether we acknowledge it or not. Ultimately, we all come from the same place, and we will all return to that same place. Why not love each other while we're here?"

Night after night, while Little Johnny slept, even though our muscles were sore and our skin dry and burnt from the day's work beneath the sun, Lenny and I loved each other silently in the dark, our perspiration mingling with our tears. But months passed, and no baby came.

Seeking advice from the mothers in the camp, I discovered the Virgen de Guadalupe, an apparition of the Virgin Mary said to have come centuries before, in the Republic. A group of women from the camp gathered and prayed the rosary to her every night. I joined them and prayed for a child, to make our family and our future whole.

But, before my prayers could be answered, they came.

At first I thought the sky was falling as jet planes thundered overhead. I'd never seen or heard them before. Like giant gleaming birds, they soared through the clouds. Then came the helicopters, buzzing and swarming like giant metallic killer bees. I streaked through the field, dropping my basket, running towards the camp, searching for my little family amidst the chaos. The ground shook as our camp burst into flames. And, out of the cloud of dust and smoke, emerged not Lenny and Little Johnny, but *Federales* wearing helmets with visors and gas masks. They were dragging field hands into giant moving trucks. A robotic voice from a loudspeaker droned on in both Spanish and English, explaining procedures. I was crammed with strangers into a dark container truck and carried away over the bumpy caliche road.

The disembodied voice clipped monotonously: "Residing without proper documentation within the Republic is not permitted.

New government criteria for legal processing as a documented alien guest worker has been ratified by the Congress, and is being universally enforced. Those deemed qualified will be supplied with a new biometric identification and data collection mechanism, and be reassigned to a labor community. Those deemed permanently invalid will be returned to their place of origin."

Returned to our place of origin? There must have been a hundred of us jammed into the dark container, but not a breath could be heard as we stood frozen in fear.

After hours of jostling and swaying in the pitch black, the transport drew to an abrupt halt. Uniformed guards in black helmets with visors separated the men from the women and guided us through different gates into a mammoth cinder-block complex. Night was falling as towering steel fences gleamed in the moonlight all around us.

"Where's my Lenny? Where's Little Johnny? What have you done with my family?" I beseeched one guard after another, but none of them would respond.

One soldier entered a code into a keypad next to a door. When it clicked open, he nudged me inside and pulled it shut.

Inside, a number of women were sitting or lying on neat rows of aluminum benches.

Behind a barred window, a dark-skinned woman clicked her fingers incessantly on a computer keyboard with such spite I wondered what it had done to her, or whether perhaps her life depended on its impending destruction.

When she noticed me, standing awkwardly by the door, she barked at me like a master to her dog: "*¡Aquí!*"

Startled, I lurched towards the window, glancing nervously over my shoulders.

She continued typing but said, "*Pon tus dedos aquí.*"

I stared vacantly at her, silent.

Impatiently, her voice tensing, the clerk urged, "*Tus dedos. Churre fee-ngerz!*"

Only then did I notice she was directing her nervous tapping at a smoked glass pad on the countertop.

Tentatively, I slid my fingers beneath the window and lay them on the pad. A sweep of blue light scanned my fingerprints, illuminating the clerk's computer screen with a stream of data.

A flash blinded me momentarily, after which my eyes focused blearily on the camera lens staring at me from beyond the glass. A printer made a loud noise and spit out a thick sheaf of papers. The woman thrust the documents beneath the glass into my hands along, with a small plastic card.

Perplexed, I slowly gathered the papers and the card. I stared quizzically back at the clerk.

Annoyed, the woman retorted, "*¿Pues, qué ves? ¡Ya! ¡Es todo!*"

I stared back, not knowing what to do next.

The clerk was exasperated, as if it physically pained her to speak English. And maybe it did. She snapped: "Go! Sit! *Guait for churre tests and churre…¿cómo se dice?…pro-see-jurre.*"

She pointed at the benches and the group of ragged women, one of whom rubbed her giant belly rhythmically as she rocked back and forth on the floor.

I edged timidly towards the waiting area, approaching the pregnant woman. Glancing back, I caught the clerk rolling her eyes towards the ceiling and shaking her head.

"*Te digo,*" the clerk muttered to no one in particular, "*Estos gringos son como niños perdidos.*"

I'd picked up enough Spanish in my months working in the fields to know "*niños*" meant children and "*perdido*" meant lost. So, this is what it came down to.

I crumpled onto the floor next to the pregnant woman, staring enviously at her bulging abdomen. She smiled weakly at me.

"You have any?" she asked, her voice hoarse.

I shook my head ruefully.

"It's my first too," she said. "They told me it's gonna be a boy. He's my little savior. Thanks to him, I'll get to stay."

"Why are the babies so important to them?" I wondered.

"They have new rules," she said. "Now they're going to make us raise the babies with their own culture and language. Of course, we'll have to learn it too, but that's okay. We'll never be able to advance, but they will. They'll get tested at birth and, depending on their genes, their smarts, their strength, they'll put 'em in a "caste," like they used to have in India. He might be a worker, or an engineer or a doctor. He'll work his whole life and, if he's lucky, he'll marry and have kids, and then their kids will get to be real citizens. Three generations is what it will take. I'll be dead or dying by then, but freedom for my children's children. It's something worth living for, no?"

I gazed back, unsure how to answer, or whether she expected a reply at all.

Shrugging, she added, "I may never know what happens, but at least I will have given them a chance, know what I mean?"

I looked at her stomach.

"You'll understand someday, sweetie." she smiled. "Everything changes when you get pregnant. You don't think about yourself no more."

"What happens to us, the ones that aren't pregnant?" I asked.

"Oh, I hear they'll do tests, put in the implant, put you back with your mate, if you have one. They'll give you a chance to reproduce. They need us, for hard labor, for the universities, for their future. They hardly have their own kids any more. They're too caught up in themselves and their precious technology."

I sighed in relief.

"Oh don't worry, honey. They're not mean-spirited. They're just fed up with us. You know, we messed up our own country pretty bad. And they still remember how we used to treat them."

I traced the stained concrete floor with my fingers. I wasn't sure how we'd treated them. That part hadn't been in the history books my mother had left me. It must not have been all that great though, from the sound of it.

***

In a white, sterile chamber, a dark-skinned nurse and doctor probed my insides with a cold machine. I'd never experienced an examination like this, and my muscles were tense. I tore into the vinyl surface of the gurney with my jagged nails. The doctor peered at a computer screen, pointing, making clinical comments to the nurse as she took notes. Finally, he pressed a silver gun-like object against the base of my neck and pulled a trigger. A shockwave rippled through me, numbing me momentarily. Then the nurse ushered me out into the hallway. As I passed through the doorway, a screen flashed red with the word "*Inválido.*"

My eyes were wide with shock and I gasped for air, turning back to ask: "What is it, doctor? What's wrong? What's wrong with me?"

Another patient slid onto the gurney as the medic shoved my file into a cabinet. A guard grabbed my arm and dragged me down the hall. The nurse glanced back at the doctor hesitantly. He nodded his consent, and the nurse followed me to the door, whispering in my ear.

"I'm sorry. Chew are not able to reproduce," she said with regret, in a thick Spanish accent. "It appears chew safferred some trauma during churre child-whoed."

As she spoke, she touched my left side, over the half-moon scar from that day at the river.

The guard punched the keypad. The door clicked open.

The nurse's deep chocolate eyes melted bitter sweetly as she whispered in a soft voice, "*Lo siento.*"

***

I never got to say goodbye to Lenny, or Little Johnny. I never saw them again, since that morning we went to work in the fields. It had been a morning like any other. We had showered and eaten a simple breakfast of scrambled eggs and corn tortillas at the little table next to the stove in our hut. It was a simple home, with no decorations or mementos to lend any sense of who we were, or where we'd come from. We could have been any family, any group of people sitting in that room, chewing our food and sipping our coffee, day after day. But we weren't. We were us. Every morning, we said a prayer at the doorway, hand in hand. We kissed Little Johnny goodbye as he joined the children to do the kind of picking that required the smallest fingers. Then my lips touched Lenny's and our eyes met before we each parted ways to work. Lenny was assigned heavy labor, causing his muscles to grow larger and the veins in his neck to protrude. I watched him walk away and climb up into the back of the truck that carried him and the other strong men to their section of the fields. As always, I waited until the cloud of swirling dust swept him away beyond the veil of crops.

I feared I might never lay eyes on them again, yet they were all I saw as I was thrust into the paddy wagon and carted to the border for my deportation. When the tailgates opened, and I was shoved to the ground by the guards and pointed towards the bridge, the vision of Little Johnny and Lenny were what held my feet to the ground, like heavy metal balls chained to my ankles. I dragged my feet because I didn't want to move away from them, wherever they were. I yearned more than ever to break free, break free and run back towards them, sure to be drawn in their direction like a magnet to its source. More than freedom, more than opportunity, more than the air I breathed, I realized what I yearned for was the loving embrace of my family.

***

I balance effortlessly again on the highest railing, the top of the bronze plaque squarely between my bleeding feet. The moon shines high overhead as the wind rips through my hair. On the grassy crests of the levee, I glimpse the lights of guards on bicycles patrolling the banks. It must be near three in the morning. Some time soon, they should be changing shifts. Upriver, maybe, just maybe, Francisco and his diminutive wife might be waiting for another obstinate alien in their battered MaxiTaxi van at the foot of the levee. Distorted music drifts through the night from the south, conflicting with the explosions of warfare to the north. In the dark, I can almost make out where the shimmering waters of the river meet the Gulf. There, Grandpa, like countless others before him, had drifted to his destiny.

I stretch out my arms as the chip in my neck scorches me deeply. I savor this last dance, in honor of my mother and father. I picture Lenny and Little Johnny toiling somewhere deep in the south, wondering where I am and whether they'll ever see me again.

I recall a string of words I once read and struggled to comprehend as a child. I'd found them buried in a book about ancient American history. I'd never forgotten the name of the man who uttered them, Patrick Henry. He'd said as he pledged his life to the Revolution, "Give me liberty or give me death."

At last I understand what he meant.

"I'm coming home," I whisper into the wind. I'm not sure if I am speaking to my departed loved ones, or to those still holding out hope for me. But I am certain that I will fight for my life until it has been torn from my clutches.

Give me liberty or give me death! I leap into the air and dive down towards the murky, shadowy waters below, hope and fear roaring through my racing heart. Tonight, I just might find both. Regardless, for a moment, suspended in midair as my body flies through the darkness, I feel free.

"The human quest for freedom and opportunity is a manifestation of our survival instinct. It is as natural as water's stubborn search for lower ground, or a vine's resilient creeping towards the sun. No man-made obstacle or law can stand in our way forever. In the end, we will persevere until we find our place of natural balance and harmony with the world in which we live."

–*Rudy Ruiz*